Rebecca M'Conkey

The Hero of Cowpens

A Centennial Sketch

Rebecca M'Conkey

The Hero of Cowpens
A Centennial Sketch

ISBN/EAN: 9783337182458

Printed in Europe, USA, Canada, Australia, Japan

Cover: Foto ©Andreas Hilbeck / pixelio.de

More available books at **www.hansebooks.com**

HERO OF COWPENS.

A CENTENNIAL SKETCH.

"A prince can mak' a belted knight,
A markis, duke and a' that,
But an honest mon's aboon his might,
Guid faith he mauna fa' that."

BURNS.

A. S. BARNES & COMPANY,
NEW YORK AND CHICAGO.

PREFACE.

THE authoress has to regret that her limited access to Revolutionary correspondence, has left her argument less exhaustive than she could desire. The point sought to be established is, that Benedict Arnold performed no essential or valuable service during our Revolutionary struggle; that he appropriated the laurels fairly won by Daniel Morgan, and has worn them for a hundred years. For facts personal to Arnold she has relied mainly upon *Sparks' Life of Arnold;* for the same for General Morgan she is indebted to *Graham's Life of Morgan.* (See page v.) For general historical conclusions, after consulting all our standard authorities and sometimes reading between the lines, she has been careful not to wander far from Bancroft's version.

If she have set her hero in a somewhat poetic light, her " offence hath this extent—no more."

BALTIMORE, August 1, 1881.

NOTE.

[So largely has *Graham's Life of Morgan* been drawn upon in the preparation of this sketch that it will not be out of place to insert the following from the preface of that work.]

"At the death of General Morgan, his papers, correspondence, etc., went into the possession of his son-in-law, General Presley Neville. During the twenty years which succeeded, many of these papers were lost or destroyed. What remained, however, were then collected, arranged and bound into two large volumes by the General's grandson, Major Morgan Neville. When he died, they became the property of his widow, who submitted them to my perusal, with the object of ascertaining whether the publication of a select portion of their contents would be advisable or not.

"This collection is a very valuable one, embracing, as it does, letters hitherto unpublished, from Washington, Greene, La Fayette, Wayne, Gates, Jefferson, Hamilton, Henry, Rutledge, and other distinguished men of the Revolutionary era. They abound in facts and circumstances which the historian has either failed or feared to notice. But what chiefly attracted my attention was the additional light which they shed upon the private character and military services of General Morgan, and upon the details of his long and eventful career. Until I saw these papers I labored under the common error of assigning him a position among the worthies of the Revolution, far below that which he deserved. After examining all the sources of information within my reach, I became convinced, that few if any of the heroes of that day, furnished larger contributions than he did to the glory of our arms, or surpassed him in the amount and value of their services. Nevertheless I found that his character and conduct had been misconceived in some cases, and misrepresented in others; and that from these causes many of our historians had been betrayed into statements at variance with facts and injurious to his fame. The absence of full and correct information regarding a man whose name and deeds furnish so rich a source for national pride, has besides tempted Fiction to make him the theme of her legends. But the fanciful pictures she has drawn, though recognizable, are not likenesses; while they fall far short of the spirit and dignity which invested the reality.

"But ample as were the materials furnished by General Morgan's MSS., much was yet to be gathered before a complete and connected chain of events could be formed. * * * A few have contributed so largely and so valuably to my collections, as to render acknowledgements a duty as well as a pleasure. The first of these is the late Dr. Wm. Hill, of Winchester, Virginia. He was one of General Morgan's personal and intimate friends. He attended him during the illness that terminated his life and preached the funeral sermon over his grave. To him I am indebted for a large collection of facts and anecdotes in relation to General Morgan which run through his entire career and which were recorded *from his own lips*. It would be difficult to estimate the advantages I derived from this valuable contribution. It explained circumstances which, without it, would have remained inexplicable Whatever of merit may be accorded to the connection of events, as displayed here and there through the work, will in a great degree be owing to the assistance I received from Dr. Hill." * * *

TABLE OF CONTENTS.

V.—1776.

THE RETREAT.

VI.—1776.

ALL'S WELL THAT ENDS WELL.

VII.—1776, 1777.

THE RIFLE REGIMENT.

VIII.—1777.

FALL OF TICONDEROGA.

Washington keeps his position near New York as Howe still threatens Philadelphia. Gates maneuvres to oust Schuyler from the command of the Northern Department. Intrigues to get the best of Washington's officers and troops. Congress direct that Morgan and the rifle regiment be sent to Gates' assistance. 76

IX.—1777.

BATTLE OF BRANDYWINE.

Washington engages Howe with a greatly superior force at the Brandywine and is defeated. Howe takes Philadelphia. Washington ventures another battle at Germantown. Loses it. He requests Gates to send back Morgan to his assistance. Gates declines to send him. Burgoyne surrenders to Gates, who still refuses to send Morgan to Washington. Washington sends Colonel Hamilton to demand the troops. 82

X.—1777.

ARNOLD BEFORE CONGRESS.

Arnold is ordered to Rhode Island to recruit a force against a threatened invasion of that coast by a British fleet. Fails to accomplish the purpose. The British entrench at Newport. Arnold determines to go to Philadelphia. On his way he hears that the British have made a raid into Connecticut to burn the stores at Danbury. The Connecticut militia; under Wooster, follow them. Arnold joins them uninvited. Fights windmills; has two horses killed under him. The British get safely away after having done all they came to do. Arnold's "exploits" reach Congress; they present him with a horse and a Major-General's commission. He is still dissatisfied. Washington offers him a post on the Hudson. He refuses it. Goes to Philadelphia to demand an inquiry. Finds that his Canadian misdeeds have told heavily against him. The spirits of Ticonderoga and Montreal will not down. He parades his services and his wounds. He is acquitted and sustained. He then presents his accounts for settlement, with enormous aggregate in his favor. Suspicions of his knavery. Congress refuse to settle. He resigns. At that moment Ticonderoga falls. Washington soothes him and urges him to join the army before Burgoyne. He goes. Undertakes the relief of Fort Stanwix, but does not do it. . . 88

XI.—1777—1780.

HORATIO GATES.

Gates assumes command of the army before Burgoyne August 19th, immediately after the battle of Bennington, by which the British were irretrievably lamed. Gates' Revolutionary career is one of intrigue, not of service. At Saratoga he appropriates laurels that belong to Morgan and others, and assumes the role of the conquering hero. After the surrender of Burgoyne Congress makes him President of the Board of War. Washington, in eclipse at Valley Forge, is now at Gates' tender mercies, which are cruel. He works the "cabal." It explodes without harm to Washington, though he "suffers exquisite pain." Gates proposes another expedition to Canada. It fails. He occupies other posts, which the tide of war does not reach. In

XII.

BATTLE OF THE COLONELS.—No. 1.—1777.

XIII.—1777.

THE SURRENDER.

XIV.—1777, 1778, 1779.

HARD SERVICE AND NO LAURELS.

XXI.—1780.

PATRIOT LEADERS OF THE SOUTH.

XXII.—1780.

BATTLE OF THE COLONELS.—No. 2.

XXIII.—1780, 1781.

MAJOR-GENERAL GREENE.

XXIV.—1780, 1781.

MORGAN TO THE RESCUE.

XXIX.—1781.

MORGAN AGAIN IN THE SERVICE.

XXX.—1781.

YORKTOWN.

XXXI.—1781.

AT LAST.

I.

DANIEL MORGAN—HERO.

"I took thee from the sheep-cote to be a prince and a ruler."

IT is no matter of regret to us, that the human origin of our hero is overhung with mystery. We like it. What a license this obscurity gives to the imagination ! The old Greeks would have set it down thus—"Son of Jupiter and ——." We moderns might do well to take a hint out of this hoar and beautiful Greek mythology, that so delighted to mix up the gods with the affairs of men.

Eternal truth ! that has bloomed into a higher meaning in our Christianity, where God in His word and in His Providence continually shows us, how He renews the world from the lowliest sources, using the things that are not, to confound the mighty, and bring to nought the things that are.

Nature disallows heredity, and hacks it with a two-edged sword. How shall we account for Luther, Shakspere, Cromwell, Napoleon or Washington ? Having them here without precedent, we thereupon build great expectations, and behold the outcome.

Nature is averse to dynasties, and when there is brave work to be done, the workmen spring into their places by the word of His power.

One person only, could have lifted the veil of mystery from his antecedents,—our hero himself,—but he declined to do it, nor did he give a reason for the silence he maintained. There was some vague hint that he was of Welsh extraction; his parents having emigrated thither somewhere between 1720 and 1730. But no reminiscence of father, mother, sister or brother, childhood or home ever escaped him. It is uncertain whether he had his birthplace in New Jersey or Pennsylvania, his family having lived on both sides of the river, alternately. His descendants give it to New Jersey about 1736. There is another misty suggestion, that he ran away from home upon some disagreement with his father. We would, however, better take him just as we find him, Daniel Morgan, "Native American" in its loftiest sense, asking no questions. We like to think that there must have been honor and virtue in the stock that sent forth such a shoot—perhaps wrong and injustice somewhere; but over all, our hero draws a pall of unbroken silence. Yet we know of a surety that the gods were there, and did set their seal to give the world assurance of a man.

These first seventeen years of Morgan's life, then, we call his prehistoric age—but from this time he begins to give account of himself. At this age he found his environments too straight, and for causes that seemed adequate to justify a hegira, he left his home. He worked his way honestly down through Pennsylvania, and in the spring of 1754, crossed into Virginia, and stopped at a small place—Charlestown, Jefferson Co. By adoption, then, Morgan was a Virginian. There were giants in Virginia in those days.

So this boy of seventeen shook off the past, and looked the world fairly in the face on his own account. He was poorly equipped as to external helps. He could barely read and write,—rude of speech and unvarnished in manner;—but he had a strong arm and a brave heart; he was honest and scorned a lie. He obtained employment immediately; his first task being to grub a piece of ground, in a primitive state. Doing this well, he presently superintended a saw-mill, and shortly after, obtained the more

lucrative and responsible post of wagoner. The savings
of two years more of honest toil, made him owner of a
wagon and team. These two years had wrought a marked
improvement in Morgan. The boy was developing a magnificent physique—over six feet in height, limbs of fine
proportion, sinews of iron—a young Hercules, with a face
full of frank intelligence ; with all, a good stock of mother
wit and practical common sense. He had found time,
too, to improve his mind, and had gained the confidence
of his neighbors.

But stirring events were at hand. The French had long
looked with jealous eyes at the vigorous young English
settlements that had climbed the Alleghanies and were
pushing rapidly towards the valley of the Ohio. French
and English blood had already crimsoned its green slopes.
French arms had wrested from the English the fort at its
head-waters, and young Colonel Washington had suffered
a defeat at "Great Meadows." The English government,
alarmed at the success of the French, sent a splendidly-
equipped army, under General Braddock, to reinstate
British interests on the Ohio. He arrived in the Potomac, disembarked and marched to Fort Cumberland. Here
the call for wagons and teams was urgent. Morgan at
once responded, and commenced his military career as a
teamster. It is on this march that we read the first characteristic anecdote of him :

"A difficulty arose between the captain of a company
of Virginia troops (to which Morgan was attached as
wagoner) and a powerful fellow, who had the reputation of
being a skillful pugilist and a great bully. It was agreed
that at the first halt the matter should be settled by a
fight. When the company halted for dinner, the captain
stepped out to meet his antagonist, when Morgan accosted
him, saying : 'Captain, you must not fight that man.'

"'Why not?'

"'Because you are our captain, and if the fellow whips

you, we shall all be disgraced.   Let me fight him, and if he whips me, it will not hurt the credit of the company.'

"The captain remonstrated, but at last yielded.   Morgan at once engaged the bully, who soon cried—'hold, enough!'"*

Soon after, followed the shameful defeat and retreat of Braddock, pursued by the French and Indians.   Most of the terrified teamsters in the rear of the army, on learning of the disaster, disencumbered their teams and drove off to the settlements.   Not Morgan,—he with a few others remained to bring off the sick and wounded.   He doubtless witnessed the burial of Braddock in the road, Washington reading the burial service and afterwards driving over the grave, as did all the wagons, to prevent its discovery by the Indians.   Here Morgan first saw Washington, who was from this time one of his chief inspirations to all goodness and nobleness.

The effect of the defeat of Braddock was to lay open the whole terrified frontier settlements of Pennsylvania and Virginia to the vengeance of the foe.   The governor of Virginia promptly raised a regiment and appointed Washington to its command.   Morgan, as teamster, was attached to the quartermaster's department.   His duty was to transport supplies to the military posts along the frontier.   This constantly exposed him to hair-breadth escapes from the lurking foe; but it was the school in which he was training for the infallible marksman he afterwards became, and to that perfect knowledge of Indian warfare so invaluable in his subsequent career. In the spring of 1757, at Fort Chiswell, occurred an event which left indelible marks upon body and mind.

"A British lieutenant, taking offence at something which Morgan had said or done, abused him in violent terms, and at length struck him with the flat of his sword.

---

* *Graham's Life of Morgan,* p. 28.

Morgan's indomitable spirit could not brook this outrage. With one blow of his clenched fist, he stretched the officer senseless on the ground. An offence so grave against military law called, of course, for summary and exemplary punishment. A drum-head court-martial sentenced Morgan to receive five hundred lashes. He was immediately stripped and tied up, and received at once the allotted number of lashes, save one. When the terrible enormity was over, the flesh of his back hung down in tags. Only such an iron constitution as his could have survived an act of cruelty so extraordinary, even in the British army of that day. The officer feeling, upon reflection, that he had been in the wrong, and regretting the consequences which had followed, made Morgan a public apology. Slight as such atonement was for so deep an injury, Morgan accepted it, and from that moment discharged from his mind all resentment towards the author of his sufferings and disgrace." *

Here crops out that incredible magnanimity which was so large an element in Morgan's character. That British whipping was, however, to be paid back with interest.

Soon after, the French and Indians came down in such numbers into Virginia that the whole garrison of Fort Edward, within twenty miles of Winchester, fell victims to their fury. So great was the consternation, that the militia was called out. Morgan promptly obeyed the call, and marched to Fort Edward. Here he makes his first appearance as a soldier. His rank we do not know, but it must have been one of, at least, temporary command. The fort was attacked by a formidable body of French and Indians. The assault was furious, but the inspiration of Morgan's presence and example resulted in the repulse and flight of the assailants. It is said that he killed four savages in as many minutes. Morgan's voice, under the

* *Graham's Life of Morgan.*

stimulus of the battlefield, was worth a regiment of men. As the savages turned and fled, he shouted at the height of his powerful voice, "Let us follow the red devils;" the garrison to a man joined in the pursuit, overtook and slaughtered the flying foe, and cleared the vicinity of their cruel presence. Here Morgan made his mark. The coolness not less than the daring, the judgment not less than the courage, above all, his influence over those he commanded, were observed and reported.

He was soon after commended to Governor Dinwiddie for a captain's commission. But the royal governor was averse to promotions—one who was but yesterday a teamster! *

The leading men of his section continued, however, to urge his advancement, in view of the value of his influence in raising recruits. There was little difficulty in getting men to enlist under Morgan. At last Dinwiddie so far yielded as to grant him an ensign's commission. He took post at once at Fort Edward.

Not long after occurred that tragic and deadly encounter with a party of Indians, where the unseen God of heroes plucked him from out the very jaws of death.

---

* In illustration of Governor Dinwiddie's arrogance, it is related that he had much offended Washington by making the king's officers always outrank the American officers of the same grade. This reduced Washington from the rank of colonel to captain. For a time Dinwiddie allowed no higher rank than captain for any American officer. Washington indignantly threw up his commission and accompanied Braddock as volunteer aid. Some time after this, Governor Sharpe, of Maryland, who greatly needed him, proposed to Washington to return to the service, with the title of colonel but the actual authority of captain. With characteristic dignity, Washington wrote, "If you think me capable of holding a commission that has neither rank nor emolument annexed to it, you must maintain a very contemptible opinion of my weakness, and believe me more empty than the commission itself." He was at this time in his twenty-third year.

On his way from one of the frontier forts with despatches for the commanding officer at Winchester, he had reached a remarkable precipice called Hanging Rock. It was a memorable place of Indian ambuscade, and had been the scene of bloody encounters between the rival tribes of Catawba and Delaware Indians. A party of Frenchmen and Indians had concealed themselves among the rocks overhanging the road, and waiting until Morgan and his escort came immediately below, they discharged their rifles, killing the escort and desperately wounding Morgan. A ball entering at the back of the neck, grazed the left side of the neck bone; it passed through the mouth near the socket of the jaw-bone, and came out through the left cheek, knocking out all the teeth on the left side. Morgan supposed himself mortally wounded ; he was bleeding profusely, and felt himself becoming helplessly weak. He was well mounted, however, and leaning forward, he grasped the neck of the noble animal and urged her into motion. Fortunately for her rider, she took the road back to the fort. A fleet Indian runner followed him for some time, expecting every moment to see him fall from his horse. Morgan's one thought was to get beyond the reach of his pursuers and so save his body from mutilation. With his last strength he urged on the animal with his heels, and putting forth all her speed, she bore him beyond the reach of the Indian, never slackening her speed until she reached the fort. Morgan was lifted from his horse perfectly insensible. He lay for months between life and death, but care and judicious treatment, with the iron fibre of his constitution, brought him again to life and strength. Notwithstanding the innumerable perils he encountered in his long military career—and his place was evermore in the fore-front of the battle, and in the hottest of the fight—this was the only wound he ever received.

"The late Morgan Neville (a grandson of Morgan), in

a biographical sketch of the general, says : 'I well remember, when a boy, hearing General Morgan describe in his powerful and graphic style, the expression of the Indian's face as he ran with open mouth and tomahawk in hand, by the side of his horse, expecting every moment to see his victim fall. But when the panting savage found the horse was fast leaving him behind, he threw his tomahawk without effect and abandoned the pursuit with a yell of disappointed rage.'" *

But the war drew to its close—a war too much crowded out of our sight and sympathy by the brilliant associations of our struggle for independence—yet a scarcely less important one, since it secured this North American continent to the custody of Anglo-Saxon Protestant civilization.

Morgan had done brave service and was home again ; but he had brought with him, besides military glory, discipline, and experience, the vices of the camp. Here begins a period of wild-oat sowing. Says his biographer, "He weighed at this time two hundred pounds, yet without an ounce of superfluous flesh." With such a constitution he could drink deeply, yet was never seen intoxicated. He gambled, and always played a winning game. His fame as an athlete went far and near, and noted pugilists came to try his skill. He kept the field. In short, we are sketching the career of one with whose name failure keeps no company. Morgan was a marvellous success from beginning to end.

It was but a brief episode in the great man's life ; for God sent his angel to him, in the form of a modest, loving, devout woman, unschooled, untrained, the daughter of a farmer of Morgan's own rank in life—by name,

* *Graham's Life of Morgan.*

Abigail Bailey.   The rustic beauty laid her maidenly spell upon the strong man and drew him gently away from his evil courses.   "The light of her eyes smote into his life," and he left all,—his tavern boon companions, the fighting ring, the gaming-table and the wine-cup, and followed her into clean paths.

Through these years of wild life, he had yet maintained his habits of thrift and industry, and was able to establish his wife in a handsome two-story dwelling—for those days—on a valuable piece of land about ten miles east of Winchester.   He called it "Soldier's Rest."

He was soon called from his quiet home by the outbreak of Pontiac's War.   During this struggle he held the rank of lieutenant, and lost nothing of his military reputation. The war was a short one, and, returning home, Morgan had nine years of happy life in the pure atmosphere of a Christian household.   Uneventful they seem in such a career as his, yet most important — years of noiseless influences, and quiet development of all the germs of virtue and nobleness in his deep, broad nature.   Abigail and two soft-eyed little girls were his household treasures. His wife's influence was most marked ; helpful alike to his moral and mental growth.   Both felt keenly their educational deficiencies, and both worked earnestly to supply the lack.   It is said that in after years, Mrs. Morgan filled with ease and dignity the high social position to which her husband advanced her.

His material interests during this period were by no means neglected.   His farming and stock-raising brought him rich returns ; while his military grants for services in the previous wars had made him a large land-owner.

In 1771, Gov. Nelson commissioned him captain of the militia of Frederick county.   Two years after we find him again in military service, on the frontier, in Lord Dunmore's war.   At its successful termination, on their return home, the division to which Morgan was attached heard of the startling events at the north, and the threatening aspect of public affairs—the closing of the Port of Boston, the appointment of a day of fasting and prayer, and the meeting of the first National Congress for deliberation, at Philadelphia.

In a sketch of Morgan's military career, written by himself, occurs the following : —"Upon learning these things, we, as an army victorious, formed ourselves into a society, pledging our word of honor to each other, to assist our brethren of Boston in case hostilities should commence."

Events followed with startling rapidity. Lexington, April 19, 1775 ; Breeds Hill, June 17 ; June 10, the Continental Congress, and on the 14th the appointment of George Washington as commander-in-chief of the twenty thousand men to be raised for the defence of American liberties. Congress also called into service ten companies of riflemen from Pennsylvania, Maryland and Virginia. Of one of the two, from Virginia, Morgan was by unanimous vote of the committee of Frederick county, chosen captain.

He had for some time intelligently watched the points in dispute between England and America and had taken his position. He saw it in its various aspects ; but most of all he weighed it as a question of justice and human rights ; whether the sham manhood of the old world should tread down the real manhood of the new. He embraced the cause of the Revolution with all the intensity of his nature.

His commission was dated June 22, 1775. In less than ten days, he left Winchester at the head of ninety-six hardy mountain yeomanry who had promptly answered to his call,—all practised marksmen with the rifle.

They marched to Boston in twenty-one days, a distance of six hundred miles, without the loss of a man, and reported to the commander-in-chief.

II.

BENEDICT ARNOLD—MOCK HERO.

" Techy and wayward was thy infancy,
Thy school-days, frightful, desperate, wild and furious,
Thy prime of manhood, daring, bold and venturous,
Thy age confirmed, proud, subtle, sly and bloody.
Shame serves thy life and doth thy death attend."

RICHARD III.

BEFORE proceeding further in Morgan's career, we must look after our mock-hero, Benedict Arnold ; for these two begin now to bear each other company, and so continue with brief intervals, until after the surrender of Burgoyne, mid-way of the war.

We shall find sharp contrasts from the very outset. We have said of Morgan that he was a marvellous success ; we have to say of Arnold that he was an unmitigated failure from first to last. Victory fled from him—honor would none of him : the way of the transgressor was hard.

The child was father to the man. Born at Norwich, Connecticut, 1740, of fine old colonial stock, which had deteriorated on the paternal side. He had an excellent mother. One of his favorite boyish amusements was, the robbing of birds' nests and mangling the young in sight of the old birds, that he might be entertained by their piteous cries. His family was in such circumstances that he enjoyed very fair opportunities of education, one of his tutors being Dr. Jewett, a teacher of celebrity; but he showed no fondness for study, and was therefore apprenticed to the brothers Lathrop,

2

druggists, at Norwich—men of wealth, energy and integrity.

They were relatives of Arnold's mother, and disposed to advance the boy's interests—the more because his father had sunk into intemperance, poverty and obscurity. But his patrons soon found they had taken a bad subject. He was ungrateful, deaf to entreaty or advice, impatient of restraint, without natural affection or conscience, utterly indifferent to good or ill report, and possessing an innate and inveterate love of *cruel mischief* and *wanton destruction*—on this wise :

" Near the drug shop was a school-house, and he would scatter in the path broken pieces of glass, taken from the crates, by which the children would cut their feet in going to and from school. Cracked and imperfect phials were perquisites of the apprentices ; an amiable fellow apprentice was in the habit of placing his share on the outside of the door and letting the small boys take them away. Arnold did the same, but when he had thus decoyed the boys, and they were busy picking them up, he would rush out, horsewhip in hand, call them thieves, and beat them without mercy.

" He was likewise fond of all feats of daring, always foremost in danger and as fearless as he was wickedly mischievous. Sometimes he took corn to a grist mill, and while waiting for the meal, he would amuse himself and astonish his playmates, by clinging to the arms of a large water-wheel and passing with it beneath and above the water." *

No marvel that such a character should have despised the monotony of the drug shop, and at sixteen enlisted in the British army without the knowledge of his friends. The grief of his mother induced her pastor Dr. Lord and others to interfere, and effect his release.

He ran away a second time, re-enlisted and was sta-

* For this and more, see "*Sparks' Life of Arnold.*"

tioned at Ticonderoga.   But garrison duty was tame—it involved restraint, discipline, and obedience, and as there was neither profit nor adventure to offset these, he deserted and returned to Norwich.   When a British officer soon after passed through the town in search of deserters, young Arnold was secreted by his friends in a cellar.   During the time of his residence in Mr. Lathrop's family, he gave infinite trouble.   Happily for her, his mother, borne down with grief and anxiety and melancholy forebodings of the future of this wayward boy, sunk broken-hearted into the grave before he reached his manhood.

At the end of his apprenticeship, the Lathrops kindly assisted him to commence the drug business in New Haven. He showed energy but no judgment, and soon embarked in shipping to the West Indies, in addition to his regular business.   He made several voyages thither, and fought one or two duels.   His turbulent, imperious manners, and his want of moral principle, continually involved him in contention and difficulty, and his speculations finally "ended in bankruptcy, under circumstances that left a stain upon his honesty and good faith."

We do not gather grapes of thorns nor figs of thistles— and the development of Arnold's subsequent villainy, seems eminently logical, consecutive and legitimate.

He is an uncanny subject to dissect; one can find nothing but foulness and deformity.   His combativeness and destructiveness were inordinate ; his dominant passion was *avarice,* which developed with frightful rapidity.   The love of mastery was strong ; his will was a cyclone ; a scheming visionary withal, and utterly without delicacy or sentiment.   No justification, apology or extenuation seem possible.   Explanation, perhaps, in the fact that he was born almost or altogether without moral sense.   The word idiot expresses one born without intellect, but it remains for our lexicographers to supply us a word for one born without moral sense.

Given the elements—with the plus and minus that went to make up Benedict Arnold—we could have no other than the miserable outcome the world got. Though we can by no means repress the loathing, we find ourselves forbidden either to hate or scorn ; human depravity, passing a certain point, excites pity rather than any other feeling. A great mystery is here wrapped up. We cannot break the seals ; "vessels of wrath," "raging waves foaming out their own shame," "wandering stars" loosed from their orbits "to whom is reserved the blackness of darkness."

Out of such volcanic forces it is clear we can get no generalship. Arnold was a military blunderer, nothing more. The war found him a ruined merchant, and as military life opened before him a prospect of adventure, distinction and profit, he eagerly entered upon it. He was captain of a New Haven company when the news of the massacre of Lexington reached the town. He assembled his company, harangued his townsmen, and proposed to lead any number of volunteers who would go with him, to Boston.

Sixty assembled the next day ; they had no ammunition. Arnold applied to the selectmen, but they refused to furnish it without higher authority. Arnold sent word that if the keys of the magazine were not forthcoming, he would break it open. The selectmen yielded.

The project of a sudden descent upon Ticonderoga had already been quietly matured at Hartford, and a party of Connecticut men had gone forward to join Ethan Allen and his Green Mountain boys. Arnold had got some hint of this, but he hoped yet to outstrip them, for immediately on reaching Cambridge he represented to the "Massachusetts Committee of Safety," in the liveliest

colors, the practicability and advantages of such an enterprise. They at once commissioned him colonel in the
Massachusetts service, furnished him one hundred pounds
in cash, with authority to draw further sums for all
necessary supplies and provisions for a body of troops
not to exceed four hundred. These he was to enlist
in the western part of the State and proceed to Ticonderoga.

Arnold hastened to the western frontier, and there
heard that the other detachment had reached Lake Champlain. He left his party, and with only one attendant,
pushed on and overtook them twenty-five miles from
Ticonderoga. He announced himself, showed his commission, and claimed the command of the expedition.
This insolent assurance of a stranger, assuming to act
under authority which they did not recognize, was
promply resented, especially by the Vermont boys, who
were warmly attached to Allen ; they refused to march a
step after the intruder.

Seeing he could not carry the point, Arnold proposed
to accompany them as a volunteer, holding his rank
in abeyance. The assault upon the fort was successful,
and Arnold *insisted upon entering the gate at Allen's left
hand.* Fairly in the fort, this meddling, masterful spirit
again asserted his right to the command of the post and
all the troops ; but as they were commissioned and paid
by Connecticut, they stoutly withstood him.

Arnold was again forced to submit, under protest, however, and he immediately sent a list of grievances to the
Massachusetts Committee. Meantime, letters had been
sent back both to Connecticut and Massachusetts concerning his insolent conduct, whereupon the legislature appointed a committee to repair to Lake Champlain to
investigate the "spirit, capacity, and conduct" of Arnold,
and if they thought it advisable, to order his immediate
return to Massachusetts, to render an account of the

money, ammunition and stores he had received, and the debts he had contracted in the name of the colony. He was also to recognize the superior authority of the officer from Connecticut.

The Committee found him at Crown Point, and laid their instructions before him. Arnold was enraged: "He said that an order to inquire into his conduct when no charge had been exhibited against him, was unprecedented; that the assumption to judge of his capacity and spirit, was an indignity: that this point ought to have been decided before they honored him with their confidence. He declared that he had already paid out of his own pocket for the public service more than one hundred pounds, and contracted debts on his personal credit in procuring necessaries for the army, which he was bound to pay or leave the post with dishonor, and finally that he would not submit to the degradation of being superseded by a junior officer. He followed this up by a formal resignation." *

He soon afterward returned to Cambridge to lodge his complaints of ill-usage against the legislature, and also to present his accounts for settlement. "His accounts were finally allowed and settled, although with a reluctance which indicated doubt and suspicion."

So much for Arnold's part in the capture of Ticonderoga, into which he had so unhandsomely thrust himself, and to which he contributed no necessary or essential part; yet he managed so to associate himself with it, before the public, that he unduly shared the prestige of the enterprise, while the waste and loss and ill feeling which he had occasioned were never weighed against him.

But his mischievous devices at this time extended farther. While on the Lakes, he wrote to Congress that

* *Sparks' Life of Arnold.*

he had sent an agent to Montreal to investigate the British force there, and discover the temper of the Canadians towards America. He wrote in high feather, sanguine that the whole of Canada could be taken with two thousand men, laid before them plans for the campaign, offering to lead the expedition and be responsible for the results. He assured Congress that the Canadians had promised to open the gates upon the appearance of an American army, and that General Carleton had not more than five hundred effective men, who were scattered at various points.

These representations were by no means without effect, though Congress was not yet prepared to act. There were doubtless weighty reasons and other advocates for the attempt, especially among the members from the New England States. Be that as it may, certes it came nigh to be a Sicilian expedition, with Arnold for its Alcibiades.

Two months later, in August, 1775, Congress ordered the attack, assigning the command, however, to Schuyler. He soon fell ill; most likely with disgust. Living in Northern New York, he knew something of the perils and impracticabilities of such an enterprise. Bancroft says, "The path across the Atlantic and up the St. Lawrence was more easily traversed than the road by land from the colonies to Quebec." The noble Montgomery succeeded Schuyler, only to be sacrificed. They were to proceed by the Lakes, to capture all intervening forts, Montreal and Quebec.

Having failed to win Congress to his schemes, Arnold, now idle at Cambridge, since resigning his Massachusetts commission, got the ear of Washington, and urged the expedition through Maine.* He showed the journal of a British officer who had made the journey, and also a manuscript map of the country watered by the Kennebec. He had been

* *Maine Hist. Society,* Vol. I, p. 341.

himself in Canada, and knew the heart of the Canadians. He was entirely satisfied of the feasibility of penetrating Maine with a division of the army, which could surprise Quebec, now so feebly garrisoned, and thus co-operate with Montgomery in the reduction of Canada. He was certain of the result, and proposed himself as the leader of the enterprise. Phaeton would drive Apollo's steeds.

Here begins that strange mastery which Arnold exerted over Washington; that incredible fascination which held and compelled the uninterrupted favor and patronage of the commander-in-chief — a fascination which nothing could disparage or impair, until the enormous villainy of West Point suddenly uncovered him.

III.—1775.

WASHINGTON AND HIS GENERALS.

WASHINGTON towered above the average humanity. Ordinary mortals could not climb to his level, or exist in his atmosphere. The faults of such a character could only be virtues in excess. The elements were so mixed in him that it is impossible to know whether judgment outweighed modesty, modesty courage, courage magnanimity, magnanimity patience, or whether integrity outweighed them all. Yet *he* knew not that "he was not as other men."

Two things he utterly lacked—self-assertion and the power to suspect. *Washington was nothing of a detective.* He was egregiously deceived in Lee, Gates and Arnold, and unaccountably continued under the delusion.

The power of an ignoble over a noble soul is as old as Eden. Othello in the toils of Iago shows it; Richard, prince of villains, with his superhuman genius of destruction, draws all about him into his current, and whirls with them down the swift steeps of ruin.

If Benedict Arnold be taken as the product of a New England puritan village, he is scarcely shamed by the parallels of such barbaric times.

Certain it is, he had succeeded in achieving a sudden reputation for brilliant military talents, and "the cause" was much in need of such. Let us see what help Washington could count upon in prosecuting the heavy work he had undertaken. "On the day of the battle of Bunker Hill, Congress had elected four Major Generals :—*Arte-*

mas Ward, a worthy man of some ability, but old and out of health ; *Charles Lee,* an Englishman, a traitor, a military adventurer, true to no cause and no man, passionate, complaining and abusive, and in time of danger, a coward. *Philip Schuyler,* a true patriot and a true man, generously using his credit, influence and resources for the cause, but he lacked nerve ; *Israel Putnam,* incompetent for such a position and too old to learn. *Horatio Gates* came next as Adjutant General, with rank of Brigadier, a place-seeker without character or military talent."

Bancroft says : "The continent took up arms with but one general officer who drew to himself the love and trust of the country, and with not one of the five below him fit to succeed to his place."

They also elected eight Brigadier Generals.

"*Seth Pomeroy.*—Well esteemed,—seventy years old.

"*Richard Montgomery.*—Seventh in rank from Washington, second in merit.

"*David Wooster.*—A man of integrity and patriotism,—sixty-five years old.

"*William Heath.*—Vain and incompetent.

"*Joseph Spencer.*—Highly esteemed, but without experience.

"*John Thomas.*—Next to Montgomery in merit.

"*John Sullivan.*—Vain, boastful and ambitious.

"*Nathaniel Greene.*—Who, after Washington; had no superior in natural resources."

These are substantially Bancroft's estimates.

This was a far more unpromising military list than any one at that time suspected ; yet Washington had urged upon Congress the appointment of both Lee and Gates, and himself gave Arnold his commission.

Congress had honored Washington with large responsibility, but the authority that should have accompanied it was reserved to itself, multiplying infinitely his labors and vexations. King George and the British army were, throughout the whole war, the least of his afflictions. While he arranged, Congress and its "Boards of War" disarranged. The cause was constantly to be saved from its friends. Besides his immediate prodigious army correspondence, he conducted another equally prodigious, with members of Congress, state governors and officers, with private individuals and with foreign courts and officials. All complaints and grievances, from all and whatever quarters, were lodged with him. It required oftentimes the whole weight of his influence to keep patriot soldiers like Schuyler and Montgomery to their posts, against the superhuman discouragements and difficulties that beset them. On one occasion, after an eloquent appeal to their patriotism, which necessitated a short essay rather than letter, he adds : " God knows there is not a difficulty that you both justly complain of, which I have not in an eminent degree experienced, that I am not this day experiencing; but we must bear up against them and make the best of mankind as they are, since we cannot have them as we wish."

He must right the wrongs of unappreciated merit, soothe the pangs of wounded ambition and adjust the jealousies of the officers among themselves.

They called for their honors in advance. Passing the sour and surly demands of pronounced traitors and place-seekers like Lee, Arnold, Gates and Burr, what a majestic patience it required for this—from Brigadier General Greene :

" LONG ISLAND, May 21, 1776.

" *Dear Sir :*—From the last accounts from Great Britain, it appears absolutely necessary that there should be an augmentation of the American forces, in consequence of which I suppose there will be several promotions. As I have no desire of quitting the service, I hope the Congress will take no measure that will lay me under the disagreeable necessity of doing it. * * *

I have ever found myself exceedingly happy under your Excellency's command. I wish my ability to deserve was equal to my inclination to merit. How far I have succeeded in my endeavors, I submit to your Excellency's better judgment. I hope I shall never be more fond of promotion than studious to merit it. * * * Modesty will ever forbid me to apply to that House for any favors. I consider myself immediately under your Excellency's protection, and look up to you for justice. Every man feels himself wounded where he finds himself neglected," etc., etc., etc.*

The campaign from August 1776 to January 1777, disclosed equally,—the stupidity of Congress, in disregarding the suggestions of Washington, and themselves undertaking to direct his military movements,—the woeful incapacity of his officers, and his own utter lack of self-assertion.

Concerning the Canadian expedition, though we nowhere find that Washington opposed it, yet we do not find that he proposed it. Three years subsequently, in 1778, when the French had come openly to our help, and Congress suggested another attempt to conquer it in the interest of the French,—Washington promptly discouraged it, urging that "it was not to the interest of the United States that a power of different race, language and religion should have a footing on this continent."

Washington at all times obeyed the orders of Congress so promptly, that they might have seemed to emanate from his own conviction. Every energy was used to bring its plans to success, or failing this, to retrieve the disaster.

Rightly estimating the demands of the campaign, he knew that the force dispatched under Montgomery was inadequate for its accomplishment. He was the more inclined to this Maine reinforcement, because he could at this time spare the troops. His own army was maintain-

---

* *Washington's Correspondence (Sparks'), Vol. I, p. 236.

ing a forced inactivity before Boston, for want of ammunition; the more trying from the fact that Congress and the War Board had repeatedly signified its desire that he should assume the offensive. He could neither act nor with safety disclose the reason of his inaction; but being more careful of the cause he served than of his reputation, he silently took the censure.

These considerations, together with the persistent counsels of the "fair-spoken and persuading" Arnold, prevailed. The reinforcement of the Canadian army by way of the wilderness of Maine was ordered, and Arnold appointed to lead it. The essentials to its success were— dispatch and secrecy. A British army would certainly arrive in Canada in the spring. It was now or never. Arnold assured Washington that the march could be made in twenty days, and maintained his assertion that two thousand men could achieve the conquest of the province. No one appears to have contradicted his assertions or questioned his estimates; for the wilderness was *terra incognita* to all but himself. Because an exploring party of British officers had penetrated this country, lightly equipped, choosing their own time and season, with no end in view but the exploration, it scarcely followed that an army could drag its supplies and military equipments through such a country at double quick, so to speak, and emerge in condition for instant assault upon the strongest position on the continent. Yet this they were expected to do.

IV.—1775, 1776.

THROUGH THE WILDERNESS.

THE force detached for service in Canada amounted to about eleven hundred men, consisting of ten companies of infantry and three of riflemen. The latter were ordered to the front, and Morgan was their leader.

"His men were armed with rifle, tomahawk and long knife. They were dressed in flannel shirts, cloth or buckskin breeches, buckskin leggins and moccasins. Over these they wore hunting-shirts made of brown linsey, or linsey-wolsey. The shirts were confined at the waists by belts in which they carried their knives and tomahawks. In the wilderness, Morgan himself, adopted the Indian dress. Part of their route was to be through a hostile Indian country, which would impose upon him an untiring vigilance in guarding against Indian ambush." *

Morgan's company wore on their caps the words "liberty or death." Neither adventure nor profit had brought him to the wilderness of Maine; of the first, his long Indian wars had given him a surfeit; for the last, he would better have found it with his flocks and herds on the slopes of the Alleghanies.

In assuming his leadership, he had received orders to "examine the country along the route, free the streams from impediments to navigation, and remove obstructions from the road; to ascertain all fords intersecting the line of march; to examine the numerous portages over which

* *Graham's Life of Arnold*, p. 63.

it would be necessary to move, and take all measures to facilitate their passage."

With all the dispatch that could be used, it was the 18th of September when they embarked at Newburyport, on transports which were to carry them as far as Gardiner, on the Kennebec. Here, two hundred batteaux, which Washington had ordered to be constructed, were waiting to receive them.

Their route was up the Kennebec, almost to its sources ; above Curritunk, they must needs traverse "the great carrying place," a distance of fifteen miles, with three small lakes intervening, before they could again embark on the Dead River, a western branch of the Kennebec,—a place of "precipitous ascents, yawning ravines, thick entangling woods, swamps and water-courses,"—the riflemen carrying the bateaux, baggage, arms and provisions.

After following the Dead River for eighty-three miles, another carrying place, over a mountain ridge, was to be passed, before they reached Lake Megantic, in Canada, crossing which, they were to enter the Chaudière, a swift, violent stream, that empties into the St. Lawrence not far from Quebec.

This journey through the wilderness, with its outcome, is the tragic-romance of the Revolution,—a presentiment of that after, greater tragedy of the French revolution, "The March to Moscow." It reads like the labors of Hercules. Arnold's twenty days dragged on to fifty-six. The distance was six hundred miles, through silent, pathless solitudes,—to this day, in part, unsettled and unexplored.

As they advanced up the Kennebec, the stream became rapid and violent over its rocky bed ; often they could not row, but must drag their heavily laden boats up the swift current, waist deep. The mountains were covered with snow, and the waters at a deadly chill. Beds of rock, falls and rapids, often forbade the passage of their boats at all. They were to be unloaded, and with their contents carried by the men, through tiresome, pathless forests, until the stream would bear them again.

Leaving the Kennebec, they dragged everything over a rough ridge and through swamps and bogs, sinking knee deep, to the Dead River. Their course now lay up this river for eighty-three miles, and no less than seventeen times, because of falls and rapids, they were forced to unload their boats, and carry them and their contents. Winter winds howled around them; their shoes were gone; rocks and briars tore their clothes from their backs; November rains drenched them; famine, disease, and death marched with them. Three companies deserted and marched back. Their commander plead a misunderstanding of Colonel Arnold's orders.

They had dragged their boats one hundred and eighty miles of the journey. Arnold in a letter to Washington writes: " You would have taken the men for amphibious animals, as they were most of the time under water." They had carried them on their shoulders forty miles, through frightful thickets, rugged mountains, and knee-deep bogs, till at last they reached the Chaudière, which goes foaming and raging down its rocky channel. Swelled by heavy storms, it whirled over and engulfed their boats and contents in its angry rapids and falls; not a boat escaped, and the men were scarcely saved. They reached their journey's end in a pitiable and almost famished condition. The first supplies that were served to the starving men, were so eagerly devoured that many of them sickened and some died from their imprudent indulgence. The Canadians looked with mingled wonder and admiration upon the men who had conquered their way through what they regarded an impassable wilderness. The troops, advancing as fast as their exhausted state would permit, assembled on November 7th, four leagues from the St. Lawrence, to the number of less than six hundred. Death, sickness and desertions, had fearfully wasted them.

Arnold had, however, effectually *ensured the failure of the enterprise*, by dispatching ahead two friendly Indians, so-called, with letters addressed to persons in Quebec, and to General Schuyler, announcing his coming. The Indians proved to be unfriendly, and the letters fell into the hands of the Lieutenant-Governor of Quebec. He made instant preparations for defence. Colonel McLean, from the Sorel, joined him with one hundred and seventy men, and crews of vessels arriving were pressed into the service of strengthening the works, while the marines of several war-vessels, lying at Quebec, to the number of nearly three hundred, manned the defences.

From the time Arnold discovered the treachery of his Indian messengers, he abandoned all idea of a surprise assault,—a mortifying disappointment to the heroes who had been nerved to their incredible labors and endurances, by the proud hope of re-enacting on the plains of Abraham the glorious deeds of Wolfe. They were still at Point Levi, for the British had secured all the boats on the opposite shore. It was November 13th before they could assemble boats and bateaux sufficient for the crossing. At nine o'clock, on the night of the 13th, Morgan and his riflemen, still leading the van, embarked. The St. Lawrence was two miles wide, the current rapid, and their course lay between a frigate and a sloop-of-war. They continued to cross safely by detachments until four o'clock, when they were discovered and fired upon.

Morgan meantime had reconnoitered the approaches to the town, and found " not a mouse stirring." He had, his life-long, accomplished what he undertook. His investigations satisfied him that the garrison were not aware of their crossing, and were not upon their guard. He thought the assault should be made at once, and so communicated his views to the officers. He had performed the eleven labors of Hercules, and now begged leave to do the twelfth. Neither Arnold nor the officers accepted his suggestions.

It was wonderful how Arnold's rashness deserted him, precisely when it was wanted. They argued that the firing on the boats had, without doubt, been heard by the garrison. Notwithstanding, they found afterward that the garrison had been entirely unaware of their crossing, and that "the entrance to the town, called St. John's Gate, had been open the whole night; the only defence of which was a single gun guarded by a drowsy watch."* During the day, Arnold paraded his whole command before the walls, offering battle, hoping to draw the British force outside; but they remembered Montcalm, and wisely remained behind their defences.

He likewise hoped that those friendly Canadians, whom he had represented as only waiting the appearance of an American army to open their gates, would now prove their sympathy for the colonies; but nothing of the kind occurred. If he had risked the assault, he would doubtless have found that sympathy within the walls. Lastly, Arnold sent an officer, under flag, with a letter to the Governor, pompously calling upon him, in the name of the American Congress, to surrender, and threatening disastrous consequences if it should be delayed. The officer with the flag was fired upon, and retired. This finished the first day before Quebec.

By this time Morgan was thoroughly disgusted with the state of affairs. From information received, it was clear that had his advice been taken, Quebec would also have been taken. Arnold's senseless bravado and meaningless parade before the town were not to his mind. It was plain to him that he had been brought upon a fool's errand. His men had also that day complained that, notwithstanding their ample supplies of flour, they were still kept upon the short allowance of a pint a day. Accom-

* *Graham's Life of Morgan, quoted from Henry's Expedition,* p. 85.

panied by two officers he waited on Arnold, represented the facts and demanded redress.

"If the matter could have been traced to its source, it would probably have been found to be a part of that system of peculation which Arnold seldom lost an opportunity of practising. He evaded at first, and then bluntly refused compliance. A violent altercation ensued, and Morgan was upon the point of striking. Language of defiance passed between them as Morgan left Arnold's quarters. The next day, however, and thereafter, the riflemen were served with a full allowance of provisions." *

Morgan was remarkable for his judicious care of his men; the effects of this care and kindness is proved in the fact that he lost but one man from his company in the passage through Maine; that one was drowned in the Chaudière.

On the 19th, Arnold marched away, and took post at Point-aux-Trembles, eight leagues from Quebec, to await Montgomery's arrival. He wrote to Washington that it would require twenty-five hundred men to take Quebec; later, he wrote it five thousand.

Meantime, Montgomery had made a brilliant campaign, taking Forts Chamblie, St. Johns, and the city of Montreal. The land rang with his praises; but Quebec remained— the key to the whole situation. After leaving garrisons at these places, and parting with those troops whose time had expired, he embarked with artillery and stores and three hundred men to join Arnold. On the 5th of December, their united forces, less than one thousand effective men, "appeared before Quebec in mid-winter to take the strongest fortified city in America, defended by two thousand cannon, and a garrison now nearly twice as large as the force of the besiegers."

* *Henry's Expedition*, p. 98.

Montgomery spoke hopefully to his men, but in his heart he knew he led a forlorn hope. To return without the capture of Quebec, was to throw away all the brave work he had done. Congress expected it; the nation waited for it; his own good name and the cause of his country alike necessitated it. Further, it must be done at once; the rigors of winter were upon them; the sufferings of the men were intolerable. Two diseases had attacked the camp—small-pox and home-sickness; also, there were discontents in the army. Arnold had quarreled with his officers, and two or three companies were ready to mutiny, but Montgomery's manly expostulation won them back to their duty.

The time of most of the men expired with the now expiring year. The assault was therefore fixed for the night of the twenty-sixth of December. "It was clear, and so cold that no man could handle his arms or scale a wall. The twenty-seventh was hazy, and the troops were put in motion, but the sky cleared, and Montgomery, tender of their lives, recalled them, to wait for a night of clouds and darkness, with a storm of wind and snow." On the thirtieth, New Year's eve, a northeast storm set in. The troops were disposed for attack at four different points. Two of these attacks were only feints: the real points of assault were reserved for Montgomery on one side of the town and Arnold on the other.

The snow had changed to driving hail, that cut the men's eyes and faces; Arnold's division advanced with heads down, and their guns under their coats to keep them dry.

They attacked with furious energy, but a musket-ball in his leg disabled Arnold at the first barricade, and he was borne to the rear. Morgan now took command, and the game was in his own hands. Cheering on his men with a voice "louder than the northeast gale," they carried battery after battery, taking their defenders prisoners.

He held now the lower part of the town, and there they watched and waited for the promised signals from Montgomery's side.

He with three hundred men and his two aides, McPherson and Cheeseman, two gallant young soldiers, had taken his course along a steep and rocky path, so slippery and dangerous from the frozen hail, that it was with difficulty they could keep their feet. On they went, Montgomery opening the path through the snow with his own hands. A battery interrupted their path—it must be taken. Montgomery ordered them to "double quick," himself leading, with the words, "Come on, brave boys, you will not fear to follow where your general leads." A flash—a well-served cannon discharge—Montgomery, McPherson and Cheeseman fell dead.

The drifted snow was the winding-sheet of the noble and the brave on the morning of the new year, 1776, before the gates of Quebec. Their leader fallen, his men made instant retreat. Morgan waited on the other side of the town for the signals they never should see. They waited too long. The enemy, now released from defending other points, surrounded and took them prisoners. So ended a noble life, and the lamentations for Montgomery were as loud and eloquent in the British Parliament as in the American Congress.

Morgan, balked in his first wish to assault Quebec, had succeeded now only too well; but let him tell his own story.

* * * * "I was appointed to the command of the forlorn hope on the river St. Charles under General Arnold. The general having been wounded in the leg while under the walls, and before we got into the town, I sent him off in the care of two of my men and took his place in the command. I had to attack a two-gun battery, supported by Captain McCloud and fifty regular troops.

"The first gun missed us; the second flashed, when I ordered the ladders, borne on the shoulders of the men, to be raised. The order was immediately obeyed, and for fear the business might not be executed with spirit, I mounted myself and leaped into the town. The first man among Captain McCloud's guard, who was panic-struck, made but a faint resistance, and ran into a house that joined the two-gun battery and platform, where the guard was posted. I lighted on the end of a great gun, which hurt me very much, and perhaps saved my life, as I fell from the gun on the platform, where the bayonets were not directed. Colonel Charles Porterfield, who was [then] a cadet in my company, was the first man that followed me, and all the men came after him as fast as they had room to jump down. All this was performed in a few seconds. I ordered the men to fire into the house and follow up with their pikes, which they did, and drove the guard into the street. I went through a sally-port at the end of the platform, met the retreating guard in the street, and ordered them to lay down their arms if they expected quarters. They took me at my word, and every man threw his arms down.

"We then charged on the battery and took it, sword in hand; pushing on, we took everything that opposed us at the point of the bayonet till we arrived at the barrier gate. Here I was ordered to wait for General Montgomery, and a fatal order it was. It prevented me taking the garrison, as I had already made half the town prisoners.

"The sally-port through the barrier was standing open; the guard had left it, and the people were running from the upper town in whole platoons, giving themselves up as prisoners. I went up to the edge of the upper town, *incog.*, with an interpreter, to see what was going on, as the firing had ceased. Finding no person in arms at all, I returned and called a council of what few officers I had with me, for the greater part of our force had missed their way and had not got into the town.

"Here I was overruled by sound judgment and good

reasoning. It was said, in the first place, that if I went on I should break orders ; in the next, that I had more prisoners than I had men, and that if I left them they might break out, retake the battery we had just captured, and cut off our retreat. It was further urged, that General Montgomery would join us in a few minutes, and that we were sure of conquest if we acted with caution and prudence.

"To these good reasons I gave up my own opinion and lost the town.* For General Montgomery, having cut down an out-picket, was marching up to a two-gun battery when an unlucky shot put an end to his existence, killing at the same time Captain Cheeseman, Major McPherson and others of his good officers. Upon this, Colonel Campbell, his quartermaster-general, undertook to order a retreat. We were then left to shift for ourselves, but did not yet know the extent of the misfortunes which had occurred, or it was still in our power to have taken the garrison."†

His detachment now found themselves surrounded by their enemies, but Morgan's spirits rose with the emergency, and he proposed to his officers to cut their way back out of the town ; but they had lost hope and preferred to surrender.

A single incident remains to be noted, which Morgan himself relates. Humanity and kindness marked the treatment of the prisoners by Carleton, but Morgan received special consideration. His conduct of the assault had impressed them with a high idea of his military ability.

"He was visited frequently by a British officer, to him unknown, but from his uniform, he belonged to the navy and was an officer of distinction. During one of his

* Several of the officers outranked Morgan, but at the fall of Arnold, not one would assume his command, but pressed it upon Morgan.

† *Graham's Life of Morgan*, p. 465.

visits, after conversing upon many topics, he asked Morgan if he did not begin to be convinced that the resistance of America was visionary. He endeavored to impress upon Morgan the disastrous consequences that must infallibly ensue if the idle attempt were persevered in, and earnestly exhorted him to renounce the ill-advised undertaking. He declared with seeming sincerity and warmth his admiration of Morgan's spirit and enterprise, which he said were worthy of nobler employment, and at last told him that if he would consent to withdraw from the American and join the British service, he was commissioned to offer him the rank and emoluments of a colonel in the royal army. Morgan rejected the proposal with disdain, and added : 'I hope, sir, you will never again insult me, in my present distressed and unfortunate situation, by making me offers which plainly imply that you think me a scoundrel." *

Here we get the true ring of his metal ; it was worthy of the "chief" himself. Perhaps nothing in Washington's career has been more admired than the manner of his rejection of the overtures of the officers, through Colonel Nicola, in 1783, proposing to him to assume the headship of the nation with the title of "King." The fine feeling is the same in both cases ; both are *personally insulted.* They receive it as a man of honor would an "unhandsome suggestion." Washington replies : "With a mixture of surprise and astonishment I have read the sentiments you have submitted to my perusal. I am much at a loss to conceive what part of my conduct should have given encouragement to such an address. If I am not deceived in the knowledge of myself, you could not have found a person to whom your schemes are more disagreeable," etc. The point of Morgan's scorn, in his Canadian prison eight years before, is not a whit less fine.

* *Graham's Life,* p. 112.

THE RETREAT.

ARNOLD, in hospital with his shattered limb, found himself, by the death of Montgomery, at the head of affairs. He wrote to Washington that it would require ten thousand men to complete the conquest of Canada, and opening a vein of modesty, adds :—"I am in hopes some experienced officer will be sent here to take command ; the service requires greater abilities and experience than I can pretend to." Montgomery in his last despatches to Congress had informed that body that it would require an army of ten thousand and a fleet of war-vessels to *keep* Canada after it was conquered. Notwithstanding this new revelation, with the disasters which had followed the attempt, Congress having entered upon it, pursued it with a stubbornness something akin to insanity.

General Wooster, a brave old patriot, had been left in command at Montreal by Montgomery, and was now the highest officer in Canada. He felt his unfitness for the position, and was anxious to be superseded by a younger and more efficient officer. He took command at Quebec April 1st, and "the garrison laughed as they saw from the ramparts the general, now venerable from age, and distinguished by his singularly large wig, walking solemnly along the walls to spy out their weak points."

New England had sent forward several regiments immediately after the fall of Montgomery, and at the end of April, Congress blindly declared itself "determined on the reduction of Quebec," and by its president urged

Washington to hasten the departure of four battalions.
A week later, though Washington was himself in urgent
need of men, arms and money, "without so much as
consulting with the commander-in-chief, they suddenly
and peremptorily ordered him to detach six additional
battalions from his army for service in Canada, and further, inquired if he could spare more. On the day he
received this order, his effective force consisted of but
eight thousand three hundred men, poorly armed and
worse clad. He detached immediately six of his best battalions—more than three thousand men—at a time when
the British ministry was directing against him more than
thirty thousand veteran troops. It was a touching spec-
tacle to see Washington resign himself to the ill-considered
votes of Congress, and send off his best troops to Canada
at their word, even though it left him bare and exposed
to the greatest dangers, saying only, 'I could wish the
army in Canada were powerfully reinforced, at the same
time, trusting New York and the Hudson River to the
handful of men remaining here, is too great a risk.'"*

To the costly life already sacrificed before Quebec, they
added now that of the next most effective officer in the
service, General Thomas of Massachusetts. He arrived
at Quebec in May, and found one-third of the troops in
hospital with small-pox, and within a month himself fell
a victim to the pestilence. "He had come to meet death
unattended by glory."

General Sullivan next succeeded. He came, and aired
his vocabulary of braggadocio, but falling into the hands
of one Frazer (of whom more anon), at Trois Rivières, was
taught modesty. Congress, by the influence of John
Adams, the special patron of Gates, now appointed that
officer as a panacea for the ills of Canada.

But the Canadian campaign was ended before he reached

* *Bancroft*, Vol. VIII, p. 421.

it. "Disasters followed fast, and followed faster." Burgoyne had arrived in the St. Lawrence with an army from England ; Arnold was now calling for a retreat as vigorously as he had called for an advance, and it was clear to all that unless that retreat was speedy, there would be no army to bring away.

The pestilence retreated with them. "The voyage over the lakes was made in leaky boats without awnings, so that the sick lay drenched in water and exposed to the July sun. Their only food was raw pork and hard bread. When, early in July, the fragments of the army had reached Crown Point, the scene of distress produced a momentary despair ; their clothes, their blankets, the air, the very ground they trod on, was infected. More than thirty new graves were made every day. In a little more than two months, the northern army had lost by desertion and death more than five thousand men." *

But we must return to the special notice of Arnold's military career in Canada. He had barely recovered from his wound when General Wooster appeared at Quebec— April 1st—and assumed command. This appointment did not please Arnold, who complained of his coldness and reserve, for Wooster neither asked nor accepted his advice or counsel.

This situation is well explained in the fact that the sturdy old patriot was a townsman and neighbor of Arnold. Just at this time, Arnold's horse stumbled with him and aggravated his wound. He asked leave to retire from Quebec, and dropped down to Montreal, where, being first in rank, he at once assumed control.

During his command there, occurred the affair of the Cedars ; not exceeded in ignominy by any event of the war. At the Cedars, about forty miles away from Montreal, a point that projected far into the river and could

* *Bancroft,* Vol. IX.

only be approached from one side, Arnold had posted five hundred men under Colonel Bedell. He was well intrenched and had two field pieces." *

Colonel Bedell heard of the approach of Captain Forster with two hundred British and Canadians, and several hundred Indians,—no American authority puts the number at over six hundred. Leaving Major Butterfield in charge, Bedell went to Montreal to give the alarm. Captain Forster had no artillery, and attacked with musketry only. After two days, but one man in the fort was wounded; but Forster terrified Butterfield into a surrender, by threats of giving the whole garrison up to the savages if any of the besiegers were wounded. The terms of the surrender were most ignominious. Meantime Arnold had dispatched Major Sherbourne with one hundred and forty men to their assistance. He approached without knowing what had happened—was surrounded by the enemy, thirty of his force tomahawked and the rest captured.

At the news of this second disaster, Arnold advanced with a force of eight hundred men. From La Chène—not far from the Cedars—he writes, May 25th, 1776 : " One of our men this moment came in who was taken at the Cedars. He made his escape this morning, and says we have lost only ten privates killed, the rest are prisoners at St. Ann's and the Cedars. *The enemy lost double that number.* They were last night within three miles of us, with three hundred savages, fifty regulars, and two hundred and fifty Canadians, with our two pieces of cannon ; *but on hearing that we had a large body of men here, they made a precipitate retreat."* †

Instead of moving at once upon the enemy, Arnold sent a party of Indians over the river with a message, demanding, in his usual bravado style, " the surrender of the American

---

* *Sparks' Correspondence of Washington,* Vol. I, p. 195.
  † *Sparks' Correspondence of Washington,* Vol. I, p 518.

prisoners, threatening, in case of refusal, or if any murders were committed, that he would sacrifice every Indian that should fall into his hands, and follow them to their towns, which he would destroy by fire and sword." "He spoke daggers, but used none."

The Indians returned as spirited a reply, promising, if he attacked, to kill all the prisoners they had, and all they should capture.

It was evening, his boats had not yet all arrived, and the darkness made it necessary for him to retire. He called a council of war, and it was unanimously decided to attack in the early morning.

At midnight, one of the imprisoned officers arrived with a flag, bringing articles for an exchange of prisoners, which had been arranged by Major Sherbourne and Captain Forster. The same ignominious terms were offered, accompanied by the threat to let loose the savages upon the prisoners, and upon Arnold, if he should attack. It was as successful with Arnold as it had been with Butterfield; nor can we see that he was more valiant. By American estimates, the enemy numbered six hundred; British estimates would perhaps reduce this. By Arnold's figures, there were about six hundred American prisoners, and he had eight hundred fresh troops. It is not to be supposed that the prisoners would fail to co-operate in event of an attempted rescue.

A very little of that rashness that was Arnold's chief military virtue, was here needed, but it again deserted him. The same threats that brought the surrender of Butterfield, now availed to scare Arnold into accepting the disgraceful terms offered.

He returned to Montreal with his eight hundred men without having struck a blow for the rescue, and writes immediately to General Schuyler, "I have ordered Colonel Bedell, his major, and Captain Young, to Sorel, for their trial." This affair led to much crimination and recrimination between the military authorities on both sides. Congress wished to repudiate the capitulation, but Washington pronounced it binding, being executed in due form by officers having proper authority. There was no honorable way out of it.

This closes the military exploits of Arnold in Canada; but there remain some other matters to be noted.

As soon as the evacuation was determined upon, he made an indiscriminate seizure of goods from the merchants of Montreal, professedly for the public service, giving certificates to their owners, who were to be paid by the military authorities of the United States.

He sent the goods to Chamblie, in charge of Colonel Hazen. This officer had been for some time associated with Arnold, but for reasons best known to himself, he declined to be implicated in any way with the transaction. The goods lay in piles on the landing exposed to the weather and the plunderer.

Their owners followed the army to Crown Point, and demanded pay for the whole amount, including the damaged and stolen. The blame fell upon Arnold; he transferred it to Hazen, who he declared had not obeyed his orders.

A court-martial followed. During its progress, the court refused to accept the testimony of one of Arnold's witnesses, who was believed to be interested in the affair. Arnold addressed a disrespectful letter to the court; they demanded an apology; he challenged them all, individually and collectively.

Such monstrous effrontery compelled the court to appeal to General Gates, commander-in-chief of the department. These two, Arnold and Gates, had already begun to exchange signs. Gates abruptly dissolved the court, and excused himself to Congress for an act so unjust and dictatorial, on the plea " that the United States could not be deprived of that excellent officer's services at that important moment."

The court, however, before its adjournment, passed judgment, acquitting Colonel Hazen—leaving Arnold, of course, under censure.

Hard upon, followed a rupture with Colonel Brown, who had been at the taking of Ticonderoga and was, perhaps, no admirer of Arnold. The latter accused Brown, in letters to Congress, of plundering the baggage of prisoners taken in Canada, during the siege of Quebec.

Colonel Brown promptly demanded a court of inquiry from General Wooster at the time, but, through evasions of Arnold, he was unable to prosecute the affair until after the evacuation of Canada. He then applied to Congress for redress, and Congress directed Gates to grant the inquiry. Gates played the dictator as before, and shielded Arnold from the inquiry.

Colonel Brown waited until the end of the campaign, and then demanded the arrest of Arnold on a series of charges running through the whole period of his command. Gates again evaded it, saying that he would lay the petition before Congress. Colonel Brown, indignant at this shuffling and baffling of justice, published the whole affair, commenting upon Arnold with unsparing severity. During all this time Arnold, safely ensconced under the wing of Gates' authority, maintained a profound silence.

Following him on the retreat of the army from Canada, we find him at Ticonderoga, actively engaged in prosecuting naval affairs. He with others urges upon Congress the building of a fleet of not less than thirty vessels for Lake defence, asking that "three hundred carpenters be immediately sent up," etc. The fleet was built and Arnold was put in command. It proved only a floating stage whereon to cut his antics before high Heaven. In retreating the army to Ticonderoga, it was thought necessary to abandon Crown Point—a measure deplored at the time, but doubtless wise, for the future policy on the Lakes was to be defensive.

One thing was certainly to be done, at all risks and all costs. Ticonderoga was to be kept. Only by holding that could the Hudson River be defended from the north ; and the possession of this river was throughout the war the supreme object of the British. A Lake fleet well-manned and judiciously maintained, would perhaps have averted the shameful surrender of the post further on. Arnold's fleet consisted of about twenty vessels, large and small, lightly built, and manned by landsmen. To attempt a battle with Carleton's fleet of heavy vessels, well-officered and manned by skillful English marines, was simply another reckless, dare-devil attempt to do the impossible.

The American fleet under Arnold "roamed the Lake without check" until October 4th, when Carleton cautiously and leisurely approached. Arnold's choice of position for battle was "warmly approved by Gates," who knew perhaps as much about a naval battle as he did about a land battle—"but one more absurd or more dangerous could not have been made."

Carleton had twice the number of vessels, with more than twice the number of guns and men. Of course the battle could end in but one way. Two-thirds of the American vessels were shattered, sunk or stranded. To save the rest from capture, Arnold ran them into a shallow creek and set them on fire, with colors flying—he the last to go ashore. Several of the smaller boats had escaped and found shelter under the guns of the fort.* The British lost three vessels.

No one denies to Arnold in this affair a magnificent energy and a death-defying courage, but to what end ?

---

* It is due to Gates to remember that Arnold acted in opposition to Gates' orders in precipitating a battle.

By the law of his nature, the irrepressible " urge " within him could manifest itself *only in destruction.* So that something was smashed, and he the smasher, with a din loud enough to reverberate with his name over the continent, it was well done. His fame rose higher than ever, and no one seemed to qualify it with the destruction of a fleet " recklessly sacrificed without public benefit." If courage is to be measured by breakage, then indeed his exceeds that of the " bull in the china shop."

Master of the Lakes, Carleton could easily have taken Ticonderoga, so inadequately was it defended and provisioned. But it was not on his programme. General Howe had failed to ascend the Hudson in time for a junction at Albany. Having secured the safety of Canada by the destruction of the fleet, Carleton retired, intending to advance to Albany in the spring.

So ends this ill-starred, ill-timed and disastrous Canadian expedition. It had involved the sacrifice of two of the most valuable officers in the service, wasted an army of ten thousand men, materially weakening Washington's force, and contributing no little to the subsequent disasters of Long Island and the Jerseys. The Congressional committee of inquiry into the causes of failure reported, " the lateness of the season," " inadequate preparation in numbers," etc, "short enlistments," "want of hard money," and " small-pox."

Congress decreed to Montgomery a monument; to honest old Wooster, a court of inquiry; to Arnold a brigadier-general's commission ; to Morgan, nothing.

VI.—1776.

"ALL'S WELL THAT ENDS WELL."

EXCEPT for the disasters in Canada, affairs had thus far gone eminently well for the Americans. They had been for more than a year in armed resistance to England. Lexington, Concord, Bunker Hill and Ticonderoga had alike witnessed to their martial spirit.

The bloodless deliverance of Boston from the British army and fleet now followed on the 17th of March. The fortification of Dorchester Heights by Washington, accomplished in a single night, "a combination concerted with faultless ability and suddenly executed, had in a few hours made their position untenable."

In the month of June, the whole country was electrified by the spirited repulse of a British fleet and army with heavy loss, from Charleston, South Carolina.

Such a series of brilliant successes had, perhaps, inspired the Americans with an extravagant estimate of their military ability. They had not sufficiently considered that England had been taken off guard by this sudden uprising of a full-grown rebellion. She was by this time, however, fairly awake, and was coming, in substantial British style, to crush it. This she hoped to do in one vigorous campaign,

Congress was so far encouraged as to sign and adopt the Declaration of Independence on the 4th of July, 1776. But in the midst of the national exultation, a courier from Washington announced to Congress that a British fleet and army were in New York harbor. "I am hopeful that we shall get some reinforcements before they are prepared to attack," he adds. The whole British force dispatched in the spring of 1776 to America, directed severally to Canada, Charleston and New York, was not less than fifty thousand of the best European fighting material that English gold could buy.

Howe, the British commander, landed on Long Island a force of upward of twenty thousand rank and file. "It was the most perfect army of its day in the world for experience, discipline, equipments and artillery ; and was supported by more than four hundred ships and transports in the bay, by ten ships of the line and twenty frigates, with other small vessels. Against this vast armament the Americans had on the Island no more than eight thousand men, most of these, volunteers or militia ; and they had not the aid of a single platoon of cavalry, nor of one ship of war." *

Here Washington felt his utmost need of the battalions he had trained and which Congress had ordered to their doom in Canada. He wrote frankly that it would be impossible to prevent the landing of the British, "but we shall attempt to harass them as much as possible, which will be all that we can do." Trumbull, of Connecticut, wrote him: "Knowing our cause righteous and trusting Heaven will support us, I do not greatly dread what they can do against us." Washington mended his theology thus: "To trust altogether in the justice of our cause without our own utmost exertions would be tempting Providence." Trumbull immediately convened his "Council of Safety" and called out nine more regiments.

It is tolerably clear that Washington fought this battle of Long Island under protest. His judgment was that the war should be carried on defensively—field actions

---

* *Bancroft*, Vol. IX, p. 85.

avoided. Others thought with him. · Jay, of New York, counselled that Long Island be laid waste, New York burned, and the army retire to the fastnesses of the Hudson.

John Adams was against "yielding the enemy an inch of ground." Congress called for the battle, and they got it. "It was the fixed purpose of Washington to obey implicitly the orders of Congress."

Just then, General Greene fell violently ill of a "raging fever," and the loss of his services was the more serious because the works he commanded were built under his eye and he best knew the environs. To Sullivan his place was assigned ; but he and Putnam blundered fearfully. The battle, at the last, proved a massacre of our brave Marylanders, who that day "won their spurs." More than half the loss fell upon Stirling's command of Maryland and Delaware troops—one-fourth on the Maryland regiment alone. A witness of their heroic but vain resistance, Washington, wrung his hands, exclaiming, "My God ! what brave men I must this day lose."

The day done, and the battle lost, Washington won immortal fame by one of the most masterly retreats ever recorded, saving his army with all its equipments in the face of an overwhelming British force. General Glover, with his brigade of mariners of Marblehead, rendered here invaluable service. But they were dark days in the American camp. The burden upon the commander-in-chief was almost beyond the limit of human endurance. "Among his major-generals there was not one on whom he could fully rely." The army knew it ; distrust and dejection prevailed ; Washington alone inspired confidence.

Congress still demanded of him impossibilities. He was expected to hold New York : but, seeing that such an attempt would be fatal to the cause, he argued the matter so clearly that they yielded in time. The British took the city, and Washington retired to White Plains, fighting, retreating, maneuvering, and so harassing, delaying, and wearing out the enemy. His policy was fruitful of good results. It was now far into September. Howe had been so long delayed that he was compelled to abandon his plan of ascending the Hudson to join Carleton,—by far the most important part of the campaign as ordered by the British ministry,—and he had frankly admitted in his despatches to England the necessity of another campaign.

Thus had Washington below, neutralized the destruction of Arnold's Lake fleet above, and enabled Gates to dispatch his pompous message to Congress, "of the retreat of Lieutenant-General Sir Guy Carleton, with his fleet and army, from Crown Point."

But still darker days were at hand. Greene having obtained the coveted Major-General's commission, for which he had stipulated, resolved to maintain his new honors at some cost. He questioned and disregarded Washington's directions;—positive orders Washington could not issue, because the Congressional Board of War were to give the final word. Greene took the liberty to differ with Washington, corresponded with the Board, expressing his opinion that Howe could not take Fort Washington, of which he had command. But within a week it was surrendered to the British, with valuable artillery and arms and twenty-six hundred prisoners, of whom one-half were well-trained soldiers. Greene never acknowledged his "errors of judgment," nor did he mend his ways; for three days after, having failed to carry out Washington's timely and positive order to remove the garrison and stores from Fort Lee, five thousand British and Hessians surprised him there. "Aroused from his bed by the report of a countryman, Greene ordered his troops under arms and took to flight, with more than two thousand men, leaving blankets and baggage, provisions, four hundred tents standing, and all his cannon, except two twelve pounders. With his utmost speed, he barely escaped being cut off. Washington, by a rapid march to his rescue, covered the retreat so that only a few stragglers were taken."—*Bancroft*, Vol. IX, p. 196.*

Nothing remained but a retreat into New Jersey and the defence of Philadelphia, now the coveted object of British ambition.

Washington's position was inexpressibly trying at this juncture. Not only was he hampered by the final word of the Congressional Board of War, but "the power to overrule the majority of his generals had not been explicitly conferred." He was expected to consult with and be outvoted by men who could do little but hinder his military operations.

John Adams, Chairman of the Board of War, "while he cultivated confidential relations with Lee and Gates, never extended the same cordial frankness to Washington, never comprehended his superior capacity for war, and never weighed his difficulties with generous consideration. Moreover, Congress was always ready to assume the conduct of the campaign and to issue impracticable resolutions. To Gates it intrusted a limited power of filling up vacancies as they occurred in his army; but it refused the same to Washington, saying, "future generals may make bad use of it." Notwithstanding the warning and entreaties of Washington after the battle of Long Island, John Adams, great man and great patriot as he was, with igno-

---

* With incredible magnanimity, Washington covered also Greene's military reputation. He never upbraided his officers. The merited "I told you so," never escaped him; though, Heaven knows, it must oftentimes have been in his thoughts. The odium of Forts Lee and Washington fell upon him, and he took it. It belonged fairly to Congress and General Greene, who from this time trusted himself less, and Washington more.

rant boldness maintained and announced, "the British force is so divided, they will do no great matter more this fall." Less than three weeks afterwards, came the fall of forts Lee and Washington.*

Little knew or thought the commander-in-chief, at this moment, that any one coveted his office. "Such is my situation," said he privately, "that if I were to wish the bitterest curse to an enemy on this side of the grave, I should put him in my stead, with my feelings"; yet, at this very time, both Gates and Lee, taking advantage of the recent disasters, were working assiduously upon Congress, and among the officers, to accomplish his removal. Gates, while in command at Ticonderoga, had thus early showed this spirit of rivalry, declining to make his reports to the commander-in-chief, and purposely communicating with Congress, claiming that he and his council of officers "were in nothing inferior to that of the commander-in-chief."

Congress had summoned Lee, as far back as August, from the South (where he was doing mad work), to join Washington, as, in event of accident, Lee would be his successor. He was now in command on the east side of the Hudson River. Some hint of the maneuvres of these two was brought to Washington's notice, yet, "neither the neglect, distrust, and interference of Congress, nor the want of faithful, able, or even competent subordinates, nor the melting away of his army by short enlistment, could make him waver in his purpose of perseverance to the end. No provocation could force from his pen one word of personal petulance, or even the momentary expression of a wish to resign." This lofty spirit

* Perilous as was the outlook, at this very time Adams asked and obtained leave of absence from Congress, and at his home in Massachusetts received the news of the disasters in New Jersey and the removal of Congress to Baltimore.

lived in a serene height to which none of these noisy little men could climb. He was neither elated nor despondent with the ebb and flow of the tide of battle, as were they.

He served a cause to which he had given all faith : who serves humanity cannot fail. He worked as " in his great Taskmaster's eye," and thus could afford to be "patient towards all men."

Things certainly looked desperate ; the British had followed Washington into New Jersey in force. As he crossed the Raritan, breaking down a part of the bridge, the Americans cannonaded Cornwallis' army across the river. One of the batteries was served by a youth named Alexander Hamilton, who was soon to become one of Washington's noblest coadjutors. The American force was scarcely three thousand. *Howe was held back by invisible hands from overwhelming the little band of heroes.* Washington, in " anguish even to tears " at the desolation of the people of New Jersey under their iron war-hoof, addressed Lee once more : " I request, and I entreat you, and this too by the advice of all the general officers with me, to march and join me with your whole force, with all possible expedition. Do come on—your arrival without delay may be the means of preserving a city."

Lee had been summoned a dozen times before to join him, but nothing was further from his intentions. Couriers and letters reached him every day, sometimes two a day, telling of the extremity of the situation ; yet he detained by far the most efficient regiments on the Hudson and declined to move. He felt himself sufficiently strong to disregard by evading the orders of Congress, writing to the Governor of Massachusetts, "Affairs appear in so important a crisis, that I think even the resolves of Congress must no longer weigh nicely with us."

The reputation of Lee was at its zenith at this time. In Congress and the New England States "his name was the mythical symbol of ability, decision, knowledge of war and success." At the disaster of Fort Washington, he spread the rumor that he had "counselled the general to draw off the garrison, and he had failed to follow it." To a member of Congress he wrote, "Your apathy makes me mad. Had I the powers, I could do you much good. *Might I but dictate for one week.* Did none of the Congress ever read the Roman history?"

At last, feeling himself compelled by authority of Congress to cross the Hudson into New Jersey, he lingered still on its western bank, determined not to join forces with Washington, but to impress into his own command all reinforcements that were now being hurried forward. In reply to Washington's mild reproof for his tardiness, he wrote only, "I shall explain my difficulties when we both have leisure." On the 4th of December, seven regiments that Schuyler had hurried onward arrived, and Lee wrote to Washington, "I shall put myself at their head to-morrow." On the 8th of December, while the commander-in-chief was painfully retreating before the army of Howe and Cornwallis with his handful of half-starved and half-clad soldiers, weak and worn with fatigue and anxiety, Lee had the audacity to announce to Congress that he had no intention to join forces with Washington, saying, "I am assured he is very strong." The courier of Washington was praying for his assistance while he penned the lie. His message to the general was, that he would aid him in so far "that he would hang on the enemy's rear and annoy them," adding that his division "amounted to four thousand noble-spirited men."

"Whom the gods would destroy they first make mad." Four days after, Lee with a small guard stopped for the night at White's tavern near Baskinridge, eight miles from his main army. The enemy were at the safe distance of eighteen miles. "The next morning he lay in bed till eight o'clock. On rising, he wasted two hours with Wilkinson, a messenger from Gates, in boasting of his own prowess and cavilling at everything done by others. It was ten o'clock before he sat down to breakfast, after which he took time in a letter to Gates to indulge his spleen towards the 'chief' in this wise:

"My dear Gates—

"The ingenious maneuvre of Fort Washington has unhinged the goodly fabric we had been building. There never was so damned a stroke. Entre nous, a certain great man is most damnably deficient. He has thrown me into a situation where I have my choice of difficulties: if I stay in this province I risk myself and my army; if I do not stay, the province is lost forever. Tories are in my front, rear, and on my flanks. In short, unless something which I do not expect turns up, we are lost. * * * * Adieu, my dear friend. God bless you.

"Charles Lee."

The paper which he signed was not yet folded when Wilkinson, at the window, cried out, " Here are the British cavalry." Something he did not expect turned up, and the cause was saved.

A young British officer with a scouting party of thirty dragoons scouring the vicinity, learned of Lee's lodgings, and made a sudden descent upon the tavern. The officer called for an immediate surrender, or the house would be fired. " Within two minutes, he who had made it his habitual boast that he would never be taken alive, sneaked out unarmed, bareheaded, in slippers and blanket-coat, his collar open, pale with fear, with the abject manner of a coward, and entreated the dragoons to spare his life. They seized him just as he was, and set him on Wilkinson's horse, which stood saddled at the door, and in four minutes from the time of their appearance they began their retreat."*

* *Bancroft*, Vol. IX, pages 209, 210.

The British declined to regard him as a prisoner, refused to exchange him, and labelled him "deserter," whereupon he proposed to desert back into the British army, and offered a plan for a British attack upon the Jerseys and capture of Philadelphia. Washington, with his illimitable magnanimity, sought to liberate him, and finally effected it by giving several British officers in exchange. It was a bad investment. He appears again at Monmouth, where his treason is unmistakably uncovered; he is court-martialed and disappears from history. It is incredible that such a combination of qualities could have become the idol of the hour with so large and respectable a faction, and that a brave, honest, puritan patriot like John Adams could have bestowed upon him a confidence which he withheld from Washington.

It would be difficult to estimate the gain to the American cause by the capture of Lee. His forces now joined Washington, who, by his masterly maneuvres, had held the whole British army at bay, slowly retreating through New Jersey for ninety miles, delaying and harassing the foe, covering as he could the terrified inhabitants, gaining time, and trusting for the "further protection of midwinter and impassable roads." Crossing the Delaware, he secured every boat for seventy miles. Gates had now joined him with five hundred New England men, led by the valiant Stark, who with Stirling, Mercer, Sullivan, Greene, Glover, Knox, Munroe and Alexander Hamilton, rendered valuable service in executing that superb stroke, the surprise of Trenton and the capture of the Hessian army. The plan included the co-operation of three detachments, crossing at different points. The one at Bristol, Washington earnestly solicited Gates to lead, "using the language of entreaty."

His own detachment began its march at three o'clock in the afternoon of Christmas day, and reached McConkey's Ferry in the winter twilight; a high wind dashed sleet and hail into their faces; the swift current swept along huge blocks and masses of ice. "At the water's edge Washington asked, 'Who will lead us on?' Glover's mariners of Marblehead, the same that had ferried Washington's army from Long Island to New York after the defeat, stepped forward to man the boats. Just then a messenger came, announcing that no help could be expected from the troops at Bristol. Soon after, Wilkinson arrived and handed a letter to Washington from General Gates. 'From General Gates?' said Washington; 'Where is he?' 'On his way to Congress,' said Wilkinson." Congress had retreated to Baltimore.

The work was accomplished without him. Brave work, fighting the elements all through that wild, stormful winter night, and snatching the victory in the gray dawn that was to turn a nation's despair into hope, and gild the gloom of night with the radiance of a new day. The enemy so interpreted it. "All our hopes," said Lord Germain, "were blasted by the unhappy affair at Trenton." Whatever might be the estimate which Congress put upon Washington's military genius, certain it is that Howe and Cornwallis had taken its true porportions. Not alone these—all Europe was watching for the outcome of this unequal wrestle. The greatest captain of the age, old Frederick the Great, recognized his distinguished ability, and from the most illustrious persons came praises and congratulations to the defenders of human liberty in the New World.

The tide of battle turned; from being the pursuers, the British now became the pursued—a panic seized them—they retreated and Washington followed, haunting the hills of New Jersey with his phantom army, hovering around homesteads and villages to protect the terrified women and children from the brutal soldiery; sweeping down upon the enemy's foraging parties like fitful winter gusts, capturing, dispersing, or compelling them to keep

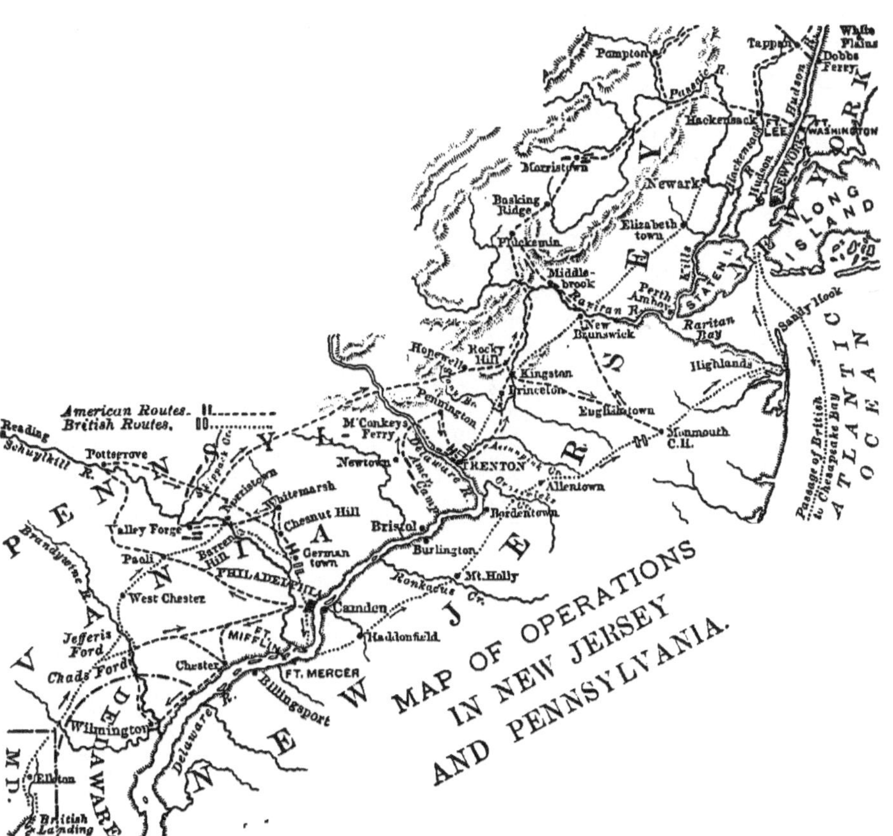

American Routes.
British Routes.
MAP OF OPERATIONS IN NEW JERSEY AND PENNSYLVANIA.
NEW YORK
LONG ISLAND
NEW JERSEY
PENNSYLVANIA
DELAWARE
MD.
ATLANTIC OCEAN
White Plains
Tappan
Dobbs Ferry
Pompton
Passaic R.
Hackensack
FT. LEE
FT. WASHINGTON
Hudson
Morristown
Newark
Basking Ridge
Elizabeth town
Pluckemin
Staten I.
Perth Amboy
Middlebrook
Raritan R.
Raritan Bay
New Brunswick
Sandy Hook
Honeybrook
Rocky Hill
Kingston
Highlands
Princeton
Englishtown
Penmington
Monmouth C.H.
M'Conkeys Ferry
Delaware R.
TRENTON
Reading
Schuylkill
Allentown
Pottsgrove
Newtown
Assunpink Cr.
Crosswicks Cr.
Shippack Cr.
Morristown
Bordentown
Whitemarsh
Chesnut Hill
Bristol
Valley Forge
Barren Hill
German town
Burlington
Paoli
PHILADELPHIA
Rancocus Cr.
Mt. Holly
West Chester
Camden
Jefferis Ford
FT. MIFFLIN
Haddonfield
Chads Ford
Chester
FT. MERCER
Brandywine R.
Billingsport
Wilmington
Delaware R.
Elkton
British Landing
Passage of British to Chesapeake Bay

within their lines; appearing where least expected, and disappearing when most wanted to remain. If assailed, leading his hungry, half-naked heroes up into some rocky fastness for safety; if followed there, creeping stealthily away like the mountain mists, to reappear in some unexpected quarter. In vain did Howe manœuvre to bring him to battle; yet with an army of twenty thousand strong, while Washington had never more than three thousand, the British general dared not march again towards Philadelphia.

The campaign of 1776 was virtually over, and the plans of the British ministry, sustained as they had been by overwhelming forces, had failed everywhere; defeat was at the last crowned with victory, and victory slunk away, dragging defeat at its heels. Carleton had not descended the Hudson, because Howe could not ascend it. Cornwallis had, indeed, overrun New Jersey and threatened Philadelphia, but was now driven back to the sea. The disastrous repulse from Charleston harbor was part of the same campaign—three simultaneous blows, which it was thought must prove mortal to the young Republic.

The possession of New York and its harbor, alone recompensed their gigantic efforts.

VII.—1776, 1777.

THE RIFLE REGIMENT.

ON the night of September 11th, 1776, five transports
sailed into New York harbor, bringing from Canada
the paroled prisoners released by the clemency of Carleton.
It was midnight, and the light of a full moon silvered the
pleasant shores and green hill slopes. From the bow of
one of the boats, as she touched the land, sprung a stal-
wart form, and casting himself down with his face to the
earth, as if to embrace it, he cried aloud, "O, my country"! It was Morgan. He reported without delay to the
commander-in-chief at the American head-quarters. He
was warmly received. He assured Washington of his determination to return to the service, as soon as he could
be released from his parole, and then he went homeward
to Abigail and the children.

Washington promptly transmitted to Congress his views
and wishes concerning Morgan, in the following letter :

"HARLEM HEIGHTS, September 20, 1776.

"SIR :—I would beg leave to recommend to the particular notice of Congress Captain Daniel Morgan, just returned among the prisoners from Canada. His conduct
as an officer, on the expedition with General Arnold last
fall, his intrepid behavior in the assault upon Quebec,
when the brave Montgomery fell, the inflexible attachment
he professed to our cause during his imprisonment, and
which he perseveres in,—all, in my opinion, entitle him to
the favor of Congress, and lead me to believe that in his

promotion the States will gain a good and valuable officer,
* * * *

> "I am, sir,
>> "Your very humble servant,
>>> "GEO. WASHINGTON."

In November, Congress acted upon Washington's suggestion and gave him a colonel's commission. About the beginning of the year he was exchanged and directed to recruit for his regiment. In February, he received an urgent summons to report with all possible dispatch to the main army,—and shortly afterwards the following characteristic letter from Patrick Henry, the Governor of Virginia, reached him:

> "WILLIAMSBURGH, March 15, 1777.

> "SIR :—I must once more address you on the subject of marching your regiment to join General Washington. There is a more pushing necessity for your aid than you are acquainted with, or than I can with propriety explain in detail. You will, therefore, surmount every obstacle, and lose not a moment, lest America receive a wound that may prove fatal.
>> "I am, sir, etc.,
>>> "PATRICK HENRY.
> "COLONEL MORGAN."

Morgan pushed on at once with what force he had collected, and by the end of March reached headquarters at Morristown. Washington, in the campaign of the previous year, had sorely suffered from the lack of a corps of sharpshooters—men of the woods and the rifle — under a leader of penetration and sagacity, upon whose prompt and correct intelligence of the enemy's movements might often turn the tide of battle. He detailed a force of five hundred picked men from his various regiments, and put

Morgan in command. As a proof of Morgan's fine discernment of character, his eight captains, appointed by himself, all rendered valuable service, and notwithstanding the severe tests to which they were subsequently subjected, not one was found wanting.

The service upon which Morgan now entered was both delicate and dangerous, involving abundant labor and anxiety, coolness or rashness, according to the emergency; prudence, judgment, and unceasing vigilance. He was the watcher, not alone for Washington's camp at Middlebrook, but also of Howe's every movement, — of which he was to give immediate intelligence to the main army, and, with his rangers, to harass, annoy and prey upon the enemy's outposts. He proved himself a " master workman " in every position in which he was placed.

Through Howe's native indolence, his sluggish Guelph blood, or through want of earnestness in the cause (so charged the home ministry), he had lost the two best fighting months—April and May. He had demanded of the ministry fifteen thousand additional troops, and the campaign of 1777 contemplated precisely what they had failed to accomplish in 1776—the capture of the Hudson River and Philadelphia.

Carleton's humanity had brought him into disgrace at home. He had been superseded by Burgoyne, who was now approaching Ticonderoga, with the expectation of Howe's co-operation from below. But Howe could not venture to ascend the Hudson, without first disposing of Washington's army. It would leave New York in peril and expose himself to be penned among the highlands of the river. He had had his tilt with Washington in its fastnesses the year before, and he had no mind to repeat the experiment. He preferred the capture of the capital of the young Republic, and preferred also to approach it by the easy lowlands of New Jersey. But here, too, he must first dispose of Washington's army before he could venture to put the Delaware behind him, and so cut off his retreat to his ships in case of disaster.

Washington had not eight thousand troops in his entire command; but he adroitly disposed them to simulate a much larger number. On the twelfth of June, Howe having received horses, tents, stores, and reinforcements, put his army of British, Hessians and Anspachers, to the number of seventeen thousand, in motion. Boats and pontoons for crossing the Delaware were collected at Brunswick. He hoped to draw Washington from his fortified camp into a field fight. He marched and maneuvred and countermarched; Washington kept six thousand intrenched in camp; with the rest, as an army of observation, he followed and watched. For himself he was night and day in the saddle, and every man slept upon his arms. Howe threw up fortifications near the American camp, and challenged attack. It was not accepted.

While the armies thus confronted, Congress adopted the present national flag of thirteen stripes, with stars, on a field of blue. They also fretted and chafed at the inactivity of the army. While Washington, with matchless prudence, was saving the cause, when to have crossed the river with his small and ill-provided force was just what Howe desired, one of his general officers wrote, " We must fight or lose our honor "; and Samuel Adams said, " I am not over-well pleased with what is called the Fabian war in America." Washington heard it, but he heeded it not; and, with undisturbed self-possession, continued to hold in check and baffle an enemy of more than twice his numbers. Howe marched again to Brunswick, feigning still an intention to cross New Jersey, closely observed by Washington. Baffled and out-maneuvred, on the twentieth, to the joy and relief of the whole State, the entire British force was in retreat for Amboy. On this retreat Morgan greatly distinguished himself. Washington had planned a joint attack by Sullivan, Maxwell and Greene, between Brunswick and Amboy. Sullivan arrived too late ; Maxwell did not receive the order sent him ; Greene was on hand, but placed his battery of heavy guns at a point too distant to be effective. But at Piscataway, Morgan and his riflemen attacked the column of Cornwallis so fiercely and persistently that Howe was forced to order up heavy artillery, before he could rid his flanks of their unerring rifle-balls and proceed upon his retreat.

The American officers were generally jubilant, declaring that the British were panic-struck. Washington did not share in this opinion, but so far yielded to their wishes as to come down from the heights with his main army. Stirling with one division pushed ahead. Howe immediately conceived the idea of getting into their rear. Hastily recalling his German battalions which had crossed to Staten Island, he made a swift march in two columns, by different routes. On the night of the twenty-sixth, Cornwallis overtook Stirling, who fired once and fled, leaving three pieces of his artillery,—brass three-pounders, but recently arrived from France. The Americans lost more than a hundred killed and prisoners ; the British less. The other column under Howe, who had aimed for Washington's division to which Morgan was attached, accomplished nothing ; they had retired promptly to the heights of Middlebrook.

The British again turned towards Amboy. On this retreat also Morgan overtook Cornwallis' division, and followed it as far as Rahway, keeping up a continual skirmish upon his flanks and rear, killing and wounding a large number. Never once had he or his party suffered a surprise, or failed to accomplish what they were expected to do.

Washington, in his reports to Congress, made honorable

mention of them, specially noting that "they constantly advanced upon an enemy far superior to them in numbers and well secured." Wayne also shared this honorable mention.

On the 30th of June, Howe evacuated New Jersey, never again, as it proved, to put foot upon its soil.

VIII.—1777.

FALL OF TICONDEROGA.

PHILADELPHIA once more breathed freely, and ventured to observe the first anniversary of independence with demonstrations rather more jubilant than if its citizens had known the calamity that was on that day impending over the northern army. A week after, the tidings fell like a sound of doom over the land. On the 5th of July fell Ticonderoga, and the northern gates of the Republic were in the hands of Burgoyne.

Washington dared not move until he could penetrate Howe's plans of summer campaign. It would be either to ascend the river and co-operate with Burgoyne, or, perhaps, to make another attack on Philadelphia. In the latter case, he might march across New Jersey as before, or embark on the fleet of Admiral Howe and by sea ascend the Delaware, or enter the Chesapeake Bay, disembark at its head, and approach the city by land. It was barely possible that he might contemplate an expedition still further; this last was not probable at so advanced a season.

Fortunately for the American cause, Howe could not rid himself of the ambition or delusion that the capture of Philadelphia was of the highest military importance. Besides, he was irritated at being out-generaled in New Jersey; and stirred with envy at the splendid success of Burgoyne, he resolved to let him for the present carve his own fortunes on the Hudson. He embarked his army and stood out to sea.

Washington ordered a strict watch along the coast.

After some days, the British fleet was seen at the mouth of the Delaware. Still Washington did not move—it might be only a maneuvre. The fleet disappeared for several days ; Washington still thought Howe would return and go up the Hudson. The commander-in-chief could not rid himself of this opinion, because it would have been Howe's highest wisdom to do so. A week later, the fleet sailed into Chesapeake Bay, and, no longer in doubt, Washington put his army in motion, and ordered the militia of Pennsylvania, Delaware, Maryland and Virginia to join him.

The conduct of the northern campaign was equally Washington's care at this time with that of his own. Discord and disorder reigned there alike, to the discomfiture of patriots and the peril of the cause. The intrigues of Gates had prevailed with Congress, and they had appointed him to supersede Schuyler in command of the northern department. Gates' ambition was pricked by his family influence. "As your son and heir," wrote his only child, "I entreat you not to tarnish the honor of your family." His uneasy and ambitious wife adds : "If you give up one iota, and condescend to be adjutant-general, I may forgive, but will never forget it."

The old patriot, Schuyler, was willing to be displaced by a man of superior ability, but not by this vain and hungry place-seeker, whom he rightly estimated.

Schuyler repaired to Congress, and in person appealed from this decision of the Board of War. After protracted debate, he was reinstated just in time to share the odium with St. Clair of the fall of Ticonderoga, and most auspiciously for Gates, who thus escaped all responsibility for the disaster. During his temporary command at the north, Gates, whose treachery against the commander-in-chief was maturing, used every effort to divert reinforcements from Washington's army to his own. Writing to Hancock, he says : "I foresee the worst of consequences from too great a proportion of the main army being drawn into the Jerseys. Request Congress, in my name, to order two troops of horse to Albany." It was done.

Washington thought that Gates should make his requisitions directly to him, or at least furnish him a duplicate; but Gates insisted upon dealing immediately with Congress, on the plea that it required less writing. He sneeringly remarked to a member of Congress, "I am not infected with a *cacoethis scribendi:* one serviceable action without doors is worth all that has been wrote since the beginning of the war." In a letter to Lovell, a New England member of Congress, he rehearses his complaints against "George Washington," urging that Congress should intervene because "Generals were like parsons, all for christening their own child first." *

In these puerile innuendoes against a spirit too lofty to entertain such sentiments, Gates lays bare his own heart, with its envious self-seeking, without an element of patriotism, or a scruple for the consequences to the cause.

Washington did not share the panic with regard to the advance of Burgoyne into the wilderness of upper New York; he rather hailed it. His prophetic forecast anticipated the disastrous termination of the invasion. Burgoyne's army was less than eight thousand. He wrote encouragingly to Schuyler, bidding him "never despair"; explaining that Burgoyne must necessarily leave adequate garrisons at every post in his rear, which would be continually menaced by the militia of New York and Vermont: that the immense labor of cutting new roads and dragging artillery and supplies through such a wilderness, would exhaust and delay their movements; that the harvests were now gathered, and the brave yeomanry of New York and New England would flock to reinforce his army, eager to avenge the shocking barbarities of Burgoyne's Indian allies. Yet at this time, "perplexed in the ex-

* *Bancroft*, Vol. IX.

treme " by Howe's maneuvres,—with the whole coast from New York to Maryland threatened ; entreaties for reinforcements and supplies continued to pour in upon him from Schuyler, from the Council of New York, from Jay and Gouverneur Morris. Schuyler was terrified out of all reason ; Washington sent Arnold the fearless, and Lincoln, who was popular with the Eastern militia. He sent also, to his own loss and discomfiture, Glover of Massachusetts, with his fine brigade of Continentals ; and wrote to the Governors of the Eastern States urging them to hasten on their militia. Things went as Washington had predicted. Burgoyne's army, supplied from Canada, began to suffer hunger. They essayed to seize the American stores at Bennington, but Stark repulsed them and won there a splendid victory and enduring fame. Another expedition for a similar purpose, in the Mohawk Valley, was repulsed near Fort Stanwix by the brave yeomanry of that valley under Herkimer, who fell in the conflict.

These were irretrievably heavy blows for the army of Burgoyne. Just after these important victories, Congress again superseded Schuyler by the appointment of Gates. "Most auspiciously for Gates," says Irving, "at this propitious moment, when everything was ready for the sickle to be put into the harvest, General Gates arrived in camp and relieved Schuyler of his command, so long the object of his aspirations, if not intrigues." Gates continued the demand for reinforcements, and Congress, against Washington's advice, who warned them that New Jersey and Pennsylvania troops were needed at home to repel Howe, granted him full powers to call on those States.

Last and heaviest loss of all to the commander-in-chief, Congress directed him to dispatch Morgan and his picked brigade, selected from his best regiments, to assist Gates against the Indians.

"Washington obeyed so promptly that the order may seem to have been his own."

"*August* 16, 1777.

"*Sir:*—After you receive this, you will march as soon as possible with the corps under your command to Peekskill, where vessels will be provided to take you to Albany. The approach of the enemy has made further reinforcements necessary, and I know of no corps so likely to check their progress in proportion to its number as that under your command.

"I have great dependence on you, your officers and your men, and I am persuaded you will do honor to yourselves and essential service to your country, etc., etc.

"I am your obedient servant,

"GEORGE WASHINGTON."

"COLONEL MORGAN."

To General Gates, Washington wrote : "I have dispatched Colonel Morgan with his riflemen to your assistance, and expect they will be with you in eight or ten days from this date. This corps I have great dependence on, and have no doubt but they will be exceedingly useful to you ; as a check given to the savages and keeping them within bounds, will prevent General Burgoyne from getting intelligence as formerly," etc., etc.

To General Putnam he wrote : "The people of the Northern army seem so intimidated by the Indians that I have determined to send up Colonel Morgan's corps. You will please have sloops ready at Peekskill to transport them, and provisions laid in, that they may not wait a moment."

To Governor Clinton : "I am forwarding as fast as possible Colonel Morgan's corps of riflemen, amounting to about five hundred. These are all chosen men, selected from the army at large, well acquainted with the rifle and with that mode of fighting which is necessary to make them a good counterpoise to the savages. *I expect the most eminent services from them*, and I shall be mistaken if their presence does not go far towards producing a general desertion among the savages."

General Gates, in reply to Washington, writes: "I cannot sufficiently thank your excellency for sending Colonel Morgan's corps to this army; they will be of the greatest service to it, for, until the late successes this way [Bennington and Fort Stanwix], the army, I am told, were quite panic-struck by the Indians and their Tory and Canadian assassins in Indian dresses." * * * *

At Albany Morgan found a letter from Gates, expressing his great satisfaction at the prospect of receiving him at headquarters. On arriving, his corps was designated as the advance of the army, and he was to receive orders only from General Gates.

These excerpts sufficiently show how rapidly Morgan had risen in the estimation of the officers of the army. The sequel proves that he was equally as good a counterpoise to the best and bravest of Burgoyne's British and Hessian officers, as to his savage allies.

IX.—1777.

BATTLE OF BRANDYWINE.

BUT how fared Washington, without the stout hearts and strong hands he had sent to Gates? Before him was another field fight with overwhelming odds, to save the city of Philadelphia. The War Boards, one would think, might by this time have digested the error of Long Island and New York. But the same spirit still adventured to direct military affairs. John Adams wrote:

"We shall rake and scrape enough to do Howe's business; the continental army under Washington is more numerous by several thousands than Howe's whole force; the enemy give out that they are eighteen thousand strong, but we know better, and that they have not ten thousand. Washington is very prudent; I should put more to risk were I in his shoes, but perhaps he is right. Gansevoort [at Stanwix] has proved that it is possible to hold a post, and Stark [at Bennington], that it is practicable even to attack lines and posts with militia. I wish the continental army would prove that anything can be done. I am weary with so much insipidity; I am sick of Fabian systems. My toast is, a short and violent war." *

Now according to returns in the British Department of States, Howe's army numbered nineteen thousand five hundred effective men, besides officers. Both officers and men were soldiers by profession, selected from the best of the British empire, and the best of the warlike race of Hesse, perfectly equipped. Washington's effective force,

* Bancroft, Vol. IX.

including militia and volunteers, was less than twelve thousand.

"Congress never exacted more from Washington, and never gave him less support ; but he indulged in no complaint, bearing himself with meekness and dignity, never forgetting the obedience and respect that were due to Congress as his civil superior. Thus he tired out evil tongues and adverse fortune, and saved his country by courage and constancy. He saw that posterity was his own." *

But such were the friends he had at his back, while his face was turned so bravely to their foes.

He never showed himself more fertile in resources than in this campaign ; but it would have required superhuman genius to overcome the blundering of his general officers—Sullivan at the fords of the Brandywine, and Greene at Germantown.   O for one hour of Morgan and his riflemen ! †

Immediately after the battle of Brandywine, Washington sent the following to Gates :

"CAMP NEAR POTTSGROVE, September 24th, 1777.

"*Sir :*—This army has not been able to oppose General Howe with the success that I wished, and needs a reinforcement.   I therefore request that, if you have been so fortunate as to oblige General Burgoyne to retreat to Ticonderoga, or if you have not, and circumstances will admit, that you will order Colonel Morgan to join me .

---

* *Bancroft,* Vol. IX.

† Colonel Heth writes to Morgan under date of September 30th : "You have been greatly wished for, since the enemy's landing at the head of Elk river."   Colonel Febriger shortly after writes : "It is generally believed that some of the severest reverses we have lately experienced, might have been obviated, could we have had the co-operation of yourself and your gallant corps."—*Graham's Life of Morgan.* p. 178.

again with his corps. I sent him up when I thought you materially wanted him, and if his services can be dispensed with now, you will direct him to return immediately. You will perceive I do not mention this by way of command, but leave you to determine upon it according to your situation, etc., etc.

"Your obedient servant,

"GEO. WASHINGTON."

"Major General GATES."

The delicate entreaty of this letter, would have been sufficient for any man, not utterly wanting in every sentiment of generosity and justice. He replied immediately, but nothing was further from his intentions than to comply with the request.

"CAMP BEHMUS HEIGHT, October 5th, 1777.

"*Sir :*—Since the action of the 19th the enemy have kept the ground they occupied the morning of that day, and fortified their camp. The advanced sentries of my picket are posted within shot of, and opposite the enemy's; neither side have given ground an inch.

"In this situation, your Excellency would not wish me *to part with the corps, the army of General Burgoyne is most afraid of.* In a fortnight at furthest I have the prospect of being able to reinforce your Excellency in a more considerable manner than by a single regiment, etc., etc., etc.

"I have the honor to be, etc.

"HORATIO GATES."

"His Excellency General WASHINGTON."

John Adams criticised the defeat at Brandywine severely, and blamed Washington for crossing the Schuylkill. "It is a very injudicious maneuvre : if he had sent one brigade of his regular troops to have headed the militia, he might have cut to pieces Howe's army in attempting to cross any of the fords. Howe will not attempt it. He will wait for his fleet in the Delaware. O ! Heaven grant us one great soul. One leading mind, would extricate the best cause from that ruin which seems to await it."— Nevertheless, Howe crossed the Schuylkill that day and spoiled the prophecy. The British Generals reached far different conclusions concerning Washington's maneuvres. The spirited attack at Germantown, October 4th, so soon after Brandywine, proved the latter rather a check than a defeat, and went far to discourage the British, and reassure the friends of America abroad. Washington lost nothing of his military prestige with them. Especially the retreat after Germantown, was pronounced "admirably conducted, as the attack had been well planned."

In both these actions, the foreign officers showed great gallantry and did excellent service ; Armand, Fleury, Pulaski, and above all La Fayette.

These noble spirits had been drawn from the ends of the earth, by the personal magnetism of Washington, and the beauty of the cause to which he had given himself. The French officers especially found themselves inspired with an admiration, at once enthusiastic and profound,—alike honorable to themselves and the commander-in-chief.

As in the campaign of 1776, Washington, by his movements below, had prevented the execution of Carleton's programme at the North, so again in 1777, after sending to Gates so many of his best troops and officers, he yet had managed to detain Howe, with an army nearly twice his own, thirty days in a march of fifty-four miles, and thus prevented his co-operation with Burgoyne.

This co-operation was included in the orders of the ministry, and Howe fully calculated to take Philadelphia in time to dispatch an adequate force to Burgoyne's assistance, after he should have reached Albany. But the second battle of Stillwater was fought three days after Germantown, and on the 18th October came swift heralds into the camp bringing news of the surrender of Burgoyne.

Washington received it as if it had been his own victory, with devout thankfulness; as "a signal stroke of Providence." "All will be well," he said, "in His own good time." Somewhere evidently, this great soul had had a Jacob's wrestle with God's angel, and they had come to an understanding.

The news of the surrender soon passed from the American into the British camp, and General Howe learned with excessive vexation the reverses of British arms at the North. He was also far from satisfied with his own position. He found that the possession of Philadelphia in no way altered the status. There was no intimidation, no panic, no yielding of purpose with the patriots. The position was likewise one of anxiety and peril.

The outcome could only be a question of "how long shall we stay here, and by what way leave?"

The British addressed themselves at once to reduce the defences of the Delaware River, as Howe foresaw that he must depend mainly upon the fleet for supplies.

In a fit of impatience he ordered the assault upon Red Bank; one of the most obstinate of the American fortifications. It was repulsed with frightful loss.

On receiving the intelligence of this victory at Red Bank, John Adams exclaimed: "Thank God! the glory is not immediately due to the commander-in-chief, or idolatry and adulation would have been so excessive as to endanger our liberties."

Not long after, Howe asked the king's leave to resign, at the same time assuring the ministry that still another campaign would be necessary for the reduction of America with larger reinforcements than they had yet dispatched.

The confidence that Congress withheld from Washington was fully given to Gates. His promises to reinforce the commander-in-chief after the surrender of Burgoyne remained purposely unfulfilled. Weeks passed, and not a soldier had been sent southward. Washington at last "dispatched Alexander Hamilton with authority to demand them." In his letter of instructions to Hamilton, Washington writes, "If you meet Colonel Morgan and his corps on their way down, let them know how essential their services are to us, and desire the Colonel to hasten his march as much as is consistent with the health of his men, after their late fatigues."* But Gates still continued to evade compliance, making an idle and insincere pretext of attack upon Ticonderoga, for he knew the British had abandoned it. He sent no report of the surrender to Washington—a marked disrespect—but to Congress :

"With an army in health, vigor, and spirits, Major-General Gates now waits the commands of the honorable Congress."

Instead of rebuking his insubordination in the matter of sending the troops to Washington, Congress forbade Washington to detach more than twenty-five hundred men, including the corps of Morgan, without first consulting Gates and Clinton. Subsequently it amended the order directing that he should not detach any troops except after such consultation, and "John and Samuel Adams, and Gerry of Massachusetts, and Marchant of Rhode Island voted for that restriction."

It was the 18th of November before Morgan with his corps arrived at Whitemarsh, Washington's headquarters, having been basely held back more than five weeks after Burgoyne's capitulation had become a certainty.

* *Graham's Life of Morgan*, p. 177.

X.—1777.

ARNOLD BEFORE CONGRESS.

WE left Arnold at Ticonderoga, after his naval battle with Carleton in October, 1776. He remained there a month, and then reported to Washington a few days before the battle of Trenton. He had missed despatches on his way down, instructing him to repair at once to Rhode Island, to concert measures to meet the threatened invasion of a heavy British fleet then hovering off the coast. He spent the winter in Rhode Island and Boston, but failed in raising an adequate force either to check the invasion or to dislodge the British from Newport, where they had landed and intrenched themselves.

In March, 1777, whilst he sojourned at Boston, Congress appointed five Major-Generals, all from Arnold's juniors in rank. He was loud in his indignation. He wrote to Gates :

> "By Heaven ! I am a villain, if I seek not
> A brave revenge for injured honor."

Washington wrote immediately a soothing letter, assuring him that there must have been some mistake, and that the matter should be investigated. This did but "plunge him into more choler."

He replied : " Congress promoting junior officers to the rank of major-generals, I view as a very civil way of requesting my resignation as unqualified for the office I hold. My commission was conferred unsolicited, and received with pleasure only as a means of serving my country. With equal pleasure I resign it, when I can no longer serve my country with honor. The person who, void of the nice feeling of honor, will tamely condescend to give up his right and retain a commission at the expense of his reputation, I hold as a disgrace to the army, and unworthy of the glorious cause in which we are engaged. When I entered the army, my character was unimpeached. I have sacrificed my interest, ease, and happiness in her cause." Here spouts up a jet of truth : *"It is rather a misfortune than a fault, that my exertions have not been crowned with success.* In justice, therefore, to my own character, and for the satisfaction of my friends, I must request a court of inquiry into my conduct," etc., etc.

Meantime Washington had, on inquiry into the affair, learned that the several States insisted on having general officers in proportion to the number of troops furnished, and Connecticut already had her quota.

He hastened to explain this to Arnold, adding : "I confess this is a strange mode of reasoning, but it may show you that the promotion due to your seniority was not overlooked for want of merit." He further dissuaded him from asking a court of inquiry, as no charge had been made against him by Congress, adding that public bodies were not responsible for their acts, and that all the satisfaction an individual could obtain was his own consciousness that he deserved better than he had received.

But this philosophy was no cure for Arnold's malady. He refused to be comforted, and still desired permission to go to Philadelphia and demand an inquiry. He had braved court-martials before, and parried their righteous judgment so successfully that he now resolved to outface Congress.

But Colonel Stark had also been omitted from the five brigadier-generals newly made by Congress, and one can scarcely refrain from wondering that Washington showed so little uneasiness for the neglect of an officer who had so recently performed the bravest and most invaluable service. He with Washington had run the ice blockade of the Delaware, and after the inspiration of the presence of the commander-in-chief, it was Stark's bayonet charge that had assured the victory at Trenton. He performed signal service afterward at Princeton, and at the same time, when the paymaster was out of both money and credit, he, with Washington and other officers, pledged his private fortune.

He had distinguished himself at Bunker Hill, and long before in the French-Indian war,—everywhere performing brilliant and valuable service. He was clearly worth all the major-generals Congress had yet appointed ; but they passed him by, because he was " self-willed," though he stood at the head of the list from New Hampshire. The great heart was hurt to the core, and on behalf of insulted manhood he left the service and went home to his plough, " where his patriotism, like the fire of the smithy when sprinkled with water, glowed more fiercely than ever." His State received him with honor, and put him at the head of all the troops soon after raised to oppose Burgoyne's approach.

But Arnold was no Cincinnatus, and had besides no plough to go to. He went to Philadelphia. On his way, passing through Connecticut, he heard of the raid of two thousand British troops under Tryon, who had landed at Campo, near Fairfax, and proceeded to Danbury to destroy the public stores thus collected. Generals Wooster and Silliman, with Connecticut militia, had gone in pursuit of them. Arnold joined himself to them *uninvited*, about four miles from Danbury, where they learned that the town and stores had been burned, and the British were retiring by the route they had come. General Wooster with his division pushed on and made a spirited attack upon their rear, taking a score of prisoners, but the brave old man fell from his horse mortally wounded. Arnold headed the other division, and made a boyish attempt to intercept their march by throwing up a barricade, behind which his party fought for fifteen minutes, when the British, four times their number, easily out-flanked them and went on their way. They, however, hung upon the enemy's rear, and Arnold fought with his usual desperate bravery—dust and splinters flying, and two horses killed under him! The British ran at the last, but embarked safely, having accomplished what they came to do with small loss.

"The news of *these exploits* soon reached Congress," and the commission of Major-General was given to him; also a horse handsomely caparisoned. Were ever honors so cheaply won? But this still left him below the five before appointed. He continued to sulk. Washington, anxious to put him in good humor, endeavored to make what amends he could for the neglect of Congress, by appointing him to the command on the North River, then considered one, if not the most honorable post an officer could hold.

He, however, declined it, and preferred to obtain from Congress an examination into his conduct. Arriving at Philadelphia, he became convinced of what he had suspected,—that the published accusations of Colonel Brown had made an impression; the spirits of Montreal and Ticonderoga "would not down."

His complaints were loud, and with an air of injured innocence he wrote to Congress : "I am exceedingly unhappy to find, that after having made every sacrifice of fortune, ease, and domestic happiness to serve my country, I am publicly impeached (in particular by Lieutenant-

Colonel Brown) of a catalogue of crimes which, if true, ought to subject me to disgrace, infamy, and the just resentment of my countrymen. Conscious of the rectitude of my intentions—however I may have erred in judgment—I must request the favor of Congress to point out some mode by which my conduct, and that of my accusers, may be inquired into, and justice done to the innocent and injured."

The case went to the "Board of War," and they acquitted him, declaring that his character had been "cruelly and groundlessly aspersed." Congress confirmed the report, but still withheld the rank for which he contended. Nor were the impressions removed from the minds of many members of Congress by the clearance of the "Board of War."

Arnold was sensible of this, and was still dissatisfied and uneasy. He next presented his accounts, which involved him in new difficulties. In fact, if the accounts had preceded the inquiry, it is doubtful if the acquittal would have been accorded. They were hopelessly confused. This confusion was no doubt largely consequent upon the want of proper organization at the beginning of hostilities. The business of purchases, payments, etc., often fell upon the commanders of detachments.

It was peculiarly the case in the Canadian campaign. "From the time Arnold left Cambridge until after the retreat to Crown Point, he had on various occasions acted as commander, commissary and paymaster. His accounts were voluminous, complicated, and in many parts without vouchers or proper certificates." This irregularity they could have condoned, but it was also discovered "that he had introduced a series of extravagant charges in his own favor, some of them dubious in their character, and others manifestly unreasonable, even if the items could have been proved, which swelled his personal claims upon the government to an enormous amount." *

* *Sparks' Life of Arnold.*

As it was pretty well known that he had entered the service without either money or credit, another "inquiry" now arose as to how, in the space of a few months spent in active military service, he could have accumulated a private fortune of such an amount as appeared in the balance of his accounts.

In short, it was clearly perceived to be a piece of insolent knavery, in which Congress was to be overreached and the public defrauded. His enemies now spoke out more emphatically, and his friends were vexed and grieved at "the hard task they had undertaken, of vindicating a man whose merits as an officer were of the highest order, and whose services they deemed invaluable to the country."

What blindness! What infatuation! What one piece of valuable service did his record show? He had certainly discovered a remarkable genius for "doing the things he should have left undone, and leaving undone those he should have done"; for running before he was sent, and where he was not needed, and bearing away laurels that others had won. Loss, failure and disaster had dogged his steps from the outset. The accounts were referred to a committee, and the matter hung.

It was now June, 1777, and Howe was again threatening to cross New Jersey. Philadelphia was astir. Arnold was sent by the "War Board" to guard the Delaware, and co-operate with Washington. But, as we have elsewhere seen, Morgan's rifle-balls, at Piscataway and Rahway, together with Washington's stubborn entrenchments, had driven Howe to decide upon approaching Philadelphia by sea. Thus Arnold had no opportunity for "new" exploits.

He returned to urge the settlement of his accounts,—a matter of prime necessity for him. But the committee seemed not at all inclined to allow them, and delayed their report. Delay and investigation were what Arnold most dreaded. He therefore broke in upon their deliberations with a tender of his resignation, declaring that he was driven to this step only by a sense of the injustice he had suffered. He protested an ardent love for his country, and his readiness again to " fight and bleed " in her cause. Just at this time, came the intelligence of the fall of Ticonderoga, and the triumphant advance of Burgoyne in the north ; also a letter from Washington, urging Congress to send Arnold to the northern army. He likewise wrote to Arnold, soothing him and persuading him to go.

His resignation was probably intended to prick the sympathies of Congress ; at all events, he was easily induced to suspend it, and he proceeded at once to join Schuyler.

Arriving at headquarters, he was put in command of a division of the army and stationed near Fort Edward. Four days after, within the limits of his command, occurred the tragedy of Jane McCrea.

Arnold's pickets were driven in, and two or three killed. Those who escaped brought an exaggerated account of the number of the savages. Arnold detached *a thousand men in pursuit,* in two divisions, one to fall upon their front and the other upon their rear. A heavy shower of rain, however, fell upon their powder, and they marched back without seeing the Indians. It proved to have been only a small party who made a swift retreat after the atrocious murder. *

The next day Schuyler and his whole army fell back to Stillwater. Meantime the question of Arnold's rank had been brought before Congress, and the vote was heavily against him,—three to one. He immediately signified to Schuyler his intention to retire ; but Schuyler besought him not to leave at that critical juncture, and he again suspended his purpose.

The next event in Arnold's military career occurred in connection with the relief of Fort Stanwix—a most important accessory to the surrender of Burgoyne. Having penetrated well into the wilderness between Fort Edward

* *Bancroft* gives only two Indians.—Vol. IX, p. 392.

and Albany, with the militia swarming in his rear, it became no longer possible for Burgoyne to feed his army from Canada. It was a necessity to draw supplies from the fruitful valley of the Mohawk. The raid upon Bennington was also planned with the view of the capture of the magazines at that point.

Burgoyne had dispatched St. Leger with eight hundred British and nearly a thousand Seneca warriors to besiege Fort Stanwix — a formidable post of well-constructed earth-works at the head-waters of the Mohawk, ably garrisoned by six hundred men under Colonel Gansevoort. A brave band of patriot freeholders of the Mohawk Valley, under. Herkimer, advanced to the relief of the garrison. Informed of their approach, the whole body of savages, carefully depositing their blankets and fur robes, left the camp naked, or with only hunting-shirts, armed with spear, musket and tomahawk for their murderous business. They were supported by Butler with his rangers, Sir John Johnson with his Yorkers, some British regulars and Canadians.

On came the patriot band, and about six miles from the fort they entered an ambuscade. They were misled as to the numbers of their foe. A fierce and bloody struggle they made of it; " the white man, born on the banks of the Mohawk, wrestled single-handed with the Seneca warrior, child of the soil, dealing mortal wounds with the bayonet or the hatchet; falling in the forest together, their left hands clinched in each other's hair, their right hand grasping in the grip of death the knife plunged in each other's bosom."* Herkimer was mortally wounded, but remained on the field giving orders to the last.

After a struggle of two hours the savages withdrew, leaving sixty of their warriors dead or wounded beneath the trees. On the other side, the blood of over one hundred and fifty of the best and bravest freeholders of the

* *Bancroft*, Vol. IX.

valley of the Mohawk, crimsoned the green sward of the forest.

During the progress of the battle, a party of two hundred and fifty sallied out from the Fort under Colonel Willett; they entered the camp and captured five British flags, private papers, all the kettles, blankets, and fur robes of the Indians, with a squad of prisoners, and returned safely.

For the first time a captured British flag floated beneath the stars and stripes.

The Indians, frantic at the slaughter of their chiefs and chilled by the loss of their blankets and furs, began to desert. They had heard of the approach of reinforcements; it might mean another Herkimer, for Schuyler had detached a brigade of eight hundred men under General Learned. Arnold, however, *volunteered to take command.* He was instructed to call out militia as he advanced, protect the settlements, and repel the enemy.

Arriving at German Flats, Arnold counted his forces, and found he had twelve hundred regulars and about one hundred militia. He also learned that St. Leger's force was seventeen hundred, including a thousand Indians. Arnold's force, with the garrison of Fort Stanwix, was quite equal to that of the enemy; but he was no Indian fighter, as the "Cedars" had proved; he therefore dispatched a messenger to General Gates, who had again superseded Schuyler, asking for a thousand light troops. He also issued a pompous and wordy proclamation full of promises to those who would submit, and direful threats to such as continued in arms against the United States. He then ventured to move forward toward Fort Stanwix.

A singular turn of affairs here occurred. A spy had been captured and brought into the American camp; an inhabitant of that vicinity. Sparks says, that Lieutenant Colonel Brooks of Massachusetts suggested that he be sent to the enemy with false intelligence; he was to report the approach of a large army; by this they hoped to stimulate the desertion of the savages. Sparks also says that "a friendly Indian advised that bullets should be shot through his clothing, to confirm his story," of escape from the Americans. His life and the security of his property was to be the reward of his faithfulness, and his brother was detained as a hostage.

His part was handsomely performed. A second messenger followed hard after, and magnified the number threefold. The ruse was perfectly successful. A panic seized the Indians, who stood not upon the order of their going, but plundered their friends, as if they had been their enemies, bearing off as their booty the clothing of the British officers, boats and provisions. The panic communicated itself to St. Leger's force, and though no man pursued, the retreat became a flight, leaving fifty-nine tents standing, with much baggage and equipage.

The news of St. Leger's retreat reached Arnold twenty-two miles from Stanwix, but this officer could by no means omit the punctilio of marching on, and in person entering the fort with colors flying, without having struck a blow.

A swift march back to Gates' army, upon which Burgoyne was now pressing down, would have been more useful, but it would have been no "exploit." Arnold's letters confirm the above statements.

"To GENERAL GATES.

"GERMAN FLATS, August 21st, 1777.

"*Dear General:*—I leave this place this morning with twelve hundred continental troops and a handful of militia, for Fort Stanwix, which is still besieged by a number equal to ours. *You shall hear of my being victorious or no more.* As soon as the safety of this part of the

5

country will permit, I will fly to your assistance. General Herkimer died yesterday.

"I am, etc.

"BENEDICT ARNOLD."

"To GENERAL GATES.

"FORT DAYTON, August 23d, 1777.

"*Dear General :*—I wrote you on the 21st from 'German Flats' and requested you to send me a reinforcement of a thousand light troops. As the enemy had made their approaches within two hundred yards of the fort, I was determined to hazard a battle rather than suffer the garrison to fall a sacrifice. This morning I marched from the German Flats for this place. Here I have met with an express, with an enclosed letter from Colonel Gansevoort, acquainting me that the enemy had yesterday retired from Fort Stanwix with precipitation. I shall immediately detach nine hundred men, and make a forced march in hopes of coming up with their rear and securing their cannon and baggage. I have sent an order for the light troops, if you have sent any, to return to you, and the militia, to go home.

"I am, etc.

"BENEDICT ARNOLD."

"To GENERAL GATES.

"GERMAN FLATS, August 28th, 1777.

"*Dear General :*—I reached Fort Stanwix on the 24th, too late after so fatiguing a march to pursue the enemy that evening. The next morning a detachment of five hundred followed them, but a heavy rain came on and obliged them to retire, except a small party who went as far as Oneida Lake *arriving just in time to see the last of the enemy going off.* There is nothing to be feared from

the enemy in this quarter. You may depend upon my
joining you as soon as possible.

"I am, etc., BENEDICT ARNOLD."

He makes no allusion to the ruse and probably knew
nothing of it, which confirms Sparks' statement concerning Colonel Brooks. But St. Leger's panic was doubtless
more largely owing to the reverberation of Stark's guns
from Bennington five days before. The spy took that
news also, from the American into the British camp,
which made the retreat a necessity. Thus victory again
gave Arnold the slip, resolved never to fold her wings on
his standards. The British Annual Register said, Gansevoort and Willet "merited the praise even of an enemy."
Washington declared, "it was Herkimer who first reversed
the gloom of the Northern campaign." The hero of the
Mohawk valley served from love of country, not for reward. He did not want a continental command or money.
He died soon after the battle and Congress decreed him a
monument ; to Gansevoort they voted thanks and a command; to Willet an elegant sword.*—Is it not competent
in this centennial recall of the fathers, that our histories
and cyclopædias should purge themselves of such errors,
by divorcing the names of Fort Stanwix and Arnold, and
identifying the real heroes with their brave deeds.

The repulse at Fort Stanwix by Herkimer was the first
great blow which fell upon Burgoyne. The second was
more disastrous still; the overwhelming defeat at Bennington, the most brilliant field fight of the war, with
the exception of Cowpens. Morgan and Stark were undoubtedly the great field executives of the Revolution.

Lamed by Herkimer and Stark, with their brave followers, Burgoyne came halting to the battles of Saratoga,
to meet his doom at the hands of Morgan and his riflemen,
with the patriot yeomanry of New York and New England.

Bancroft, Vol. IX.

XI.—1777–1780.

HORATIO GATES.

THE northern army lay encamped nine miles above Albany, near the mouth of the Mohawk. On the 19th August, 1777, General Gates assumed command and General Schuyler retired.

Who was this man Gates? English by birth. All authorities agree that his mother was housekeeper for the second Duke of Leeds. Irving says his father was a captain in the British army ; Sargent says he was a respectable victualler of Kensington. That whiff of unwholesome atmosphere put a virus into his blood that he never had the stamina to throw off, though transplanted into the mountain air of freedom that nourished Patrick Henry, Morgan, Jefferson, and Washington. He had accompanied Braddock upon his expedition to Fort Duquesne, and was wounded in the battle ; he returned to England, but, dissatisfied with his prospects of promotion, he sold his commission in the British army and emigrated to Virginia.

Here he renewed his acquaintance with Washington. His military career, through the war of Revolution, was one of intrigue rather than of service. His exploits can be more than reckoned on the fingers of one hand. In fact, Saratoga and Camden include all that could be called active military service.

Appointed Adjutant-General, with rank of Brigadier-General, he accompanied Washington to Cambridge in June 1775. He began at once to clamor for an independent command. He was appointed to Canada the next year ; but the expedition was dead, and he met the retreating army at Crown Point, July 1776.

The only military event that marks his administration there, was the building and afterwards the splintering and burning of the Lake fleet under Arnold.

A few weeks after that, though entreated to co-operate with him, he left Washington in his dire extremity at the passage of the Delaware and hurried on to Congress, then sitting at Baltimore, to push his own fortunes. Again, in the spring of 1777, Washington entreated Gates to come to his aid, as he was doing nothing,—but vainly; he was still maneuvering for an independent command of the northern department.

He succeeded, and jostled the old patriot Schuyler from his post. Schuyler appealed personally to Congress and was re-instated. But after the fall of Ticonderoga, July 5th, 1777, Gates, with the New England influence, directed the odium of the disaster upon Schuyler, and Congress again superseded him. On August 19th, immediately following the important victories of Stanwix and Bennington, Gates took command of an army ably officered and largely outnumbering the British forces.

Here he assumes the role of the conquering hero and crowns his own brows with stolen laurels.

After the surrender of Burgoyne, Congress makes him President of the Board of War, thus virtually putting Washington—in eclipse at Valley Forge—at his mercy. Gates is now emboldened to the infamous work of the " cabal," which had some strong supporters in Congress. Great efforts were made by the conspirators to win over Patrick Henry, then Governor of Virginia, and Laurens, President of Congress. But their proposals were met with disdain—the people and the army stood loyally to the " chief "; Congress had salt enough to save it, and the " cabal " returned to plague its inventors.

The same fate befell a projected expedition to Canada, proposed by Gates at this time, without consulting Washington, and to the command of which he appointed La Fayette, with a hope of drawing him away from his allegiance to Washington. So unmitigated a failure resulted in Congress directing Gates to undertake nothing further without previously consulting the commander-in-chief, who stood now higher than ever in all estimations. La Fayette writes to his beloved friend in an exquisitely charming manner :

" FLEMINGTON, February 9, 1778.

"*My Dear General :*— I cannot let my guide go without taking this opportunity of writing to your Excellency, though I had not yet public business to speak of. I go on very slowly, sometimes drenched by rain, sometimes covered by snow, and not entertaining many handsome thoughts about the projected incursion into Canada.

If successes were to be had, it would surprise me in a most agreeable manner. Lake Champlain is too cold for producing the least bit of laurel, and if I am not starved, I shall be as proud as if I had gained three battles.

"Mr. Duer had given to me a rendezvous at a tavern, but *nobody was to be found there.* I fancy he will be with Mr. Conway sooner than he told me. They will perhaps *conquer Canada before my arrival,* and I expect to meet them at the governor's house in Quebec.

Could I believe, for one single instant, that this pompous *command of a northern army* will let your Excellency forget a little your absent friend, I would send the project to the place it comes from. It is a very melancholy idea for me that I cannot follow your fortunes as near your person as I could wish ; but my heart will take very sincerely its part of everything which can happen to you, and I am already thinking of the agreeable moment when I may come down to assure your Excellency of the most tender affection and highest respect."

Again, under date of March 25, 1778 :

"*Dear General :*—I am very sensible of the goodness which tries to dissipate my fears about that *ridiculous Canadian expedition.* At the present time, we know which was the aim of the 'Honorable Board,' and for which project three or four men have rushed the country into a great expense, and risked the reputation of our arms and the life of many hundred men, had the general (your deceived friend), been as rash and foolish as they seem to have expected. O, American freedom! what shall become of you, if you are in such hands? However, you know I have wrote to Congress, and as soon as their leave will come, I shall let Conway have the command of these few regiments, and I shall immediately join my respectable friend. My only desire is to join you, and the only favor I have asked of your commissioners in France has been, not to be under any orders but those of General Washington.

"With the utmost respect and affection,
"I have the honor to be,
"LA FAYETTE." *

After this Gates occupied a post on the Hudson, but the tide of war did not reach it. In 1779, he obtained leave of absence and went home to Virginia to look after his private affairs. In June, 1780, he was ordered by Congress to take the command of the Southern department, then overrun by, and in possession of, the British.

He went to Camden August 1780, and there, undertaking to fight his own battle,—Camden pricks the bubble of Saratoga, and he gets his quietus.

* *Sparks' Correspondence,* Vol. II.

XII.—1777.

THE BATTLE OF THE COLONELS.

"A century before Burgoyne's campaign, Frontenac, ablest of French colonial commanders, had proposed to move against the colony of New York by the same route followed by Burgoyne in 1777. France saw that upon that very theatre of war where Britain had wrested from her the control of this continent, her ancient enemy had been beaten by the new power which was springing up into existence. To the French government this victory had a significance that no like victory could have had upon other fields."

LITTLE thought the brave spirits that marched out on that 19th of September, 1777, to arrest the advance of Burgoyne's army, that that battle, with the final one so soon to follow, were to be remembered among the great, decisive battles of the ages : with Marathon, Metaurus, Tours, Orleans, Lützen, and Waterloo. "They builded better than they knew." It was the turning tide that was to lead on to victory, securing a vast continent dowered with every physical essential of a great nation ; immeasurable areas of virgin soil, grand forests, matchless rivers and lakes, and countless harbors, vast coal fields and inexhaustible mountain storehouses of metallic wealth,—a magnificent theatre for the fifth act of the great drama of the race.

> " Westward the course of empire takes its way ;
> The first four acts already past,
> A fifth shall close the drama with the day,—
> Time's noblest offspring is its last."

Up out of this ponderous natural foundation was to rise a political fabric, resting on its stately pillars of liberty and law, which should environ and defend a social system recognizing the equal brotherhood of man, and, discarding hereditary privileges, secure absolute intellectual freedom, and, in things spiritual, absolute tolerance of everything but intolerance. The world was to see, for the first time, a government attempted to be administered according to the tenets of the New Testament.

The Declaration of Independence had fallen like a thunderbolt out of the clear heavens upon the rotten systems of the old world—a word of final doom to them, but to the peoples a word of eternal hope. A nation "born in a day" was to illustrate it before the race.

The old spirit stirred, and tyrants whispered: "If we let it thus alone all men will believe it, and what shall become of our place and nation"? It was a stone of stumbling, a rock of offence—whosoever should fall upon it should be broken, and upon whomsoever it should fall, it would grind him to powder.

One thing only lent it grace to the eyes of the European governments. The loss of her colonies would effectually cripple England, now grown so powerful and arrogant that all envied and hated her. And they looked on anxiously watching for the outcome of her proud efforts to crush the young giant in its cradle. Especially did they watch the fate of this expedition of Burgoyne into the very heart of the colonies. France and Spain waited only for its discomfiture, to arm against England, and thus secure the independence of the new transatlantic power.

Had the shock of battle resulted only in checking Burgoyne's progress—had he safely effected his retreat to the Lakes, it would not have sufficed to assure Europe of the final triumph of American arms. The attempt would undoubtedly have been repeated; but the total defeat, rout, and capture of this splendid army, in fair and open field fight, after such fashion as compelled the admiration of even their enemies, closed all controversy; they no longer hesitated to espouse the cause of a people who had proved themselves so strong in self-defence.

The reverses of the British arms were as sudden as they were disastrous. But two months before, the English court and ministry were intoxicated with the brilliant successes of the expedition. Worst of all, they were themselves intoxicated with their own achievements, and could not sufficiently express their contempt of their provincial foes.

From Canada to Ticonderoga, had been a swift procession of easy victories; the Lakes and fortresses, keys of the North, were in their hands.

They had reached the banks of the Hudson, not far from Albany, object so long desired; they imagined that their toils were over, and anticipated an easy and agreeable descent to New York. So confident were they, that the Baroness Reidesel, Lady Acland, and other officers' wives, did not hesitate to accompany their husbands. The army was a picked one; the finest military organizations of England and the continent had contributed their ablest fighting material; its equipment, from the best arsenals of Europe, left nothing to be desired. There was no question of the personal bravery of Burgoyne—of this he had made proof in his late campaigns in Portugal—but judgment is an element as essential as courage, for high generalship, and this he lacked.

His forces were half English and half German. The German officers Reidesel, Breyman, Baum, Specht, and Gall had proved their skill and courage beyond cavil. He was most ably supported by his English officers, Sir John Dyke Acland, Sir Francis Clarke, the Earl Balcarras, Generals Phillips and Hamilton, Captains Williams and Jones of the artillery, and notably by General Frazer, at once the charm and inspiration of the British army. He it was who, on that fatal night assault of Montgomery upon Quebec, going his midnight-rounds, had with his eagle eye perceived the fuses, the American signals of attack, and without waiting further orders, caused the drums to beat the garrison to arms ;* he who further on at Trois Rivières, had defeated Thompson and confounded Sullivan ; foremost in the late attack upon Ticonderoga, he had afterward chased the retreating army of St. Clair, and with Reidesel, harried and captured many, destroying baggage and arms.

He came now, at last, to meet his doom at the hands of "a foeman worthy of his steel," a foeman "thrice armed" because he had "his quarrel just."

Frazer with Tarleton were the only British officers, throughout the whole war, who showed *military genius.* These two undoubtedly possessed it. Both were out-generalled and put to shame by Daniel Morgan.

This man Frazer, the Highlander, fought under the spur of a powerful motive. A scion of the house of Lovatt, which had embraced the cause of the last Stuart Pretender, and whose fortunes went down with that dynasty on the field of Culloden 1745. This gifted and ambitious descendant entered the British army, and rose rapidly to distinction. He had obtained the rank of Brigadier General, and was specially selected to command a division of Burgoyne's army. He had also received assurance that the successful issue of the expedition would avail to revoke the attaint still cleaving to his house, and restore its honors and estates. True to the traditions of his ancestry, he girded on his sword and went forth to battle against the rights of humanity.

But from out the forest of the New World came the fearless spirit appointed to arrest and end his brilliant career. No scion he, of an illustrious house. Though only a century ago, we know as little of his ancestry as of that of the prophet of Horeb, far off in the misty dawn.

* *Botta's Hist. American Revolution.*

Enough! he was son of God, who is able to raise up his children from the stones.

It was meet that a representative of the new dispensation of manhood should shiver the lance of this "belted knight" of man's making. Morgan was a splendid presentiment of the new order of noblemen—of the "mill boys" and "rail splitters" of the young Republic.

Burgoyne's forces by various estimates approximated eight thousand,—about four thousand British, three thousand Germans and a thousand Canadian loyalists and Indians. He had left a thousand to garrison Ticonderoga—a too heavy drain; his lack of judgment was now shown in sending off his heavy Brunswick mercenaries under Baum, to be surrounded and bayoneted by Stark's lightly equipped yeomanry, brimful of enthusiasm and patriotism, by which he suffered a loss of nearly two hundred killed and four hundred prisoners. Burgoyne's army decreased daily; the American camp was reinforced daily. Burgoyne's army was a splendid machine; the American army was a living, breathing, burning soul, moving like Ezekiel's wheels, by the spirit of the living creature.

From the beginning of the campaign early in May, until the middle of August, the British had met no adversary who had in the least intimidated them; and even now, notwithstanding the rebuke of Herkimer and the disaster of Bennington, Burgoyne injudiciously ventured, September 13th, to cross the Hudson on a bridge of boats, with his splendid train of artillery, thus compromising his chances of retreat should it become necessary. He encamped on the heights of Saratoga on the banks of the Hudson, near where it receives the waters of the Mohawk.

On the 8th of September Gates' army left their encampment at "Sunset," and on the 12th occupied "Behmus Heights," which were at once strongly fortified, under the direction of Kosciusko. But a few miles now intervened between the opposing armies. Washington, when he dispatched Colonel Morgan to Gates' assistance, said : "A check given to the savages and keeping them within bounds, will prevent General Burgoyne from getting intelligence." It proved so. Morgan was kept far in advance of the army, watching the movements of the enemy, "with the liberty of attacking whenever he judged prudent." *

His presence had inspired so wholesome a terror among the Canadians and Indians that they were deserting by hundreds, while the British regulars could not show themselves beyond their camp, without provoking a shower of rifle-balls. Burgoyne remained in painful ignorance throughout the remainder of his campaign of the numbers, position, and movements of the Americans, while his own were well understood by his enemy.

The Baroness Reidesel, in her interesting notes of this campaign, naively writes : "The Americans anticipate all our movements and expect us whenever we arrive; this, of course, injures our affairs."

On the morning of the 19th, Burgoyne put his army in motion in three columns, a half mile apart. The right led by Frazer, the centre by himself. and the left marched by the river road under Reidesel.

Morgan was ordered forward to develop their intentions. Two companies under Major Morris were sent ahead, and Morgan followed with the main body of his corps. He was always watchful of the rear, "to see that every man did his duty, and that cowards did not lag behind while brave men fought in front." Morris, a most spirited officer, however, pushed on too rapidly, and came suddenly upon a strong picket of the enemy, occupying a log-house ; he announced himself by a volley of rifle-balls, but the enemy replied from their covert with so brisk a fire that the Americans quickly fell back toward their main column,

* *Graham's Life of Morgan*, p. 142.

leaving several killed and wounded, and even thought it necessary to disperse. Morgan's prudence equalled his courage; he was never rash until the fulness of time, then nothing could exceed the fierceness and impetuosity of his assault. Coming up at this instant, he fully realized the gravity of the situation. "But to retreat or advance, to flee or pursue, to disperse or collect, were the tactics of this celebrated corps." Morgan's signal was an instrument made from a turkey-bone for decoying wild turkey. In a few moments the dispersed column gathered to their leader, and the whole regiment advanced upon a large body of the enemy. Morgan attacked with such vigor that the British fell back to an eminence fronting an open piece of ground called Freeman's Fields. The wrestle was for the possession of this cleared ground. Burgoyne's centre column being reinforced, the struggle was fierce and bloody; Frazer with his right wing now wheeled and dashed his column against Morgan, who was forced to give ground and take his corps to the shelter of the woods. Gates, however, hearing of the extent of the action, had dispatched the regiments of Colonels Scammell and Cilley. They took the left of the rifle corps, and finding himself secure on the right by impenetrable thickets and a marshy ravine, Morgan again advanced and renewed the action with redoubled fury.

The iron hail of six hundred marksmen forced back both columns of the British army, leaving the ground covered with dead and wounded, and their artillery. This, however, the Americans could neither bring off, by reason of the nature of the ground, nor turn against the enemy, because they had taken away the lintstocks. The British quickly rallied and came down again. By this time Gates had reinforced Morgan with five additional regiments, who were now opposed to the combined forces of Frazer and Burgoyne.

The Americans numbered two thousand five hundred; the British about three thousand, with artillery, of which the Americans had none. The battle raged along the whole line for more than an hour ; but the hottest was at the American right, where Morgan opposed Frazer. Again and again he had driven the British back upon the eminence beyond the clearing. Their cannon were become almost useless, for their artillerists had all been picked off. Morgan now made the most desperate effort to charge up the eminence, drive them over the hill, and turn their left flank. But here Greek met Greek, and Morgan was sensible of a *point de resistance* which he could not overcome. So they swayed back and forward, alternately giving and taking, and the British, amid the heaps of their dead and wounded, at last began to show signs of yielding, when Reidesel, pushing through the woods, brought his column to the timely rescue of his general, and saved the army from a rout. Frazer and Breyman were now eager for a bayonet charge with their fresh troops, which would have inevitably turned the fortunes of the day ; but Burgoyne ordered a retreat. His officers were chagrined, and Frazer and Reidesel told him plainly that he did not know how to avail himself of his advantages.

General Learned, with his brigade, at sunset came upon the field ; but the fire had slackened and the battle was done. The Americans returned to their camp, taking their wounded and one hundred prisoners. The British bivouacked on the battle-field, and claimed the victory—a claim which could scarcely be sustained. The American loss was slightly over three hundred killed and wounded, while that of the British exceeded six hundred, besides a heavy desertion of Canadians and Indians after the battle.

Also it was the purpose and necessity of the British to advance, and the object of the Americans to prevent their advance. This was fully accomplished. Furthermore, both Frazer and Reidesel, officers of great judgment as well as bravery, now counseled Burgoyne to a speedy retreat across the Hudson. They knew that another such victory would be their ruin, and had no wish for a second tilt with these American colonels.

The day after the battle, one of the rifle corps brought down an Indian, and found in his shot-pouch a letter from Burgoyne to General Powell.

"Camp near Stillwater, September 20, 1777.

"*Dear Sir :*—I take the first opportunity to inform you that we have had a very smart and honorable action, and are now encamped in front of the field, which must demonstrate our victory beyond the power of an American news-writer to explain away. The loss on each side cannot be particularly ascertained.

"Your obedient servant,   J. Burgoyne."

General Gates dispatched the following to Hon. J. Hancock, President of Congress :

" Behmis Heights, September 22, 1777.

" Friday I was informed by my reconnoitering parties that the enemy were moving toward our left. I immediately detached Colonel Morgan's corps, consisting of the rifle regiment and the light infantry of the army, to observe their direction and harass their advance. This party, at half-past twelve, fell in with a picket of the enemy, which they immediately drove ; but the enemy being reinforced, after a brisk conflict, they were in turn obliged to retire.

" This skirmish drew the main body of the enemy, and a brigade from my left, to support the action which, after a short cessation, was renewed with great warmth and violence. At this time, hearing from prisoners that the whole British force and a division of foreigners had engaged our party, I reinforced with four more regiments. This continued the action till the close of the day, when both armies retired from the field.

"Enclosed is a return of our loss, and I am well assured,

by the concurrent testimony of prisoners and deserters of various characters, that General Burgoyne, who commanded in person, received a wound in his left shoulder ; that the sixty-second regiment was cut to pieces, and that the enemy suffered severely in every quarter where they were engaged. The general good behavior of the troops, on this important occasion, cannot be surpassed by the most veteran army : to discriminate in praise of the officers would be injustice, as they all deserved the honor and applause of Congress. Lieutenant-Colonel Colburn and Lieutenant-Colonel Adams, with the rest of the unfortunate brave who fell in their country's cause, leave a lasting memorial to their glory. The armies remain encamped within two miles of each other." *

Very adroitly put, certainly. Only the harmless dead men have mention ; not a word for the living Morgan, whom, a few days after, he excuses himself from sending back to Washington, with the plea, " in this situation your Excellency would not wish me to part with the corps the army of General Burgoyne is most afraid of."

" Morgan's corps bore the brunt of the day's perils, and should reap the greater share of its glories. The sixty-second regiment of Hamilton's brigade, against which his regiment contended, lost nearly two hundred men, and of the forty-eight who composed the artillery corps, and were likewise arrayed against him, but twelve left the field uninjured. During one of the most obstinately contested actions of the war, in which nearly seven thousand men were engaged, not a single officer, above the rank of a colonel, appeared upon the field until night began to close upon the combatants, when General Learned arrived. Arnold never appeared upon the ground. General Wil-

* Copied from *Graham's Life of Morgan*, p. 152.

kinson states that he was expressly forbidden by Gates to visit the field or *direct* operations. The credit of this glorious action, so generally accorded either to Arnold or Gates, properly belongs to neither. It should go to enrich the memory of those gallant men who, unassisted by the directing hand of either of their commanders, fought the battle and won the day. Historic truth requires this explanation, and public justice will give the laurels to those who won them.

"Among this glorious band of heroes, it is no injustice to assert that Morgan was pre-eminently distinguished. His regiment was first in the field and last out of it. Where it was engaged, the strife was more deadly than in any other position. Its loss was greater, in proportion to its numbers, than that of any other regiment, while the number of the enemy which fell by its hands, was nearly one-half of that admitted by Burgoyne to have fallen in the battle. Though Morgan was denied the merited mention in Gates' communication to Congress, justice claims for him the foremost position among those who shared the glories of that day. Posterity will freely accord him this, and hail him, as did his friends and neighbors on his return home a few months after, as 'the hero of Saratoga.'

"The news of this victory was received with great demonstrations of joy throughout the country, and Gates and Arnold reaped a rich harvest of undeserved honors and applause." *

Bancroft says: "On the British side, three major-generals came on the field; on the American side, not one, nor a brigadier, until near its close. Praise justly fell upon Morgan of Virginia and Scammel of New Hampshire; none offered their lives more freely than the Continental regiment of Cilley and the Connecticut militia of Cook. The American loss, including the wounded and missing, was less than three hundred and twenty. This battle

* *Graham's Life of Morgan*, p. 151.

crippled the British force irretrievably. Their loss exceeded six hundred. Of the sixty-second regiment (handled by Morgan's corps), which left Canada five hundred strong, there remained less than sixty men and four or five officers. A rifle-shot meant for Burgoyne struck an officer at his side." *

Sparks, in his Life of Arnold, says : "That officer was neither ordered out, nor permitted to go out, to take any part in the action." Hildreth makes no mention of him in the first battle, and Arnold's own letters confirm his absence.

Yet the error moves on, and to this day Gates and Arnold wear their unearned honors.

One is pained to find that in that very handsome contribution to recent historic literature, " Fifteen Decisive Battles of the World," so eminent an English scholar as Professor Creasy, falls into the same error by following the Italian historian " Botta," whose history, though in many respects a very noble statement of our Revolutionary period, was yet written too near the date of the events described. The smoke of the battle-field had not sufficiently cleared away to disclose the true role of the actors. To give the glory of this battle to Gates or Arnold, would not be a greater error than to ascribe the honor of Metaurus to Livius rather than to Nero.

More mournful still it is to read in the centennial year of grace 1877, in one of our foremost monthlies, in an article dedicated to the memory of this most important military event : " By four o'clock, the action had become general; Arnold, with nine continental regiments and Morgan's corps, had completely engaged the whole force of Burgoyne and Frazer;" and most mournful of all, to find that the orators of the late centennial celebration (1877) on the battle-field—we believe without exception— make Arnold the " hero of Saratoga."

Arnold was absent by express command of Gates, who

* Vol. IX, p. 413.

wanted no rivals. He had realized his long ambition of independent command; but it was to be only a stepping-stone to a higher place. The conspiracy against Washington was maturing in his mind. He meant to jostle him from his post as he had done Schuyler. A year ago, we saw him baffling justice to shield Arnold, of whose service he then stood in need; but now having Morgan, to whose skill he safely confided his reputation, he had no need of Arnold, and obviously wished to keep him in eclipse. Arnold was at this time Gates' equal in military rank, and had won a reputation far more brilliant. Both were thoroughly selfish and alike intent upon pushing each his own fortunes. They were equally wanting in magnanimity. Arnold had more will, energy and impetus; a more incredible audacity, and was utterly without scruple or conscience. His chief hope being the patronage of Washington, Gates knew he had no prospect of drawing him from his allegiance to the commander-in-chief. Neither did Gates share in the general enthusiasm concerning Arnold's military ability. Wilkinson, Gates' aid-de-camp, says, he forbade him to go upon the field "lest he should do some rash thing." Had he needed him, he would doubtless have made use of him.

We do not forget that upon the arrival of Morgan's corps at headquarters, Gates had reinforced it with a battalion of light infantry, designated it as the advance of the army, and directed that it should receive orders only from himself. After the action of the 19th, the returns were accordingly made directly to Gates. Arnold was incensed, and still more at finding that the report to Congress left his name and that of his division unmentioned, stating only that the battle had been fought by detachments from the army. "Had my division behaved ill," said he, "the other division of the army would have thought it extremely hard to have been amenable for their conduct."

Resolved to appropriate the prestige of Morgan's corps to himself, Arnold continued to issue orders for their movements, which drew from Gates the following general order :

" Colonel Morgan's corps, not being attached to any brigade or division of the army, he is to make returns and reports to headquarters only, from whence alone he is to receive orders."

A high altercation now arose between the two generals, during which Gates informed Arnold " that he thought him of little consequence in the army, and that when General Lincoln arrived he should give to him the command of a division."

A correspondence followed, hot and wrathful on Arnold's part, arrogant and unyielding on the part of Gates. Arnold demanded a pass for himself and suite to the commander-in-chief. Gates promptly gave it.

Arnold found he did not want it. He feared the odium which would fall upon him for retiring from service at this critical juncture, when another battle was in hourly expectation. He therefore remained in camp *without command and without employment.* Lincoln arriving at this time, Gates gave him the right wing, and himself assumed charge of the left. Morgan and the rifle regiment were his special property.

All the better for this falling out of the rogues went matters in the American camp. The country had interpreted the battle of the 19th as a great victory. The militia of New York and New England reinforced the camp daily. Gates' numbers now nearly doubled those of Burgoyne. Hope and confidence inspired every heart.

They smelled the battle and scented the victory ; they stood "like greyhounds in the slips, straining upon the start."

XIII.—1777.

THE SURRENDER.

IN the British camp the hearts of the keepers trembled, brave men though they were. Burgoyne had abandoned all intention of a further advance until intelligence could be received from Clinton below. He proceeded to intrench on the field of the late battle, throwing up strong works to the right, which he called the "Great Redoubt"; it was a final stronghold and was placed under Frazer's command. He extended his intrenchments leftward to the river bank; here the Germans were posted and Burgoyne's headquarters were between and in the rear. A deep ditch ran along the entire front for nine hundred paces.

So vigilant were the American marksmen that the British remained close prisoners within their camp and in profound ignorance of our affairs. The journal of one of their officers says: "We could hear his morning and evening guns, his drums and other noises of his camp, yet we knew not where he stood, how he was posted, much less how strong he was; a rare case in such a situation."

On the night of September 23d, British ears were startled with such shouts of exultation that they supposed the Americans were celebrating some holiday. A few days after a released prisoner carried to them the news of the gallant exploits of Colonel Brown at Ticonderoga; and Burgoyne was chagrined to find himself "indebted to his enemy in front, for the news of disasters at his own posts in his rear."

It was the same Colonel Brown who had so promptly met Arnold's unhandsome charges against him, and afterwards published a full account of that officer's misdemeanors in Canada. He wrote thus to Gates:

"LAKE GEORGE, September 18th, 1777.

"*Dear General:*—With great fatigue after marching all last night, I arrived at this place at break of day and immediately began the attack, and in a few minutes carried the place.

"I find myself in possession of two hundred and ninety-three prisoners exclusive of one hundred of ours released. I have taken one hundred and fifty bateaux above the falls, fifty in Lake Champlain, several large gun-boats, an armed sloop, and a few cannon." * * * *

This reverse was keenly felt in the British army, where affairs grew daily more distressing and depressing. Their horses were starving, the soldiers' rations had been reduced to a minimum, and they were heavily encumbered with their sick and wounded.—The only ray of hope came from the lower Hudson. A messenger from Clinton had made his way with great difficulty into the camp, informing Burgoyne that he was about to attack the forts and defences of the river. Burgoyne dispatched the messenger back bearing earnest entreaties for Clinton's speedy co-operation, stating that he could hold out until October 10th, but after that, hunger would compel him to retreat to Lake Champlain.

On the 5th of October Burgoyne called a council of war.

Frazer and Reidesel urged a speedy retreat to their old position on the east bank of the Hudson.

But Burgoyne's pride would not be advised. The boast had been too often on his lips " Britons never retreat."

He recalled, also, that Germain had censured Carleton because he would " hazard nothing." Re-reading his instructions in which his orders were peremptory, and taking counsel only with himself, he resolved once more to try the fate of battle. In fact it had become a choice of evils, to either advance or retreat.

It was now the 7th of October. Burgoyne strained his ear towards the river, but caught no sound from Clinton's army. This General had on October 6th, the day before the battle, captured the forts, and passed the defences of the river, and a detachment of his army did actually approach within forty miles of Albany. Fortunately, each remained in ignorance of the other's movements.

Burgoyne delayed the attack until three o'clock, so that in case of disaster, night at least would come to their relief. The plan of battle was much as before; they advanced in three columns. Frazer with the infantry under Balcarras on the right, the Germans in the centre. and Acland's grenadiers on the left, with artillery posted at intervals along the whole line.

The rifle corps discovered the movement and it was immediately communicated to Gates, who dispatched Wilkinson to " order on Morgan to begin the game," by pushing forward his corps in front. But Morgan judged otherwise. Knowing the lay of the land to its minutest features, and having informed himself of the disposition of the enemy's forces, he submitted his own plan of attack, which Gates immediately accepted.

General Lincoln was to watch the right of the American lines, cover the camp, and take care of the commander. General Poor's brigade was directed to advance and simultaneously attack the centre and left wing; Morgan re-

served for himself the British right wing under Frazer
and Balcarras. It rested on a fence, and beyond on the
right rose abruptly a thickly wooded hill. Morgan's regiment made a swift and silent push up through these
woods;—gaining the hill top, he was confirmed in his
judgment, and felt assured of a speedy victory. He
quickly put his troops in position. Dearborn's infantry
were ordered to incline to the front, the riflemen to the
flank and rear.

The first fire from Poor's brigade upon the British left
was the appointed signal; Morgan swept down from the
hill like a tornado; the crack of six hundred rifles sent
their messengers of death into rank and file, strewing the
ground with the dead and wounded. For a moment the
column staggered, but recovered. Morgan now ordered
Dearborn to fire and charge with the bayonet while the
rifles reloaded. They charged grandly. In another moment the rifles poured in again, on flanks and rear. The
British broke and fled. It was the work of a few minutes.
Frazer who had been held in reserve, seeing the mischief,
advanced with his infantry to the rescue. "He met the
whole wing flying in disorder, fiercely pursued by Morgan
and his men." He threw himself between the flying
column and their pursuers and covered their retreat to the
rear, where they rallied. Having pushed back the British
right, the tide of battle now rolled toward the centre, and
the whole American force was turned upon it. Seeing
the danger, Burgoyne ordered Frazer to the rescue at that
point.

Morgan had observed this officer closely. It was he
against whom, in the battle of the 19th, he had so desperately pushed, and who had so desperately pushed back
upon him. *He was the invincible.** He had watched him
on this day, a noble-looking officer, mounted upon a

* This account of Frazer's death is mainly from *Graham's Life of
Morgan.*

6

splendid black charger dashing from one end of the line to the other, wherever the danger was greatest, and by his courage and activity restoring and rallying the wavering columns.

While he lived, Morgan considered the issue of the contest doubtful; he therefore sternly resolved to seek for victory in his death. He selected twelve of his most unerring marksmen, led them to a favorable position, pointed out the doomed man, and bid them, when he next came within range, to fire. The only remark that fell from Morgan, beyond these directions, was: " He is a brave man, but he must die." How often had he thrown himself across the track of a righteous cause ? It was enough —its triumphant wheels must this day roll on over his mangled body.

Morgan told afterwards how attentively and anxiously he observed his marksmen when, in a few minutes, he saw them raise their rifles and aim. A ball cut through his horse's mane and another through the crupper. His aid implored Frazer to change his position. " My duty forbids me to fly from danger." In another moment a rifleball tore through his body, and he fell mortally wounded.

With Frazer's fall, fell all ; there was no longer a pretence of resisting ; dismay seized all hearts. The Americans at this moment, reinforced by fresh regiments, charged furiously along the whole line.

Burgoyne ordered a retreat to the " Great Redoubt," in imminent peril of not safely effecting even this ; leaving all his cannon, four hundred killed and wounded, including the flower of his officers—Frazer, Acland, Williams, Sir Francis Clarke and others.

But the victorious army were at their heels. Morgan pursued the defeated right division, under Balcarrus, into their intrenchments ; but, checked by a furious discharge of cannon, he sheltered his corps in a piece of woods at hand, and continued his murderous fire upon their artillerists. The field battle won, the Americans now stormed the British works. For an hour the firing and fierce assaults continued. At length the ardor of the rifle-corps, no longer brooking restraint, dashed into the intrenchments of Balcarras within the "Great Redoubt." A hand-to-hand struggle here took place. The British light infantry were on the point of giving way, when they were strongly reinforced and threatened a bayonet charge. Morgan, in his moments of highest battle exaltation, never lost his presence of mind or his prudence. He ordered a retreat. Meantime the reinforcements drawn off to strengthen the right against Morgan, had weakened the British centre; here Colonel Brooks broke through the German lines, and at this crisis, General Learned coming up, they put the whole division to rout: they fled, leaving their killed, wounded, tents, baggage and artillery, with the dead body of their brave General Breyman.

Burgoyne ordered the position to be retaken; but night was coming on, or they had no heart to attempt it, and Colonel Brooks and General Learned established themselves within the enemy's works. This Colonel Brooks was .he who had sent the spy into St. Leger's camp at Stanwix. He was afterwards Governor of Massachusetts.

Up to this time, the English at home had never been brought to admit the fighting qualities of the Americans. This illusion was now to be dispelled. If these battles of Saratoga were the work of American colonels and patriot yeomanry (and who can disprove it?) they were on the British side pre-eminently the battles of great generals— their bravest and best. There is, probably, no other instance of such splendid leadership in proportion to the number of its rank and file. General Burgoyne, on his return to England, opened their eyes, in his " Record of the Evidence before the House of Commons," on his " Campaign and Surrender." Referring to Morgan's rifle-corps *driving picked British infantry from the field* and afterwards storming the "Great Redoubt," he observes : "If there be any person who, after considering that circumstance, and the subsequent obstinacy in the attack on the post of Lord Balcarras, with various other actions of the day, continues to doubt that the Americans possess the *quality* and *faculty* of fighting, they are of a prejudice that it would be very absurd longer to contend with."

On Burgoyne's introduction to Morgan after the capitulation, he took him warmly by the hand and said : " Sir, you command the finest regiment in the world." *

Night closed on the battered, beaten, out-generaled, discomfited British army. The American camp rang with shouts of exultation ; the people crowded in from miles around as the news of victory spread.

Morgan coming, grimed with the dust and sweat of battle, to headquarters, was met by Gates, who embraced him, exclaiming : "Morgan, you have done wonders this day ; you have immortalized yourself and honored your country—if *you are not promoted immediately, I will not serve another day.*" Morgan merely replied : " For Heaven's sake, General, forbear this stuff, and give me something to eat and drink, for I am ready to die with hunger and exhaustion." † Morgan was a man of marvellous penetration, and had doubtless taken the General's measure.

Gates had not appeared on the field. Wilkinson says he remained at his quarters, conversing with Sir Francis Clarke, who was brought in, early in the action, mortally wounded, and laid upon Gates' bed.

Where was Arnold ? Sparks says that after the quarrel, he had remained with the army, without authority or command, and without communication with Gates.

When the second battle commenced, Arnold, still forbidden to take part, became infuriated. "He continued *in camp some time*, but at length rode off, in full gallop, to the field without permission. This being told to Gates, he sent Major Armstrong after him with orders to return."*

As soon as Arnold saw Armstrong, anticipating the purport of his message, he put spurs to his horse. Armstrong pursued, following the *erratic movements* of Arnold, without being able to get near enough to speak to him. He moved incessantly on the field, giving orders in every direction, and sometimes in direct opposition to those of the officers." "He behaved," says Samuel Woodruff, a sergeant in the battle, "more like a madman than a discreet officer." It was the opinion of many that he was intoxicated; some thought with brandy, some with opium, —more likely with pride, rage and desperation. He had lost all command of himself; was scarcely conscious of, or responsible for, his actions, and certainly in no condition to give orders to others.

But a word concerning the duration of the battle. It began about three o'clock. Bancroft says : "Just twenty minutes after the beginning of the attack, the British lines wavered and broke, and Burgoyne gave the order to retreat." The Baroness Reidesel, *in her quarters, far to the rear*, says : "About four o'clock they brought in to me poor General Frazer, mortally wounded." Even extending the time of the field-fight to a half-hour or longer, what had Arnold to do with it ? He did not leave the American camp for " some time after the battle commenced." † Indeed, no authority makes mention of him until the attack upon the British intrenchments. Then Major Armstrong pursued him "for half an hour," Arnold dashing hither and thither, without aim or object, except to evade his pursuer and his message—everywhere, and nowhere to any useful purpose. He dashed in after Morgan

* *Sparks.* † *Sparks.*

into Balcarras' works and out again; then into the German lines after Colonel Brooks, and the last volley of the retreating Brunswickers shattered his leg and killed his horse. Major Armstrong only then overtook him, and succeeded in delivering Gates' order for him to return to camp. But his fame was secure!!! "His madness resulted most fortunately for himself. The wound he received at the moment of rushing into the very arms of danger and death, added fresh lustre to his military glory, and was a new claim to public favor and applause."*

His only well-authenticated field performance, was striking an American officer on the head with his sword; "the next day, when the officer demanded redress, Arnold declared his ignorance of the act and expressed regret."

In the face of these admitted facts, can any one maintain that this man was capable of issuing an intelligent military-order? Wilkinson, who was on the battle-field, and whose attention was specially directed to Arnold's movements, says: "It is certain that he neither rendered service nor deserved credit on that day; and *the wound he received alone saved him from being overshadowed by Gates' popularity.* On such caprices of fortune does the bubble of military reputation depend." The exulting cry of the victors had reached his ears, and maddened him; he determined to share with them the fruits of that victory, rushing in at the close of the action, and identifying himself with the glories of the day. The very horse upon which he rode into the field, he stole.†

---

* *Sparks.*

† The animal, a beautiful Spanish horse, the property of Colonel Lewis, was borrowed by Arnold on this occasion. A short time after the action, Colonel Lewis called on him and requested a certificate of the horse having been killed, that he might obtain the value of him, according to usage, from the public treasury. Arnold declined

But the conclusion of the whole matter is, that both Gates and Arnold were only, and solely, accidental figure-heads in this important military crisis. It was certainly fortunate for the cause that Gates remained at head-quarters. Though not altogether wanting in military knowledge he was, from personal cowardice, *nothing on the field;* and perhaps no one knew this better than him-self. The only movement ordered by him, two days after the battle, when Burgoyne was attempting a general

giving the certificate, saying it would have an ill appearance for a Major-general to sign a certificate for a horse that had been shot under him in battle. Lewis said no more till Arnold was about to leave the camp, when he insisted on being allowed a proper compensa-tion for the loss of his horse. Arnold still assigned motives of delicacy for refusing a certificate, but told Lewis that he had a fine Narragansett mare in the public stables, which he would give him in the place of his horse, and immediately wrote an order to the keeper of the stables, directing him to deliver the mare to Colonel Lewis. Meantime Arnold left, and a few days after the order was presented. The keeper said there was no mare belonging to Gen-eral Arnold, in the stables. There had been one of that description some time before, but she had been sold to another officer. It was subsequently ascertained that Arnold had sent in a certificate and had received pay from the government for the horse that had been shot.

Again, at the close of the war, when on the point of sailing for England, Arnold borrowed two hundred dollars from Captain Camp-bell in the British service, for which he gave him an order on Cap-tain Lewis, saying that Lewis owed him for a mare purchased three years before. Captain Campbell being a friend of Colonel Lewis, and expecting to see him again, took the order as a safe equivalent and loaned the money to Arnold. When the news of peace arrived in New York, Colonel Campbell was, by permission of General Washington, dispatched by the British commander at New York by land, with the intelligence, to the Governor of Canada. On his way, he stopped to visit his friend Lewis in Albany, and presented Arnold's order. Their mutual surprise may be imagined, both being equal sufferers by this refinement of knavery.* Thus he ad-dressed himself with equal gusto to small, as to great villainies.

* *Sparks.*

retreat, well-nigh resulted in disgrace and disaster to the American army.

"The action was the battle of the husbandmen. So many of the rank and file were freeholders or freeholders' sons, that they gave character to the whole army. Next to the generous care of Washington in detaching to that army troops destined against Howe, victory was due to the enthusiasm of the soldiers. Their common zeal created a harmonious correspondence of movement and baffled the high officers and veterans opposed to them." *

On this decisive day, men of New York, New England, and men of the valley of Virginia, led by the lion-hearted Morgan, fought together in a common cause.

The British General might yet have saved the remnants of his army, by a rapid flight on the night following the battle ; but he contented himself with transferring his camp to the heights on his rear, and the dawning day revealed the misery and hopelessness of his situation. Delay was fatal to Burgoyne ; the Baroness Reidesel says : " A retreat was spoken of, but there was not the least movement made toward it. We learned that General Burgoyne intended to fulfil the last wish of General Frazer, to have him buried at six o'clock in the evening at the place designated by him. This occasioned a delay to which part of the misfortunes of the army was owing."

The death of Frazer, aside from the defeat, would have hung the British camp in gloom, so closely had he drawn all hearts to himself. "He questioned the surgeon eagerly as to his wound, and when he found that he must go from wife and children ; that fame and promotion and life were

* *Bancroft*, Vol. IX.

gliding from before his eyes, he cried out in his agony : 'Damned ambition.' "

● "At sunset of the 8th, as his body, attended by the officers and his family, was borne by soldiers of his corps to the Great Redoubt above the Hudson, where he had asked to be buried, the three Major Generals, and none beside, joined the train. Amidst the ceaseless booming of the American artillery, the order prescribed for the burial of the dead was strictly observed, in the twilight, over his grave. Never more shall he chase the red deer through the heather of Strath Errick, or guide the skiff across the fathomless lake of central Scotland, or muse over the ruin of the Stuarts on the moor of Drum-mossie, or dream of glory beside the crystal waters of the Ness. Death in itself is not terrible, but he came to America for selfish advancement, and though bravely true as a soldier, he died unconsoled."*

As soon as the funeral services were over, the order for retreat was given, but through a night of pouring rain, it was all too slow. The continual rain of the next day compelled a halt, and by the 10th it was impossible to attempt the crossing of the Hudson. The Americans had taken position on the opposite side on the banks of the Batten Kill. Burgoyne ordered his army to reoccupy their former camp on the heights of Saratoga.

The lay of the land resembled a vast amphitheatre with the British in the arena, and the Americans posted upon the rising elevations around. Burgoyne's fortified camp extended a half mile along the river, with his artillery on an elevated plateau.

Morgan and his sharpshooters were posted on still higher ground in his rear, and to the west. Opposite, on the eastern bank of the Hudson, Fellowes with three thousand was intrenched. Gates with the main army occupied the height south of Fish Creek. Stark the invincible, with

* *Bancroft*, Vol. IX.

two thousand men, held the river at Fort Edward. Between him and Lake George the Americans had a strongly fortified camp, and the river on both sides was lined with bodies of militia, who flocked from all quarters, to bag the game. The condition of the British army was pitiable in the extreme. The soldiers were worn down by weeks of incessant toil, privation, sickness, and desperate fighting.

Their losses included their highest officers and best fighting material. Deserted by their Canadian and Indian allies, their hospitals crowded with sick and wounded, their effective force was less than one half the number Burgoyne had brought from Canada.

In the depths of a gloomy wilderness, they were invested by a victorious army, more than twice their number, who encircled them with a wall of steel; an enemy who declined to fight, and who in their high intrenchments defied attack. "The trap which Reidesel and Frazer had foreseen was sprung."

"In this helpless condition, obliged to be constantly under arms while the enemy's cannon played on every part of their camp and their rifle-balls whistled through the lines, the troops of Burgoyne retained their firmness, and while sinking under a hard necessity they showed themselves worthy of a better fate." *

On the 13th, starvation was imminent, and the officers in council urged Burgoyne to capitulate. On the 15th, the articles of capitulation were barely concluded, when a messenger brought to Burgoyne news of Clinton's success on the Hudson, and that part of his forces were within fifty miles of the camp. Too late—their faith was pledged. The Americans also had heard from below, and would have attacked immediately.

On the 17th of October, the convention of Saratoga was carried into effect by which five thousand, seven hundred and ninety surrendered themselves prisoners,

* *Botta.*

with forty-two pieces of the best brass ordnance then known, forty-six hundred muskets, and a large amount of ammunition.

Much has been said and written concerning the magnanimity and delicacy shown by Gates to his vanquished foe; the over-generous terms granted to Burgoyne, which gave infinite dissatisfaction to Congress and the country, and which were finally disallowed; his ordering his whole army out of sight while the British stacked their arms, at the command of their own officers; also the spectacular arrangement for the surrender of Burgoyne's sword, etc., etc.

On that day Gates dined and wined the officers, and many compliments and fair speeches were exchanged. Burgoyne finally proposed a toast to General Washington, which it must have irked Gates to swallow, who in turn drained a glass to King George. By pre-arrangement, as the British army filed past headquarters, the two generals stepped out in front of the tent, and, in sight of both armies, Burgoyne handed his sword to Gates, who immediately returned it.

It was scarcely magnanimity, seeing that magnanimity is not a garment to be worn to-day and folded up as a vesture to-morrow; that it is no respecter of persons, but is debtor to all mankind; that it is a quality of the soul, which inheres; the exquisite bloom and aroma of the character, that unconsciously and inevitably colors and perfumes every thought and deed of its possessor.

It was more likely that unhandsome thing which we call toadyism, since it was only exercised towards the enemies of his country. At that very instant he had none for the noble spirits who had contributed so largely to secure his present exaltation. We have already seen how persistently he held back Washington's own forces, even after the surrender, when he no longer needed them.

He forgot that the pompous message dispatched to

Congress, instead of to the commander-in-chief, was made possible only by the generosity of Washington, in stripping himself of his best officers and men to reinforce the army of the Hudson, while he skilfully kept at bay nearly twice his own numbers on the Delaware.

Who does not see that Gates, handicapped with Sullivan and Greene, and Washington, supported by Stark and Morgan, with any approach to equality of forces, would have given a surrender at Philadelphia instead of Saratoga. We should have held the Delaware and lost the Hudson—a calamity which the commander-in-chief foresaw and provided against.

Gates' course towards Arnold, odious as he appears, was equally wanting in justice and generosity; and from an extravagant appreciation and a fawning patronage of Morgan, he suddenly assumed towards him a haughty and disdainful demeanor. Notwithstanding the splendid service he had rendered, Morgan's name had only a passing notice in the early despatches, and was not even mentioned in Gates' official account of the surrender, to which he had so largely contributed.

This sudden fall from the General's favor was marked by the officers, as Gates had given Morgan the most unmistakable proofs of his confidence and esteem from the moment of his arrival in camp. Morgan kept silence, and the matter remained a mystery at the time, but was afterward satisfactorily explained.

" Immediately after the surrender, Morgan visited Gates on business, when he was taken aside by the General and confidentially informed that the main army was extremely dissatisfied with the conduct of the war by the commander-in-chief, and that several of the best officers threatened to resign unless a change took place. Morgan perfectly comprehended the motives of Gates, although he did not then know of the correspondence he had been holding with Conway, and he sternly replied : 'I have one favor to ask of you, sir, which is, never to mention that detestable subject to me again, for under no other man than Washington, as commander-in-chief, would I ever serve.' A day or two after the foregoing interchange of views, General Gates gave a dinner to the principal officers of the British army, to which a number of American officers were also invited. Morgan was not among the number. Before the evening was over, the petty indignity recoiled upon its author. Morgan had occasion to see Gates upon official business. He was ushered into the dining-room, where they still sat at table. Having attended to the matter in hand, he was allowed to withdraw, without even the empty ceremony of an introduction. Struck by the commanding figure and noble mien of the colonel, they inquired his name, and on learning that it was Colonel Morgan, they left the table, and, following him, took him by the hand, made themselves known to him, frankly declaring at the same time that they had felt him severely in the field." * They had only a dining-room acquaintance with Gates.

Salvos of cannon announced the glorious tidings of the surrender all over the country. Congress gave thanks to the army, the coveted full rank of major-general to Arnold, a medal of gold to Gates—to Morgan, nothing.

And do we, in these holy centennial days, living in the rich fruitage of the noble planting of those mighty spirits, —do we still confirm the old injustice, and still consent to fraud and villainy, by raising statues and carving marbles to Gates and Arnold?

* Graham's Life of Morgan. Dr. Hill's MSS.

HARD SERVICE AND NO LAURELS.

MORGAN moved with all haste to join Washington at Whitemarsh, a strong position. in the vicinity of Philadelphia, which he reached November 18th, 1777.

At that time a party were clamoring for the commander-in-chief to attack Howe, but, as he had less than eight thousand effective men and Howe was well intrenched with twice that number, he declined so rash a movement, notwithstanding the unhandsome innuendoes levelled at him. He strengthened his own position, and compelled Howe to the initiative.

On the night of December 4th, that officer moved out from his lines with fourteen thousand men, and the next morning advanced to Chestnut Hill, about three miles from the right wing of the American army.

The Pennsylvania militia were ordered forward to skirmish with the enemy, but after a short engagement, they fled in disorder, leaving their commander, General Irvine, wounded and a prisoner. The British, during the night, changed their ground, and now menaced the American left, advancing within a mile of their lines. Every appearance indicated a serious intention of battle, which Washington determined not to decline. On the morning of the 8th, Morgan was ordered to the front with his corps. General Gist and a body of Maryland militia were also thrown forward a short distance to the right.

Morgan put his men in motion towards a very considerable body of the enemy. As soon as he heard the firing in the direction of the Maryland militia, he gave the word, and his corps delivered a well-aimed discharge, and rushed forward with their usual impetuosity. A second and third volley of balls, in rapid succession, thinned out the British ranks; they fired without effect, broke and fled in disorder. Morgan pursued the flying foe until they reached a body of British infantry, who were moving to their support. They rallied and the contest was renewed with vigor. Nothing daunted by the presence of thrice their numbers, the riflemen sheltered themselves among the trees and continued to pour in upon the British an unceasing fire, every ball carrying its message of wounds or death.

Unfortunately, General Gist had been compelled to give ground before his opponents, who now turned upon Morgan. Finding himself threatened upon flank and rear, he signalled a retreat; they drew off in perfect order, nor did the British venture a step in pursuit, so heavy was their loss.

The engagement, though short, had been exceedingly spirited, and, for the time and numbers engaged, the slaughter of the British was incredible. Their loss in this encounter with the rifle corps was not less than two hundred.

Howe had now maneuvred for three days before Washington's army and lost during that time not less than three hundred and fifty in killed and wounded—the majority of them in a skirmish of less than an hour with the rifle corps.

Such an admonition was not lost upon a commander like Howe. The next day he marched with his whole force back to Philadelphia, and did not again repeat the experiment. It was fortunate; for Washington's army, pinched with hunger and nakedness, was *hors-du combat.*

The rifle corps had suffered severely in the affair of Chestnut Hill, twenty-seven killed and wounded; among them the brave Major Morris, beloved by all. He died a few days after. Here we get a glimpse of that rare and beautiful spirit that brooded over our cause, our battle-fields and camps, like an angel of mercy, dropping the balm of sympathy where it was most sorely needed.

The brave instinctively draw to the brave. Upon the arrival of Morgan's corps from the North, LaFayette had expressed the greatest interest in their movements, and had sought the friendship of its officers. Between Morgan and himself, this friendship ripened into an intimacy that ceased only with life.

LaFayette had commanded part of the corps in a little skirmish a day or two before the fight at Chestnut Hill, and, in his account to Washington, was enthusiastic in their praise.

They had attacked a picket-guard of three hundred and fifty Hessians, with their field-pieces, who, after a few minutes hard fighting, were compelled to fly. He wrote : " British reinforcements came twice to their aid, but very far from recovering their ground, they always retreated." The pursuit was pushed to their camp, with the loss, on the American side, of only one killed and six wounded. The marquis extolled the riflemen : " I never saw men so merry, so spirited, and so desirous to go on to the enemy, whatever force they might meet, as that small party in this little fight."

For Major Morris the marquis entertained the most generous affection. The fact that his wife and children were left unprovided for, by his death, pained LaFayette deeply, and drew from him the following proposal, so exquisite in delicacy of feeling and expression :

" *Dear Sir :*—I just now received your favor concerning our late friend Major Morris, and I need not repeat to you how much I am concerned in the interests of his family. I spoke the other day to his Excellency on the subject, and I shall write to Congress a very particular letter, where you will be mentioned.

"I intend to speak as in your name, and that of all your corps, and as being myself honored with their confidence.

"It is my opinion that a decent estate might be given to the family, as a mark of gratefulness from their country, and that his son must be promoted as soon as possible.

"But, my dear sir, you know how long Congress waive any matter whatsoever before a decision, and as Mrs. Morris may be in some want before that time, I am going to trouble you with a commission which I beg you will execute with the greatest secrecy.

"If she wanted to borrow any sum of money, in expecting the arrangements of Congress, it would not become a stranger unknown to her, to offer himself for that purpose. But you could (as from yourself) tell her that you had friends who, being in the army, don't know what to do with their money; and as they are not in the mercantile or husbandry way, would willingly let her have one or many thousands of dollars, which she might give again in three or four years.

"One other way would be, to let her believe that you have got, or borrowed, the money from any town or body you will be pleased to mention ; or it would be needless to mention where it comes from.

"In a word, my dear sir, if with the greatest secrecy and the most minute regard for that lady's delicacy, you may find a manner of being useful to her, I beg you would communicate to me immediately. I shall, as soon as possible, let you know the answer of Congress, whenever an answer will be got, and in expecting the pleasure to hear from you, I have the honor to be, very sincerely,

"Your most obedient servant,

"MARQUIS DE LAFAYETTE.

"To Colonel MORGAN, of the Rifle Corps."

Persuaded that Howe had now abandoned all intention of battle, Washington conducted his tatterdemalion army into winter-quarters at Valley Forge; a position secure from attack and favorable to such a disposition of the American forces as would best prevent the foraging of the British army. General Armstrong kept the old camp at Whitemarsh; General Smallwood took post at Wilmington; Major Jameson with cavalry guarded the east, and Captain Lee the west side of the Schuylkill; Morgan was in advance of these, on the west side of the river, charged to watch every movement of the enemy and detect their purpose.

Soon the vigilance of his American keepers made it necessary for Howe to detach a British brigade to steal a sheep; the fleet of Admiral Howe was taxed to supply the army, and the witticism of Dr. Franklin was justified, "instead of the British taking Philadelphia, Philadelphia had taken them."

Much of the service to which Morgan was now appointed was of the severest character, invaluable to the cause but unattended with glory or remuneration; nevertheless, that unknown, unseen, unappreciated work which, faithfully performed, best strengthens the fibre of heroic souls.

In advance, as usual, and so near the enemy's post, their vigilance was never to slumber nor sleep,—frosty night watches succeeded the labors of the day; the cold was intense, yet oftentimes they dared not build fires; without shelter and most scantily fed, they saved themselves from perishing only by keeping in constant motion.

Here sets in a stretch of eighteen months of much such service. Even his Herculean physique was beginning to succumb. Wherever skill, vigilance, penetration, judgment or daring was most wanted, thither went this Agamemnon, shepherd of the people. Not once was he surprised; not once did he bring false intelligence.

His services at the time of the evacuation of Philadelphia in the summer of 1778 were invaluable—the following brief letters among many testify to it:

"HEAD QUARTERS, VALLEY FORGE, May 17, 1778.

"*Dear Sir:*—His Excellency is much obliged to you for your information. There is little room to doubt of their intentions to evacuate the city.   *   *   *   *

"I am, with much respect,
          "Your humble servant,
                    "JAMES McHENRY."
"Colonel MORGAN, at Radnor."

"HEAD QUARTERS, May 30, 1778.

"*Dear Sir:*—Your letter concerning Sir Henry Clinton is received. His Excellency is highly pleased with your conduct upon this occasion, etc.   *   *   *   *

"I am your obedient servant,
          "JOHN FITZGERALD, A. D. C."
"Colonel MORGAN."

Certain it is, that Morgan was rising to fame and honor with the army and with its ablest officers, though his name had not yet penetrated "the dull cold ear" of Congress. They did not know this great combination, that reminds us by turns of Hercules and Ajax and Agamemnon and old Bunyan's "Great Heart." History says that Belisarius had a voice, like that with which we know Morgan led on his men, when he stormed Quebec, and rushed into the "Great Redoubt" at Saratoga, and rode down Ban Tarleton on the field of Cowpens.

There was one thing, however, which this heroic soul could *not do,* with all the power of that matchless voice. *He couldn't blow his own trumpet.* No heroic soul ever did. Perhaps, like Washington, he thought posterity would blow it for him ; meantime he served a *cause* and not *himself.* That he felt the neglect is equally certain, and this, with other considerations, undoubtedly led to his retirement in June 1779.

He remained long enough to see the fruit of his labors at Saratoga. The French king's ambassadors had been received by Congress, and the French king's armies and navies were in our waters, and had necessitated the evacuation of Philadelphia. Spain and Holland were likewise arrayed against England, and they were crossing swords in every quarter of the world, for it seemed that the birth-throes of the Young Republic were to shake the globe. The cause, Morgan thought, was now assured—it no longer needed him. He knew perfectly the value of the services he had performed, and he knew that others were wearing the laurels that rightfully belonged to him. He constantly saw his inferiors, either by their own importunities or those of their friends, or through favoritism or still less worthy motives, pass above him.

Gates filled a huge space in public favor, and Arnold was at this moment installed in splendor in Philadelphia, the pampered pet of society and of the commander-in-chief—hatching "treasons, stratagems, and spoils."

In this continued lack of recognition and acknowledgment, this great spirit at last realized that *manhood was insulted in his person*, and, to his eternal honor, he resigned and went home.

It was shortly before this that the Marquis de La Fayette, under whose orders Morgan's corps had so often served, was about to embark for France to offer his sword to his king, who had come to open rupture with England by the recognition of the independence of America. On the point of sailing he had been seized at Boston with a violent fever and barely escaped with his life. The following letter was in reply to one from Morgan:

" FISHKILL, November 28, 1778.

"*Dear Sir:*—Your most kind and obliging letter arrived

safe into my hands, but I was then too ill for thinking of answering it. However, though it was at that time, out of my power to express anything, I did feel all the sentiments of gratitude for the friendship and the good idea you are pleased to entertain of me. Both are extremely dear to my heart, and I do assure you my dear sir, that the true regard and esteem, and the sincere affection you have inspired to me, will last for ever.

"The strength of youth and a good constitution, have brought me again to health and to the enjoyments of this world. Dying in a shameful bed, after having essayed some more honorable occasions in the field, would have been for me, the most cruel disappointment.

"I am just setting out for France and hope to be there in a short time. My country is at war, and I think it my duty to go myself for offering my services to her. However, I am very far from leaving the American service, and I have merely a furlough from Congress. I am much inclined to think that the king will have no objection to my returning here ; so that I am almost convinced that I shall have the pleasure to see you next spring.

"I most earnestly beg you to present my best compliments to the gentlemen officers in my division. I shall for all my life, feel pleased and proud, in the idea that I have had the honor to be entrusted with such a division. I anticipate the happiness of finding them next campaign, and I dare flatter myself that these gentlemen will not forget a friend and fellow soldier, who entertains for them all the sentiments of affection and esteem.

"Farewell my dear sir ; don't forget your friend on the other side of the great water and believe me ever.

"Your affectionate

"LA FAYETTE.

"Colonel MORGAN."

It is worth while to inquire for the secret of the esprit

of this matchless rifle corps, whose fame had gone through the land and crossed the seas. Old Frederick the Great had observed their tactics with profoundest interest, and introduced into his own army bodies of sharpshooters.

Coming to a close scrutiny of its soul and inspiration,—this great, massive, granite character,—we find it exquisitely veined with tenderness, delicacy, and sensibility.

Morgan's capacity for commanding was "singular, rather than rare." His own conduct furnished the best example for the imitation of his men, and inspired them equally with the profoundest respect and the most affectionate regard.

"In the government of his regiment the stern and severe system of the army was unknown. He appealed to the pride rather than to the fears of his men, and obtained from them a prompt performance of their duty.

"He held himself accessible to them on all necessary occasions, and encouraged them to come to him whenever they had just cause of complaint. He knew what every soldier was entitled to, and would never suffer them to be wronged or imposed upon. He took great pains to have them provided at all times with a sufficiency of provisions, clothing and everything necessary to their comfort. The wounded and sick experienced his constant care and attention. Thus officers and men came to regard themselves as a band of brothers, among whom none of the austerities of strict discipline were observed. The affection of his men for Morgan is shown in the fact, that almost every one who marched with him through the wilderness to Quebec and survived its disasters, was found afterwards in the ranks of his regiment.

"He never permitted any of them to be brought before a court-martial, or to be punished by whipping. [That sword had once entered his own soul.] When one of

them was charged with an offence which called for punishment, the accused, if guilty, was taken by Morgan to
some secluded place, where no one could witness what
might occur, and there, after a lecture on the impropriety
of his conduct, would receive a thumping, more or less
severe, according to the nature of his offence.

"It once happened, when Morgan was away from his
camp, that one of his favorite riflemen, who had committed some misdemeanor, was brought before a court-martial, condemned and whipped in the face of the whole
regiment. When Morgan returned, and was informed of
what had happened, he was so moved that he wept. He
declared that he would not have had the offended whipped
upon any consideration whatever; that he was a high-
spirited and efficient soldier, respected at home, and now
he must be so lowered in his own esteem as to be unable
ever to recover his former self-respect and pride of manhood.

"Another instance of his manner of governing. On one
occasion, a rough piece of road was to be repaired; a
party of his men were accordingly sent, under an ensign,
to execute the work. While thus engaged, Morgan rode
up and saw two of them heaving at a large rock, the removal of which was evidently beyond their strength. The
ensign stood and looked on but offered no assistance.
'Why don't you lay hold and help those men?' inquired
Morgan of the ensign. 'Sir,' replied the latter, 'I am
an officer.' 'I beg your pardon,' responded Morgan;
'I did not think of that.' Instantly alighting from his
horse, he approached the rock, seizing hold of which, he
exclaimed to the men, 'Now heave hard, my boys.' The
rock was soon displaced, and Morgan, without another
word, mounted and rode off." *

We have alluded to other circumstances that conduced
to Morgan's resignation. The depreciation of the cur-

* *Graham's Life of Morgan*, p. 200.

rency, and the poverty of the military chest, had for some time left the officers without adequate support. Many efficient officers had quit the service, because they could no longer make a decent appearance. Morgan had long been drawing upon his private revenues, while his interests were suffering seriously by his protracted absence from home.

A graver compulsion, however, was the impaired state of his health. The unparalleled severities of that ill-starred Canadian expedition ; that winter wading through the rivers and marshes of Maine, with the subsequent hard service before Quebec; had induced a rheumatic affection, which at times developed into a torturing sciatica.

The services of the rifle corps, for the eighteen months following the surrender at Saratoga, had also involved more peril, privation and fatigue than that of any other regiment in the army.

Their incessant reconnoissances and manœuvres before the enemy's outposts, their innumerable picket fights and skirmishes, unrecorded, lost to history and now forgotten, were attended by more privation and danger than regular field engagements.

In June, 1779, he communicated his intentions to Washington and asked permission to wait upon Congress with his resignation. Washington received his proposition with much concern, and endeavored to dissuade him, while he admitted the gravity of the causes for such a step.

Morgan, however, adhered to his resolution, and presented to Congress, a few days after, the following from the commander-in-chief :

"To the PRESIDENT OF CONGRESS.

Sir :—Colonel Morgan, of the Virginia line, who waits on Congress with his resignation, will have the honor of delivering this to you. I cannot, in justice, avoid mentioning him as a very valuable officer, who has rendered a series of important services, and distinguished himself on several occasions.

"I am, sir, very respectfully,
"Your obedient servant,
"Geo. Washington."

ARNOLD AT PHILADELPHIA.

ARNOLD, by this time, was moving swiftly to the consummation of his villainies. After the "Surrender," October 1777, he had lain some months in hospital, at Albany, with his shattered limb. Here he accepted and appropriated the compliments of General Burgoyne for his bravery and military skill, especially *in the action of the 19th September*, of which he got the whole credit.

Congress had so far relented as to permit Washington to commission him to the full rank for which he had so valiantly contended with that body. There is little doubt that the injustice of Gates toward Arnold still further quickened the sympathies of the commander-in-chief, who accompanied the commission with a letter saying, "As soon as your situation will permit, I request you will repair to this army, it being my earnest wish to have your services the ensuing campaign."

In the spring of 1778, he journeyed homeward to New Haven. Near that place, he received unmistakable demonstrations of the public appreciation of his services, being met and escorted into the town by several military companies with leading citizens, while his arrival was announced by thirteen discharges of cannon. He received while here a further compliment from Washington, in the gift of a handsome set of epaulettes and sword knot, "as a testimony of sincere regard and approbation of his conduct." These had been sent to Washington from one of his French admirers, with the request that he would wear one, and present the other to any gentleman he might select.

At the end of May 1778, Arnold joined Washington at Valley Forge. The condition of his wound still forbidding active service, Washington decided to appoint him to the command at Philadelphia, as soon as the British should evacuate it.

A more injudicious appointment was, perhaps, never made. Nothing could more forcibly illustrate how completely Washington's eyes were holden in regard to Arnold's character and qualifications. A military commandant was scarcely necessary, as only a handful of militia remained in the city ; but, otherwise, the post involved the settlement of the nicest and most intricate questions, requiring the utmost tact, delicacy, judgment and integrity.

During the British occupation of Philadelphia, many of doubtful patriotism had flocked thither, and still remained, holding large quantities of merchandise ; this naturally led to disputed ownership and gave opportunities for fraudulent transactions.

The difficulty was further complicated by the indefinable powers of the military commander. How far did his authority extend, and where clash with the civil government of Pennsylvania, whose laws its citizens were bound to obey?

Arnold's instructions from Washington could only be expressed in general terms, leaving far too much to his own discretion in their execution.

His proclamation upon entering the city, prohibiting the sale of any and all goods until a joint committee of Congress and Pennsylvania should decide their ownership, brought upon him at once an odium that his haughtiness and arrogance could only increase.

Before a month, this restless spirit conceived a sudden design of obtaining the command of the navy, and with that intent wrote to consult the commander-in-chief, saying that his friends had proposed such a position for him.

The Chief, in reply, declined to advise him in the matter, urging his ignorance of naval concerns.

As there is nowhere any record of any such offer being suggested for or made to Arnold, except in this letter to Washington, it was doubtless a matter of his own invention, and he thought to obtain the influence of Washington to further his plans.

He was most likely induced to the project by avarice— it opened a fine prospect of rich prizes and plunder. Money was becoming an absolute necessity, for he was at this time in the greatest pecuniary straits.

In assuming the command of the city, he had installed himself in a style of splendid extravagance, out of all proportion to his revenues. He took a handsome house, formerly the Penn mansion, furnished it extravagantly, and drove a coach and four. When the French Ambassador arrived in Philadelphia, he and his suite were Arnold's guests for some time.

Likewise, he had married the young and beautiful daughter of Mr. Edwin Shippen, afterwards Chief Justice of Pennsylvania—pronounced royalists. The lady had been on terms of intimacy with the British officers during their occupation of the city; she had adorned the fête of the Mischianza, inaugurated in honor of the departing heroes, and afterwards corresponded with Major André. Social relations, so intimate, with the royalist circles of Philadelphia, doubtless gave stimulus and direction to Arnold's villainy.

A few months after the "naval" project subsided, Arnold conceived a design of obtaining a grant of land in Western New York, as a place of settlement for officers and soldiers who had served under him, and others—whosoever would. It received the sanction and favor of some of the best men of that State ; but this project necessitated a genius for building up—creating something—bringing something to pass. Arnold's genius was one of destruction only; he could only pull down and destroy. The scheme fell through. What was wrapped up in that project no man knows. Most likely it was a presentiment of such treason as that subsequently attempted by Aaron Burr.

From the time of Arnold's arrival in Philadelphia, he had been involved in constant disputes and difficulties with the "Council of Pennsylvania," which resulted, seven months after, about January 1779, in the passage by that body of a severe public censure upon his conduct. The Attorney General was directed to prosecute him in their courts of law for his illegal and oppressive acts.

As Arnold was a United States officer, it was thought proper to appeal to Congress, and accordingly they laid their charges before that body. These documents were in time referred to a "committee of inquiry," who vindicated Arnold from all criminality on the charges brought before them. But it came to be known that the "Congressional Committee" had not received the full testimony offered by the "Council of Pennsylvania," so that their report was not accepted by Congress, but referred anew to another joint committee of the two bodies.

The affair dragged on for months, and it was finally proposed to refer it to the commander-in-chief and to a military tribunal.

Arnold considered himself very unhandsomely dealt with by Congress, which had declined to confirm the acquittal of their own "Committee," and he charged them with sacrificing him to maintain amicable relations with the "Council of Pennsylvania."

The court-martial was about to assemble, June 1st, 1779, at Middlebrook, when the British army threatened a movement upon the Hudson, or, it might be, into the Jerseys; the court was adjourned.

Arnold had, by permission of Washington, resigned his command some months before ; he, however, still retained his commission and continued to reside in Philadelphia.

Detested by the always keen-sighted populace, he was one day assaulted in the streets by a mob. He immediately complained to Congress and requested that body to order him a guard of continental troops, adding, "this request, I presume, will not be denied to a man who has so often fought and bled in the defence of the liberties of his country."

Congress declined to interfere, and referred him to the civil authorities of Pennsylvania for redress. He renewed his request for a guard of twenty men, declaring that his life was in danger from a " mad, ignorant, deluded rabble," again reminding them of his rank and services. Congress turned a deaf ear to the wily Pisistratus.

THE COURT-MARTIAL.

THE fall of 1779 wore away in military maneuvres, and in the winter Washington announced that a court-martial would assemble December 20. It sat until January 26th, 1780, when it pronounced its verdict.

Arnold's defence of himself was "vigorous, elaborate and characteristic," especially when he made his usual parade of his "patriotism, services, sacrifices and wounds, and enumerated his real and imaginary wrongs." This over-done, weakened the force of his arguments, and it was clearly seen how adroitly he manœuvred to divert the attention of the court from essential to irrelevant points.

He spoke thus : "When the present necessary war with Great Britain commenced, I was in easy circumstances, happy in domestic connections, blessed with a rising family who claimed my care and attention. The liberties of my country were in danger. She called on all her faithful sons to join in her defence. I obeyed the call. I sacrificed domestic ease and happiness to the service of my country, and in her service have I sacrificed a great part of a handsome fortune. I was one of the first in the field, and from that time to the present hour I have not abandoned her service. My time, my person and my fortune have been devoted to my country in this war, and if the sentiments of those who are supreme in the United States in civil and military affairs have any weight, my time, my fortune and my person have not been devoted in vain. * * * * I have often bled in this service ; the marks that I bear are sufficient evidence of my conduct. The impartial public will judge of my services, and whether the returns I have met with are not tinctured with the basest ingratitude." He bitterly denounced his persecutors, as he was pleased to call his prosecutors, and added : "In the hour of danger, when the affairs of America wore a gloomy aspect, when our illustrious General was retreating through New Jersey with a handful of men, I did not propose to my associates basely to quit the General and sacrifice the cause of my country to my personal safety, by going over to the enemy and making my peace."

Says Sparks : "The boastfulness and malignity of these declarations are obvious enough ; but their consummate hypocrisy can be understood only by knowing the fact that, at the moment they were uttered, he had been eight months in secret correspondence with the enemy, and was prepared, when the first opportunity should offer, to desert and betray his country." Notwithstanding this elaborate defence, the court found him guilty of two of the four charges, and sentenced him to be reprimanded by the commander-in-chief.

The language of Washington was preserved by M. Marbois, secretary of the French legation : "Our profession is the chastest of all. The shadow of a fault tarnishes our most brilliant actions. The least inadvertence may cause us to lose that public favor which is so hard to be gained. I reprimand you for having forgotten that, in proportion as you had rendered yourself formidable to our enemies, you should have shown moderation to our citizens. Exhibit again those splendid qualities which have placed you in the rank of our most distinguished generals. As far as it shall be in my power, I will myself furnish you with opportunities for regaining the esteem which you have formerly enjoyed."

Washington's tenderness and delicacy were as pearls

thrown to swine. He received the reprimand with sullen reserve, and from this time devoted himself to such maturing of his treasonable designs as should bring him the largest pecuniary results. He asked leave of absence for the summer, on the plea of attending to his private affairs, but continued to reside in Philadelphia. He was at that time concerned in petty speculations, privateering enterprises and commercial ventures, in which he had his usual ill-luck — "the losses outweighing the profits." Also, shortly after the trial, he again pressed Congress for a settlement of his old disputed accounts, with such effrontery as to confirm his enemies in their disgusts and wear out the patience of his friends. His claims were not allowed.

His next move was to offer himself for sale to the French envoy, M. de la Luzerne. That minister, taking the public estimate of his distinguished services, had treated him with great kindness even after the censure of the court-martial. Arnold wished to turn the Frenchman's amenities into cash, and to that end he unbosomed himself without reserve, making the usual parade of his "services, sacrifices and wounds, the ingratitude of his country, the injustice of Congress, and the malice of his enemies."

The war, he said, had swamped his fortunes; he was harassed by his creditors, and, unless he could effect a loan to the amount of his debts, he should be compelled to quit his profession from poverty. He set before the minister the great advantage that would accrue to his sovereign, the French king, to secure to his service an American general of a rank and influence so high as his.

The Frenchman was a man of clean hands and noble sentiments; he listened to the American with pain, and frankly answered : "You desire of me a service which it would be easy for me to render, but which would degrade us both. When the envoy of a foreign power gives, or, if you will, lends money, it is ordinarily to corrupt those who receive it, and to make them the creatures of the sovereign whom he serves ; or, rather, he corrupts without persuading ; he buys and does not secure.

"But the firm league entered into between the King and the United States, is the work of justice and of the wisest policy. It has for its basis, a reciprocal interest and good will. In the mission with which I am charged, my true glory consists, in fulfilling it without intrigue or cabal ; without resorting to secret practices, and by the force alone of the conditions of the alliance."

Furthermore, hoping to win back to paths of duty and rectitude so illustrious a soldier, he "addressed him in the language of expostulation and advice, reminding him that murmurs and resentments at the acts of public bodies and the persecutions of political opponents, were evidences of a weak rather than of a great mind, resting on its own dignity and power, and that a consciousness of innocence was his best support. He recurred to the renown of his former exploits, appealed to his sense of patriotism and honor, his love of glory, and represented in the most attractive colors the wide field of action yet before him, if he would suppress his anger, bear his troubles with fortitude, and unite heart and hand with his compatriots in the great work in which he had already labored with so much credit to himself, and benefit to his country." *

The pitch of such sentiments was away above and out of Arnold's inner sense of hearing ; the one only thing he wanted was money. The advice of the French minister was not appreciated, and Arnold left him, indignant at his ill success, and at the rebuff he had received.

Arnold's talents show to the highest advantage in the matter of the treason ; in devising mischiefs he was in his element. The plan was matured with skill, caution, deliberation, and matchless ability, up to a certain point ; for at the last, always, " the devil is an ass."

* *Sparks' Life of Arnold.*

He had been for eighteen months in communication with the enemy under assumed names. The correspondence with Major André, still maintained by Mrs. Arnold after her marriage, afforded facilities which Arnold so managed as not even to excite her suspicions. Through this channel he communicated directly with Sir Henry Clinton. He was in British pay, and had already furnished valuable information.

It was now midsummer of 1780, and certain movements of the French and English fleets, newly arrived in our waters, made it desirable to consummate the treason.

We have already explained that from the commencement of hostilities, the possession of the Hudson River had been the supreme object of the British. Arnold's supreme necessity was money, and he knew that West Point would bring the largest price in the British market; this booty, so rich, he hoped might be further enhanced by the betrayal into the enemy's hands of the person of his friend and benefactor, the commander-in-chief.*

* The following letter from the chivalrous young Laurens expresses the sentiment of the day on this point:

"PHILADELPHIA, October 4, 1780.

"*Sir:*—With the triumph of a republican and the more tender emotions of one who sincerely loves his General, I congratulate your Excellency on your late providential escape. I congratulate my country, whose safety is so intimately united with yours, and who may regard this miraculous rescue of her champion, as an assurance that Heaven approves her choice of a defender, and is propitious to her cause. In fact, all the ascendency that could be given by virtue, genius and valor, would only have furnished a deplorable example of unfortunate merit, if, by the Divine interposition, you had not prevailed over the most impenetrable perfidy that has yet disgraced mankind. This happy event must inspire every virtuous citizen of America with new confidence, and transfix her enemies with awful terror. I need not inform your Excellency, how I have languished in so long a separation from you, and how anxious I am to assure you, in person, of the veneration and attachment of your faithful aid,

"JOHN LAURENS."

Such were the relations between Arnold and Washington, that it was only to ask and have; he therefore addressed himself at once to obtain the command of that post.

He had up to this time pleaded the state of his wounds, in justification of his long furlough from active service. He now suddenly represented himself ready and solicitous to resume military duty. Washington, from certain indications, anticipating a stirring campaign, intended to give him command of the left wing of the army, hoping he would here find an opportunity to retrieve his popularity by some brilliant stroke. Arnold at first maneuvred indirectly through Schuyler and Livingston to obtain the coveted command, but Washington esteemed the post he had assigned him, so important and honorable, that he declined to act upon their suggestions. Meantime Arnold arrived at headquarters, and learning from General Tilghman of his appointment to the left wing, his countenance fell. He seemed embarrassed and ill at ease. He sought the commander-in-chief and represented to him that his wounds still disabled him from field service, and that at West Point only, could he do himself justice and his country service.

Washington was puzzled. He could not comprehend how a man of Arnold's temperament and enthusiasm, should decline a post that offered active service and rare opportunity for his special abilities, and ask for one of quiet garrison duty, with no prospect of enterprise or glory.

Not a shadow of suspicion, however, seems to have crossed his mind, and being convinced that Arnold really desired it, he made out his instructions August 3d, 1780, and Arnold immediately assumed command at West Point. This included all the fortifications in the Highlands.

"Four years before, Washington had sailed between the Highlands where nature blends mountains and valleys, and the deep river in exceeding beauty; and he had selected for fortification the points best adapted to command the passage. Now it was covered with fortresses and artillery. Fort Defiance alone was defended by a hundred and twenty pieces of cannon, and was believed to be impregnable. Here were magazines of powder and ammunition, completely filled, for the use not only of that post, but of the whole army. These fortifications seemingly represented a vast outlay of money. With prodigious labor, huge trunks of trees, and enormous hewn stones were piled up on steep rocks.

"All this had been done without cost to the state, by the hands of American soldiers who were pervaded by a spirit as enthusiastic and as determined as that of the bravest and most cultivated of their leaders. These works, of which every stone was a monument of humble disinterested patriotism, were to be betrayed to the enemy, with all their garrisons." *

Clinton caught eagerly at the prospect of so magnificent a prize as West Point, with its opulent military magazines, cannon, garrisons, vessels, boats, and stores. The home ministry as eagerly supported him, directing him to incur any expense within reason, for the successful issue of the gigantic scheme.

* Bancroft, Vol. X.

XVII.—1780.

TREASON.

" Being remiss, most generous, and free from all contriving."

HAMLET.

AND now, the treason having taken shape, Arnold drew across its " blackness of darkness," a line of sudden radiance ;—himself selected the costly victim to adorn the odious tragedy about to be enacted. He demanded that André, the grace and idol of Clinton's army, whom Sir Henry loved as his own son, should be sent to consummate the foul treachery,—André, whose name for all knightly virtues and accomplishments, might have gone down the ages linked with that of Sir Philip Sidney, had he, like him, *given* his life in the cause of human liberty. But alack ! he could urge nothing but " an honest zeal in the service of his king," * and the successful issue of the affair was to bring him rank and emolument. Without duplicity, or even ordinary caution, André was the last man to be sent upon such an errand, and it is certain that he did not seek the service.

Clinton had dispatched him upon his dangerous mission with three distinct charges : not to pass within the American lines; not to change his dress, and upon no account to take papers. Arnold compelled him to all three.

The British ship " Vulture" had been sent up the Hudson and anchored off Tellers Point, to facilitate the affair.

* *Letters to General Washington and Sir Henry Clinton.*

Dobb's Ferry had been first designated as the place of meeting. André arriving there and finding no message or messenger from Arnold, afterwards ascended the river and reached the "Vulture" at 7 o'clock on the evening of September 20.

He confidently expected to meet Arnold there the same night, "according to the tenor of his letter"; but that coward-villain had no intention of coming on board the "Vulture." He had resolved that André and not he, should take the risks of the meeting.

André waited anxiously through the night, and in the morning dispatched a letter to Sir Henry, in rather despondent tone, "saying that this was the second excursion he had made without any ostensible reason, and a third would infallibly fix suspicions. He thought it best, therefore, to stay where he was, under pretence of sickness, and try further expedients." An opportunity occurred the next day to send a letter ashore under flag. It reached Arnold safely, and he now addressed himself to arrange for bringing André on shore.

Arnold had no accomplice—he bore the whole burden of infamy alone—but he had managed to win to sundry nefarious transactions, a man named Joshua Smith. Seeing his susceptibility as a tool, Arnold had flattered him with civilities, invited him to headquarters, etc. Smith served him, and asked no questions.

The difficulty was to get two boatmen willing to go with Smith at midnight, with muffled oars, to the "Vulture." Two brothers named Colquhoun were selected, but they stoutly refused, saying they would willingly go by daylight under flag, but declined the night service. Arnold argued with them that the morning would be too late—there was a gentleman on board whom he must see immediately upon business of highest importance to the public interest, and they were no patriots if they refused their services. They still drew back. Further appeals to their patriotism failed; the men were obdurate.

Arnold, at last, threatened to put them under arrest, as disaffected to their country's cause. They then consented to *obey his orders.* He promised them fifty pounds of flour as an encouragement, which, it is almost needless to add, they never received.

At midnight of the 21st a boat with muffled oars approached the "Vulture," and a letter signified to André that he was expected to come ashore. It illustrates André's character, that he at once prepared to comply with the summons, with no security for his safety but "the word of a man who was seeking to betray his country." "Remissness" could go no further.

He was strongly dissuaded from so doing ; but such was his eagerness to accomplish the object, that he seemed indifferent to the risks of such a step.

He wore his uniform, but over it a blue overcoat, which concealed all. He entered the boat, and the oarsmen rowed, a silent party, to the shore, called Long Clove, on the western bank of the river, about six miles below Stony Point.

It was the precise point that Arnold had designated, and, in a few moments after the boat touched the river side, Smith and André groped their way up the bank through the darkness and found the traitor concealed in a clump of thick bushes. Smith returned to the boat at Arnold's request, but full of vexation and disgust, as he expected to be present at the interview, after the trouble it had cost him to bring the parties together.

Some hours passed. The honest oarsmen slept heavily, but a troubled conscience kept Smith uneasy and wakeful. With the first streak of dawn he approached and admonished Arnold that the boat must leave its present station before day.

But the affair was yet far from concluded. Arnold gave consent for the boat to return up the river, and he, with André, mounted horses which had been provided and rode several miles to Smith's house. "It was still dark, and the voice of the sentinel, demanding the counter-sign, was the first intimation to André that he was within the American lines. "* Marshall also says, that André had peremptorily refused to be carried within the American lines ; but the promise made him by Arnold, to respect this objection, was not observed. André was startled, and perfectly realized the peril of his situation. It was too late, however, except to nerve himself to meet the exigency now upon him.

Their consultations were resumed upon arriving at Smith's house. Shortly after daylight, their attention was attracted by the sound of a cannonade, and André saw from his windows, with anxious heart, the "Vulture" hoist anchor and drop down the river out of range of the shot from an American cannon at Verplanck's Point.

Before noon of September 22d, the plot, with all its conditions and details, was consummated and ready for execution. The day was fixed. Much of these details has never seen the light. It is not known for how many pieces of silver Arnold agreed to sell his country. But, as avarice was his stimulating motive, and the prize was of priceless value to the purchaser, the sum demanded by Arnold *upon the successful issue of the plot,* must have been fabulous.

The business concluded, André's concern now was a safe and speedy return to the "Vulture." He insisted that he should be put on board of the "Vulture." Ar-nold pretended to assent, but at the same time suggested many objections to it, and advised the return by land as much safer. André adhered to his determination to re-turn as he came. This could not be accomplished until nightfall.

In André's own account of his capture, he says : "Arnold quitted me, having himself made me put the papers I

* *Sparks' Life of Arnold.*

bore, between my stockings and feet. Whilst he did it, he expressed a wish, in case of any accident befalling me, that they should be destroyed; which I said of course would be the case, as when I went into the boat I should have them tied about with a string and a stone. Before we parted, some mention had been made of my crossing the river and going another route; but I objected much to it, and thought it was settled, that in the way I came, I was to return."

Arnold left André about eleven o'clock in the morning, entered his barge and went up the river to his headquarters. It was just here that the gods smote him blind, and he could not see that his own safety and that of the whole affair was wrapped up in the personal safety and assured return of André to New York.

The extreme caution and skill which had characterized him in the entire conduct of the treachery up to this point, seemed suddenly to desert him. The important documents placed by him in André's stockings were in Arnold's undisguised handwriting, and endorsed by him. Having, as he thought, secured his own personal safety, he, with a blind insensibility, sent André to his doom.

This view of Arnold's treachery· to André is sustained by André's own statements in his letters to Washington and to Sir Henry Clinton. To Washington he wrote: * * * "I came up in the 'Vulture' man-of-war, and was fetched from the ship to the beach. Being here, I was told that the approach of day would prevent my return, and that I must be concealed until the next night. I was in my regimentals and had fairly risked my person. Against my stipulations, my intentions, and without my knowledge beforehand, I was conducted within one of your posts. Your excellency may conceive my sensation on this occasion, and will imagine how much more must I have been affected, by a refusal to reconduct me back the next night as I had been brought.

"Thus become a *prisoner*, I had to concert my escape. I quitted my uniform and was passed another way in the night, without the American posts, to neutral ground, and informed I was beyond all armed parties, and left to press for New York. Thus, as I have the honor to relate, was I *betrayed* into the vile condition of an enemy in disguise within your posts."

To Sir Henry Clinton he wrote: * * * "The events of coming within the enemy's posts and of changing my dress, which led to my present situation, were contrary to my own intentions, as they were to your orders; and the circuitous route which I took to return, was *imposed* without alternative upon me."

But to continue:

Upon leaving André, Arnold wrote and gave to Smith two passports, one authorizing him to go by water and the other by land. A third passport ran: "Permit Mr. John Anderson (André's assumed name) to pass the guards to the White Plains, or below," etc. This last was the one which he presented to his three captors.

André wearied through an anxious day, and at sundown became impatient to set off. What were his feelings upon learning from Smith that he had made no arrangements for returning to the "Vulture," and that he had no intention of so doing. All André's entreaties were without avail, and nothing remained but to submit to the hard necessity of his situation and take the land route.

Arnold had impressed upon him the absolute necessity of changing his dress, in event of returning by land. Smith therefore furnished him a citizen's coat, and his military coat was left behind. Arnold had even lulled Smith's suspicious about the British uniform, by representing to him, that it was the pride and vanity of "Anderson," who wished to make a figure as a man of consequence, and had borrowed a coat from a military acquaintance.

Smith accompanied him to within a short distance of
White Plains. He then left him and returned to report
to Arnold. Every school-boy knows the rest: how André
after passing all the American lines, through the dangerous
neutral ground, had almost reached the first British post,
when three poor, obscure, but incorruptible patriots—John
Paulding, David Williams, and Isaac Van Wert—there,
by the Eternal decrees, emerged from the wayside and
called the handsome horseman to halt.

A thorough search brought all to light. André's rich
offers of his purse, his horse, his watch, with further
rewards and honors from the British commander at New
York, failed to corrupt his captors.

"Thus in the very moment when one of the most distinguished chiefs of the American army—a man celebrated
throughout the world for his brilliant exploits—betrayed,
out of a base vengeance, the country he had served, and
sold it for a purse of gold, three common soldiers preferred the honest to the useful, and fidelity to fortune."*

Brought to trial, André preserved a most noble and
dignified deportment, "he answered every question
promptly, discovered no embarrassment, sought no disguise, stated with frankness and truth everything that
related to himself, and used no words to explain, palliate
or defend any part of his conduct." His knightly scorn
of a lie compelled the tragic verdict which the court pronounced and executed. At his death, the lamentations
of his enemies mingled with the wail of his friends.

Yet Bancroft well says: "His king did right in offering honorable rank to his brother, and in giving pensions
to his mother and sisters; but not in raising a memorial
to his name in Westminster Abbey—such honor belongs
to other enterprises and other deeds. The tablet has no
fit place in a sanctuary, dear, from its monuments, to
every friend of genius and mankind."

* *Botta's American Revolution.*

XVIII.—1780, 1781.

ARNOLD'S SMALL VILLAINIES.

" The name of the wicked shall rot."
PROVERBS.

THE colossal, even in crime, overawes us, and invests the perpetrator with a certain dignity. We have therefore, as far as possible, abridged the details of Arnold's great villainy, preferring to bring to the front his smaller villainies. He has been too much estimated by this one deed of shame ; too much regarded as a fallen man. He did not fall. His brazen impudence blazed out in a letter of threats to Washington, as soon as he had reached the British lines,—it contained these words : "I beg leave to assure your Excellency that I am actuated by the same principle which has ever been the governing rule of my conduct in this unhappy contest." He spoke better than he knew.

Colonel Hamilton, in a letter to Washington immediately following the treason, writes : "This man is in every sense despicable. In addition to the knavery and prostitution during his command in Philadelphia, which the late seizure of his papers has unfolded, the history of his command at West Point, is a history of little as well as great villainies. He practised every dirty act of peculation, and even stooped to connections with sutlers of the garrison to defraud the public."

Immediately upon his capture, André, not regarding the case in the serious light it afterwards assumed, and far less apprehending the fate which awaited him, seemed only anxious to provide for Arnold's safety.

The blundering stupidity of the commandant of the American post to which he was first taken, served his generous impulse, for André induced him to dispatch a messenger up the river to inform Arnold that the man " Anderson " had been captured.

Arnold received the intelligence as he sat at breakfast table. Comprehending the full danger that menaced him, he stayed no longer than to give a hurried word of farewell to his young wife, but recently a mother, and fled to take refuge on board the " Vulture," still lying anchored in the stream.

Riding with hot speed to the landing, he entered a boat and ordered the oarsmen to push out from the shore. Six rowers promptly obeyed the command. Arnold stimulated their lusty oar-strokes with a promise of two gallons of rum if they made a quick passage to the " Vulture," representing the extreme importance of the business to be dispatched.

He passed the shore batteries in safety, by waving his white handkerchief as a flag, and arriving on board the " Vulture " announced himself to Captain Southerland. He then sent for the leader of the boatmen to come into the cabin, when he informed him that he and his fellow-boatmen were prisoners.

The man was an intelligent and spirited fellow ; he declared they were no prisoners, that they had come on board under protection of a flag, and he turned to Captain Southerland for justice and honor. The British sailor felt extreme disgust at the affair, and though he could not countermand the order of Arnold, he took the boatman's parole and allowed him to go ashore for clothes and money. On their arrival at New York the following day, Sir Henry Clinton, with scorn of the meanness, at once set them all at liberty. British honor acquired a new lustre from Clinton at this time.

With his heart full of anguish at the impending fate of

André, and humiliation at the total miscarriage of so magnificent a scheme, it was distinctly intimated to Clinton, from the highest sources, that there was one way, and one only, to save André—that was, to exchange him for the traitor Arnold. He wrung his own heart in returning the answer, that " to give up a man who had deserted from the enemy, and openly espoused the king's cause, was such a violation of honor and of every military principle, that he would not for a moment entertain the idea." An unspeakable disgust filled the mind of every British officer and man of honor, at the sight of this betrayer of his country, and prime cause of the death of the man they idolized. Yet Clinton was compelled to give him the specified high rank in his majesty's army, and receive him at his military counsels. British officers "hated to serve with him, under him, or over him."

Arnold made haste to present also his claims for indemnity for loss incurred by coming over. The sum demanded was between thirty and forty thousand dollars. It was simply obtaining money under false pretences, for he left behind nothing but debts, and his creditors were the only losers.

To the American cause, his defection was immense gain, and he speedily became as mischievous and pestilent to British interests as he had been to American.

The expectation that Arnold would have an extensive following of deserters, was doomed to disappointment. His windy and audacious addresses to the American people, and to the American army, with the proffer of bounties of English gold, failed to draw a single officer or private from their country's standards. A few refugees and discontented spirits, already in New York, were given him as a nucleus for a regiment, which was never filled.

He took all his native impudence with him, and, nettled by his failure, ascribed it to the insufficient bounty offered by Sir Henry Clinton; passing by his commander's authority, he wrote himself to the ministry, urging that the bounty be increased. It was done, but with the same ill success. The more honorable to those he sought to corrupt, as at that time the continental currency was at its worst.

Also, in his letters to the ministry, he had greatly misrepresented the real status of American affairs, stating that the resources of Congress were utterly exhausted, notwithstanding the late favorable alliance with the French ; that the cause was becoming more and more unpopular with the people, who ardently desired a reconciliation with England, etc. So eager were the ministry at this time to listen to any word of hope, that they greedily swallowed the assurance of a man who had stood so high in military councils from the very beginning of the war, and had so eminently enjoyed the confidence of the commander-in-chief. It caused the ministry to relax their efforts at the very moment when they should have renewed them, to the manifest detriment of Clinton's military plans.

It was, perhaps, the first real service he had performed for his country. Furthermore, his restive ambition led him again to pass the authority of his commander General Clinton, and he wrote to Germain submitting a plan by which West Point might be taken with ease, if not by a *coup-de-main,* yet by a few days regular attack. This caused Lord Germain to prick the sides of Clinton's military intent, in a manner that implied "censure, either upon his discernment or his enterprise."

Clinton returned for answer, that the scheme was visionary and impracticable with the present strength and vigilance of the so-recently-menaced posts, and concluded : "As to Major-General Arnold's opinion, I can only say that, whatever he may have represented to your Lordship, nothing he has yet communicated to me, has convinced me that the rebel posts in the Highlands can be reduced by a 'few days' regular attack.' But, if he convinces me now that such a thing is practicable (for to fail would be death to our cause in the present state of the war), I shall most likely be induced to make the attempt. I have, therefore, required that general officer to send his plan of operation to me without delay, and to follow, or accompany it, himself."

It was as visionary as had been his plan for the capture of Quebec, but the prudence of Clinton prevented the disastrous attempt. Nothing more was ever heard of it, and Arnold idled through the summer without a command.

He had left his military fame behind him. His new friends did not share the American enthusiasm for his soldierly abilities. They had a truer gauge, and, estimating him with remarkable penetration, they appointed him only to the work of a thief and a robber.

In the winter of 1781, they sent him on a plundering and burning expedition to Virginia [it was the very time that Daniel Morgan was at Cowpens]; but so little did Clinton trust him, that he sent with him two officers, of tried ability and honor, with the express command that he was to undertake nothing without their counsel and consent.

A gale scattered the fleet at the mouth of the Chesapeake, and Arnold, without waiting to reassemble, pushed on up the James River to Richmond. Here he thought to cheat his new masters, for "he offered to spare Richmond if he might carry off unmolested its vast stores of tobacco"; but they rejected the proposition with scorn, and he burned all. He was soon compelled to retreat, and was recalled to New York by Clinton.*

* It was at this time that Arnold attempted to correspond with La Fayette by flag of truce. But La Fayette refused to read the letter and sent it back unopened. When Cornwallis came into Virginia, he took the first opportunity to send him down to Ports-

One more and the last of his "exploits." His ravages of the shores of Connecticut; and, from his knowledge of the locality, it is believed that the expedition originated with him.

It was in the golden September 1781, while Washington and La Fayette were before Yorktown. He burned towns and vessels, immense magazines of public property, and butchered, with savage ferocity, the garrison at Fort Griswold, after they had surrendered. It is said that "he stood in the belfry of a steeple and witnessed the confla-gration, and what adds to the enormity is, that he stood almost in sight of the spot where he drew his first breath; and that many of the dying whose groans assailed his ears, and of the living whose houses and effects he saw devoured by the flames, were his early friends—the friends of his father and mother—and that these wanton acts were without provocation on the part of the sufferers." * He might even have seen the little school-house, around which, in his boyish iniquity, he used to strew the pieces of broken glass that the children might cut their feet on going and returning from school. The boy was father of the man.

With the surrender of Cornwallis, Arnold found his military occupation gone; shunned by his fellow officers, he asked permission of Clinton to sail for England. Arriving there, he found a deeper scorn and contempt awaiting him. There was only one "so poor to do him

mouth, out of his sight and association. It was also at this time that Arnold asked an American officer who had been taken prisoner, what they would do with him if he should fall into their hands. He replied, " We would cut off the leg which was wounded while you fought in the cause of liberty, and bury it with the honors of war, and hang the rest of your body on the gibbet."

* *Sparks' Life of Arnold.*

reverence." His Majesty, the Third George, was perforce his friend.

The invective of Lord Lauderdale resulted in a duel; while Lord Surrey, rising to speak one day in the House of Commons, saw Arnold enter the gallery; he sat down quickly, pointing to him and exclaiming: "I will not speak while that man is in the House."

Again and again, he solicited a command in the British service, but it was not granted. All he obtained was a contract for supplying the British troops and provisions; he afterwards received a gift of land in Canada for his services in the West Indies. At St. Johns, New Brunswick, he carried on an extensive business, occupying two large warehouses. Upon one of these he procured insurance for a large amount. It soon after took fire and was entirely consumed with all it contained. His two sons, who slept in the warehouse escaped, but could give no account of the origin of the fire.

It was generally believed that it had been insured for an amount far beyond the value of the goods stored in it, and was set afire. Proof, however, could not be furnished, and Arnold received the full value of the merchandise insured.

To illustrate the sentiment of the public in the matter: Monson, Arnold's partner, accused him of having instigated the fire; Arnold brought suit against him for libel, and obtained a verdict of two-and-sixpence.

Fortune continued to desert him to the last, until, twenty years after his treason, in 1801, in shame, obscurity and poverty, he sank into a dishonored grave,—an unanswerable argument for the doctrine of native depravity.

TIDE OF BATTLE FLOWS SOUTHWARD.

MEANTIME the tide of battle had rolled southward. The British had good reasons for shifting the theatre of war. Sentiment was more equally divided there. The republicans scarcely out-numbered the tories. It must be said, however, that as a rule the virtuous and intelligent adhered to the cause of independence, while the ignorant and vicious, with the hope of plunder and adventure, flocked to the king's standards.

The coast abounded in good harbors and the country was a rich plain, watered by navigable rivers, by which they could penetrate to the very heart of the provinces.

Among the reasons given by Tarleton, who accompanied Sir Henry Clinton on his expedition to South Carolina, were : "The mildness of the climate, richness of the country, its vicinity to Georgia [already in the power of the British] and *its distance from Washington.*"

From the midsummer of 1775, the ablest commanders in the British service, Generals Gage, Howe, Burgoyne, Cornwallis, and Clinton, had been successively out-generalled, out-maneuvred and put to shame, by his matchless combinations. They had thought to uproot the American rebellion by striking at Boston, " the hot-bed of treason "; but in a few months they were driven from its harbor. They then fancied to decapitate it, by seizing the Hudson river and thus dividing the eastern from the middle colonies. They were foiled on the plains of Saratoga, and the surrender of Burgoyne was the consequence. In 1777 they had indeed established themselves in the city of the Continental Congress, but only to yield it up in the following year. In the summer of 1778, coming again upon White Plains, Washington wrote : "After two years maneuvering, and the strangest vicissitudes, both armies are brought back to the very point they set out from, and the offending party is now reduced to the use of the spade and pickaxe for safety. The hand of Providence has been so conspicuous in all this, that he must be worse than an infidel that lacks faith, and more than wicked, that has not gratitude enough to acknowledge his obligations."

Had Washington been an unbeliever, consulting only the "stars" for his omens, he would still have been a formidable antagonist ; but, with his splendid military instinct—holding fast by the hand of his God—saying continually : "Thou wilt guide me with *thine eye*," he had become to his enemies, *the unconquerable*.

As early as 1778, the coast of Georgia had been ravaged by British troops, from their station in Florida, joined by Indian tribes who were bought by British agents with costly presents to enter their service.

In 1779 Colonel Campbell was dispatched from New York with three thousand troops to take Savannah. It was feebly defended by the American General Howe. Guided through a swamp by a negro, Campbell turned Howe's position. Vigorously attacked on all sides, he capitulated, and the capital with nearly five hundred prisoners, forty-eight pieces of cannon, the fort with large military stores and much provision fell to the British with a loss to them of only twenty-four killed and wounded.

Having established themselves in Savannah, the British ranged at will through southern Georgia ; pushing northward, they fortified Augusta and opened communication with the savage tribes of upper Georgia.

The delegates of South Carolina requested Congress to

send Major General Lincoln, to command their forces; a man highly esteemed for his integrity and private virtues, but without a stir of military instinct. Disaster followed fast and followed faster. In September 1779 the chivalric but impetuous Frenchman D'Estaing suddenly appeared upon the coast of Georgia with fleet and army, and signified his purpose to assist in retaking Savannah.

Autumnal gales approaching, he precipitated the mad assault, which was repulsed with frightful slaughter.

Among the slain, were the brave Polander Pulaski and Sergeant Jasper. Three years before Jasper had earned immortal fame at the defence of Fort Moultrie in the harbor of Charleston. A ball from the enemy's ship shot away the flagstaff; Jasper leaped from the wall, upon the beach, caught up the stars of liberty, and climbing the breastwork, through a storm of bullets, fixed the flag upon the point of his spontoon, and gave it again to the breeze, crying, "God save liberty and my country forever." After the enemy had retired discomfited, Governor Rutledge, in presence of the whole regiment, took his sword from his side and with his own hand presented it to Jasper.

He offered him a commission also, but this high heroic soul declined it. He was only one of God's noblemen and modestly said: "I am greatly obliged to you Governor, but I had rather not have a commission; as I am, I pass very well with such company as a poor sergeant has a right to keep. If I took a commission, I should be forced to keep higher company, and then, as I don't know how to read, I should only be putting myself in a way to be laughed at."

The fair daughters of Charleston were also gathered there to thank their brave defenders, and Mrs. Colonel

Elliot presented the regiment with fresh colors, embroidered in gold and silver with her own hand. They were delivered to Jasper, who "vowed never to give them up but with his life."

Now, under the fatal walls of Savannah, he made good his vow. Through all that day of carnage Jasper had remained unhurt, but when the retreat was sounded he rushed forward to seize and bring off his colors, when a fatal ball entered his lungs.

In an old time-worn book, a specimen of the southern literature of more than half a century ago, entitled "Weems and Horry's Life of Marion," may be found a page or two, describing the death of this brave man. It has an exquisite touch of poetry and pathos, equal to anything that ever fell from the pen of Dickens, albeit the death of "Poor Joe" or "Little Paul." Thus:

"As he passed by me with the colors in his hand, I observed he had a bad limp in his walk.

" 'You are not much hurt, I hope, Jasper,' said I.

" 'Yes, Major, I believe I've got my furlough.'

" 'Pshaw,' quoth I, 'furlough for what?'

" 'Why to go home to Heaven, I hope.'

"His words made such an impression on me, that as soon as duty permitted I went to see him. As I entered the tent, he lifted his eyes to me, but their fire was almost quenched. Stretching his feeble hand he said, with perfect tranquillity: 'Well, Major, I told you I had got my furlough.'

" 'I hope not,' I replied.

" 'O, yes! I am going, and very fast too; but thank God, I am not afraid to go.'

"I told him, I knew he was too brave to fear death, and too honest to be alarmed about its consequences.

" 'Why as to that matter, sir, I won't brag; but I have my hopes. I am but a poor ignorant body, but somehow or other I have always built my hopes of what

God may do for me *hereafter*, on what he has done for me here.'

"I told him I thought he was correct in that.

"'Now, Major, here's the way I comfort myself. Fifty years ago (I say to myself) I was *nothing*, and had no thought that there was any such grand and beautiful world as this. But, notwithstanding, there *was* such a world, and here God has brought me into it. Now can't He in fifty years more, or indeed in fifty minutes more, bring me into another world, as much above this as this is above that state of *nothing* in which I was fifty years ago?'

"I told him I thought it was a very happy way of reasoning, and such as suited the goodness and greatness of God.

"'I think so, Major, and I trust I shall find it so,' he continued; 'though I have been a man of blood, yet, thank God, I have always lived with an eye to that *great hope*. My mother was a good woman, and when I sat, a child, on her knee, she talked to me of God, and told me it was God who built this great world, with all its riches and good things, and not for *Himself* but for *me!* and that if I would but do His will, in that only acceptable way—a good life—he would do still greater and better things for me hereafter. These things went so deep into my heart, Major, that they never could be taken away from me. I have hardly ever gone to bed or got up again without my prayers. I have honored my father and mother, and, thank God, I have been *strictly honest*.'

"He continued, with tears in his eyes and with much effort, that he had a good hope he was going where he should not do what he had been obliged to do in this world.

"'I've killed men in my time, Major, but not in malice, but in what I thought a just war for my country; and as I bore no malice against those I killed, neither do I bear any against those who have killed me ; and I heartily trust in God, for Christ's sake, that we shall one day meet together where we shall forgive, and love one another like brothers. And now, my good friend, as I have but a little time to live, I beg you will do a few things for me when I am gone.

" 'You see that sword—it is the one Governor Rutledge presented to me for my services at Fort Moultrie—give that sword to my father, and tell him I never dishonored it. If he should weep for me, tell him his son died in hope of a better life.

" 'If you should see that great gentlewoman, Mrs. Elliot, tell her I lost my life in saving the colors she gave to our regiment. And if you should come across poor Jones and his wife and little boy, tell them Jasper is gone ; but the remembrance of the hard battle which he once fought for their sakes, brought a secret joy to his heart just as it was about to stop its motion forever.' * He spoke these last words in a livelier tone than before; but it was like the last kindling of the taper in its oilless socket; instantly the paleness of death overspread his face—he sank back and expired."

Lincoln led the remnants of his maimed and shattered army into Charleston. Reinforcements from the Carolinas and Virginia, with large military stores and provisions, were crowded into a city which could not be defended. The brave men industriously strengthened its fortifications; it was but to build their own graves.

In January of 1780, Sir Henry Clinton had sailed from New York with eight thousand five hundred men, fully equipped. He encountered outrageous storms; his ordnance-ship foundered ; of his transports, many were either captured or lost, and his cavalry horses all perished. It

---

* He had, at fearful odds, rescued them from the murderous hands of a brutal soldiery, and saved their lives.

was the end of February before the fleet reassembled off the island of Tybee. Clinton found his whole force in Georgia and Carolina, not far from ten thousand, and, so soon as he could remount his cavalry, he commenced a cautious and leisurely March along the coast into South Carolina, firmly establishing his posts as he advanced. April 9th, his fleet gained the harbor of Charleston without loss, and on the 10th of April he summoned Lincoln to surrender.

THE SCOURGE OF THE CAROLINAS.

THERE accompanied Clinton on this expedition an officer of exceptional military genius, who was speedily to become the scourge and terror of these unhappy provinces. Some critics have pronounced him a presentiment of the new system of military tactics—taking Braddock and the Howes as representatives of the old. "Tarleton's operations were characteristic of that new system, which gained fresh spirit during the French Revolution, and afterwards distinguished Napoleon I."*

Yet the same elements have characterized all great soldiers,—Alexander, Cæsar, Gaston de Foix, Adolphus, Marlborough, and Morgan. That fine equipoise of judgment and daring—swiftness, celerity, suppleness, ingenuity, ubiquity—persistent sledge-hammer blows, as long and as many as needful to accomplish a result, adjourning sleep and food, and filling the twenty-four hours with valors.

Tarleton needed only a great opportunity and unlimited command. Well for our cause he was only a colonel, and but poorly generaled. It must be said that he was utterly without the quality of mercy. A few specimens of his work will best illustrate the worker. We left Lincoln penned up in Charleston, with all the military resources of the Carolinas, having been, on April 10th, summoned by Clinton to surrender. The city was almost completely invested ; but the American cavalry, under General Huger

* *Carrington's " Battles of the American Revolution."*

and Colonel Washington, both fine officers, held a position at Monk's Corner, thirty miles above Charleston, which maintained a communication with the upper country for supplies for the garrison, and covered a way of retreat out of the city.

A swift night march, April 12th, and Tarleton had them in his grip. Huger and Washington fled to the swamp and secreted themselves, as did all who could.

Tarleton took a hundred prisoners—officers, dragoons and huzzars—fifty wagons of clothing, ammunition, etc., and, most valuable of all to the British at that time, four hundred horses, with equipments. He also took possession of the ferry and all the boats. This completed the investment of Charleston. British loss—one officer and two men wounded, and five horses killed." *

May 6th, Tarleton totally surprised an American detachment under Colonels Washington and White, at Lenew's Ferry.—" Resistance and slaughter soon ceased." The two colonels saved themselves this time by swimming. American loss—five officers and thirty-six men killed and wounded ; seven officers and sixty dragoons prisoners, with all the horses, arms and equipments. Tarleton lost two dragoons and four horses, but, returning to Lord Cornwallis' camp the same evening, twenty horses expired with fatigue. More of this kind of work in its place.

Charleston passed to the British May 12th, 1780. By including all the male adults, old and infirm, in his list, Clinton could report five thousand prisoners. The spoil was not less than a million and a half in our money. The British army became a band of plunderers, and "the dividend of a major-general was four thousand guineas." †

The negroes were the most valuable part of this spoil. The slaves of rebels, not excepting those who threw themselves upon the British for protection, were immediately

* *Tarleton's Campaign.*   † *Bancroft,* Vol. X.

shipped to the West Indies, where they brought a high price.

A ban of indiscriminate confiscation was prepared for the whole country. Protection could only be obtained in return for unconditional and *active loyalty.* Clinton determined to crush out the spirit of liberty, and compel every man, capable of bearing arms, into British service.

The male inhabitants of the various districts were enrolled, and either British or tory officers (far more dreaded of the two), were appointed, "with civil as well as military powers." All over forty years of age, were to preserve the king's authority at home; all under that age, were to serve six months of the year in the royal armies. The Carolinas were to become a vast British camp.

After the issue of this proclamation, any Carolinian taken in arms, was liable to death for desertion and bearing arms against his country. Lord Rawdon, in command on the Santee, issued the following order : " If any person shall meet a soldier straggling, and shall not secure him, or spread an alarm for that purpose; or if any person shall shelter or guide a soldier straggling, they shall be punished by whipping, imprisonment or be sent to serve in the West Indies. I will give ten guineas for the head of any deserter belonging to the volunteers of Ireland, and five guineas *only,* if they bring him in alive." Thus were these proud and high-spirited people forced to become the agents of their own subjection.

Stunned by their military disasters and by the savage cruelty of their oppressors, their energies were for the time paralyzed—yet the people of the Carolinas remained unconquered.

Clinton sent a detachment to strengthen Augusta ; another to Ninety-six, and a third under Cornwallis to Camden. These important posts held the two States, Georgia and South Carolina, in present subjection.

The only armed American force yet in the field was a

portion of the Virginia line, which arrived too late to join the garrison in Charleston, and they had retreated northward toward North Carolina. Tarleton was dispatched after them, May 29th. He forced a march of one hundred and five miles in fifty-four hours, and came up with them on the borders of the State. "Colonel Buford, with about one hundred, saved themselves by a precipitate flight, the rest sued for quarter, but one hundred and fifteen were killed on the spot, a hundred and fifty were too badly · hacked to be moved; only fifty-three could be brought away as prisoners." *

Tarleton's own account of it is: "One hundred officers and men killed and wounded, two hundred prisoners, fifty-five barrels of powder, and twenty-six wagons of clothing, arms and camp-equipage, with a British loss of sixteen killed and wounded and thirty-one horses."

Sir Henry Clinton announced that Tarleton "had killed, wounded, and taken prisoner, more than his own force." Cornwallis in his despatches to the ministry writes: "I add the highest encomiums of Lieutenant-Colonel Tarleton. It will give me most sensible satisfaction to hear that your Excellency has obtained for him some distinguished mark of His Majesty's favor." †

The people of America called it a cold-blooded massacre, and "Tarleton's quarters" became a by-word of horror.

General Clinton now returned to New York and left Cornwallis and Tarleton to complete the subjugation of the South. Their cruelty was overdone and worked the other way. Marion rejoiced when he heard of the sufferings of the people; "'tis a harsh medicine, but it is necessary. Our country is like a man who has swallowed a mortal poison, and unless they are well worked and scoured of their partiality to the English, they are lost."

In Congress, Houston, the delegate from Georgia, said: "Our misfortunes are, under God, the source of our

* *Bancroft*, Vol. X.   † *Tarleton's Campaign.*

safety." The people, wrought up to fury and desperation, and compelled to fight, now rallied to the standards of their own country.

The fall of Charleston had reverberated like a sound of doom over the land. Not since the fall of Ticonderoga had the cause of the republic received so severe a blow;— "but worse remained behind."

Washington had detached southward from his army, the splendid continental brigade of Maryland and Delaware troops, under the able General De Kalb.

General Greene solicited from Washington the command of the Southern Department, and would have obtained it, but Congress ignoring his preference and still "joined to its idol," appointed General Gates, whose "high blown pride was so soon to break under him." It was a fatal amendment to the judicious appointment of the modest, brave, and experienced De Kalb. Not only so, but they unhandsomely made Gates independent of the commander-in-chief. He was to receive orders from and report only to Congress. It might have been his own stipulation. He was destined, however, to a brief and inglorious career, with the large authority granted him by that body. In two short months he had the infelicity to report to Congress from the ignominious field of Camden, "Headquarters in the saddle,"—flying.

Gates had received the announcement of his appointment to the Southern Department at his home in Virginia, June 1780.

His first thought was to obtain Morgan's services, and he immediately solicited of Congress a commission for him as Brigadier General in the continental service.

Shortly before this, he had sought an interview with Morgan, when the cause of their estrangement was reviewed. Morgan proudly reminded him of the services he had performed during the campaign of Burgoyne, and of their importance in compelling his surrender. He reminded Gates of the ingratitude and injustice of not even naming him in his official account of that most momentous affair of the war.

What amends Gates could make, he attempted, and Morgan from that time, with his usual magnanimity, dismissed the matter from his mind and accepted Gates' overtures of friendship.

Congress, however, recalled Morgan into the service as Colonel only; but to his eternal honor he asserted his dignity by declining to go. Besides the sense of injustice he felt, a weighty reason for this course remained. The Southern States had been divided into military districts, in each of which, officers had been appointed by State authority. He would be outranked by these, and subject continually to the orders of his inferiors in military experience and ability. Throughout his whole previous career, except when acting under the commander-in-chief, Morgan had contended with this disadvantage,—so "no more of that." His health also, though much improved, was far from re-established.

Gates was fain to go without him and fight his own battle. Conceit and self-assurance went with him, however; the blind led the blind. On his way through Virginia he met his old friend Lee, the traitor, now in private life, who warned Gates that he would find Cornwallis a tough piece of English beef. "Tough, sir," replied Gates, "tough! then begad I'll tender him. I'll make *pilos* of him in three hours after I set eyes upon him."

"Aye! will you, indeed," returned Lee; "then send for me and I will come and help you eat him."

Gates smiled an adieu and rode off, but Lee called after him: "Take care, Gates, take care, lest your Northern laurels turn to Southern willows."

" Gates, though a Chesterfield at court, was but a Paris in camp. He was of that fool-hardy and crazy-brained quality to whom it is a misfortune to be fortunate. He could never bring himself to believe that Lord Cornwallis would ' dare to look him in the face.' So confident was he of victory that on the morning before the fatal day of Camden he ordered Marion and myself [Horry] to hasten to Santee river, and destroy every scow, boat, and canoe, that could assist an Englishman in his flight toward Charleston." *

Gates, in superseding De Kalb, had declined to take his counsel, and instead of proceeding by the way De Kalb and his officers advised, through a salubrious and well-provisioned country, he led his army through a pine barren where they were fain to feed upon unripe peaches and green corn, with molasses and water for beverage. They marched under a July sun, and upon arriving near Camden, were fitter for the hospital than the battle-field.

Marion and Horry, before departing, presented themselves to take leave of the brave old De Kalb, with whom they had been serving as aids, and between whom a warm friendship had sprung up. The good old man said : " I part with you with the more regret, because I feel a presentiment that we part to meet no more."

" ' We hoped for better things.'

" ' O, no,' he replied, ' it is impossible. War is a game, and has its fixed rules. To-morrow, it seems, the die is to be cast, and, in my judgment, without the least chance on our side. The militia will, I suppose, as usual, play the back game—that is, get out of the scrape as fast as their legs can carry them. But that, you know, won't do for me. I am an old soldier and cannot run ; and I believe I have some brave fellows with me who will stand by me till the last. When you hear of our battle, you will probably hear that your old friend De Kalb is at rest.'

* *Horry and Weems' Life of Marion.*

"I looked at Marion, and the tears stood in his eyes. De Kalb saw it, and taking us by the hand, with a look of animation, said : ' No, gentlemen, no emotions for me but those of congratulation. I am happy. To die is the irrevocable decree for all ; then what joy to be able to meet death without dismay ! This, thank God, is my case. The happiness of man is my wish—that happiness I deem inconsistent with *slavery*. To avert so great an evil from an innocent people. I will gladly meet the British to-morrow, at any odds whatever.'

" As he spoke, I saw something in his look which demonstrated the divinity of virtue and the immortality of the soul."

Tarleton was a good critic as well as a good fighter. He points out in his " Campaign," Lincoln's mistake of shutting himself up in Charleston to be captured, instead of doing as Washington did " when he abandoned New York for the Jerseys and yielded Philadelphia to the English, as a contrary course would have unavoidably re-established the sovereignty of Great Britain in America."

Of Gates, he said : " He had not sufficient penetration to perceive that by a forced march up the creek, he could have passed Lord Rawdon's flank and reached Camden, which would have been an easy conquest and a fatal blow to the British, for their hospital, baggage, provisions and ammunition were there under a weak guard."

Instead of this, Gates made an unmeaning halt of two days, which enabled the British to reinforce and secure a favorable position. On the night of the fifteenth of August, at ten o'clock, Gates put his army on the march, and at two next morning they stumbled upon the British, advancing to meet them.

The advance of Gates' army were militia, who had never

"paraded together before." Some shots were exchanged, but both sides adjourned action until daylight. Besides the detachment under Marion to destroy the boats on the Santee, Sumter had come into camp with four hundred men and asked for four hundred more to intercept a British convoy of stores and provisions on the road from Charleston to the camp at Camden. It was granted.

Gates found himself with but three thousand and fifty, fit for duty. He pompously exclaimed; "These are enough for our purpose." Cornwallis had less than two thousand.

Gates had no plan of battle, and took his own place well in the rear. De Kalb, at the last moment, advised that the army should fall back to Rugley's Mills, where they could occupy an excellent position and await the British attack.

Gates not only rejected the counsel, but hinted that it was prompted by cowardice; whereupon the brave old General leaped from his horse and, placing himself at the head of his command, retorted with warmth : " Well, sir ! a few hours will let us see who are the brave."

Gates issued no order for the battle to begin; one of his officers suggested that the brigade of Stevens' militia, the weakest of the army, should attack; but Cornwallis' very best troops, under the able Colonel Webster, were thrown against them, and the battle really commenced with the flight of the militia; Tarleton, with his cavalry, pursued them thirty miles, cutting them down without mercy. Gates fled with them, nor did he halt until he reached Hillsborough, North Carolina, and it was said "that he killed three horses in his flight."

The flying wing composed two-thirds of the army. De Kalb and his Maryland and Delaware troops *remained to save American honor*. The whole British army now turned upon them. Never was better fighting done, and the British lost nearly five hundred before the Americans yielded. De Kalb fell, pierced by eleven wounds. He died, a few days after, a prisoner, but "the unconquered friend of liberty."

A British officer condoled with him for his misfortune; he replied: "I thank you, sir, for your generous sympathy, but I die the death I always prayed for—the death of a soldier fighting for the rights of man."

By all accounts, both British and American, Gates had done everything in his power to ensure the victory of Cornwallis. The omission and the commission were perfect. In a letter from General Nash of North Carolina to Washington, immediately after the disaster of Camden, he reviews the situation. The oppressed people were just beginning to lift up their heads after the fall of Charleston. De Kalb's army had advanced to Pedee River, and by this had recovered from the enemy one of the most fruitful regions of the State. Besides this, the militia of the two States, under their leaders — Marion, Sumter, Pickens, and Williams, had had nine several skirmishes with the enemy, and had been successful in all. Affairs were beginning to wear a most favorable aspect, had not Gates rashly decided to risk the fate of the two Carolinas on a single battle. "I think I am justified in saying that he put all to risk,—because no previous effectual measures were taken to save the baggage; nor do I learn that any place was assigned for the army to retreat to in case of misfortune. At the flight of the militia, if the regulars had been ordered to retreat to Rugley's Mills, five miles in their rear, possibly all might have been saved. I am told that with one hundred men the pass could have been defended against the whole British army. * * * * Sir, we had expended upwards of twenty-five millions of dollars on that army; we had drained every source and exhausted every fund in purchasing tents, wagons, horses, arms, ammunition, provisions, spirits, sugar, coffee, camp-equipage—in short, everything appertaining to an army, and in a single half hour all was completely lost and the army annihilated. The militia scattered to their homes, spreading terror as they went; the regulars retreated on after their General to Hillsborough, two hundred and fifty miles from the place of action, where General Gates arrived three days after the battle, leaving all the country open to the ravages of the enemy." *

The vanquished General, though only required to report to Congress, reported a few days afterward to the commander-in-chief : " If I am yet to render good service to the United States, it will be necessary it should be seen that I have the support of Congress and your Excellency, otherwise some may think they please my superiors by blaming me, and thus recommend themselves to favor. But you, sir, will be too generous to lend an ear to such men, if such there be, and will show your greatness of soul rather by protecting than slighting the unfortunate." †

But the disaster did not finish with the day of Camden. Tarleton, returning from the pursuit of Gates' flying army, learned that Sumter had intercepted and captured the convoy of forty wagons of British supplies and taken a hundred prisoners. Sumter, havng heard of the defeat of Gates, had retreated up the Wateree. Tarleton was quickly upon his track. Sumter, supposing, probably, that the British cavalry would take a day of rest after the battle, and having himself made a march of forty miles, halted at the midday heat, for his own rest and refreshment and fell fast asleep in the shade of a wagon. Tarleton, by forced marches, pounced suddenly upon them, dispersed and destroyed the detachment, killing one hundred and fifty on the spot, taking three hundred prisoners, releasing all the British and tory prisoners, and recovering all the wagons Sumter had captured. Tarleton lost one officer

---

* *Sparks' Cor. with Washington*, Vol. III, p. 110.
† *Sparks' Cor. with Washington*, Vol. III, p. 70.

and twenty-nine killed and wounded.   Cornwallis, reporting this affair, says : "This action is too brilliant to need any comment of mine, and will, I doubt not, highly recommend Lieutenant Colonel Tarleton to his Majesty's favor." *

This was Sumter's first encounter with Tarleton. "Two days after, he rode into Charlotte alone, without hat or saddle." †

* *Tarleton's Campaign*, p. 138.   † *Bancroft*, Vol. **X**.

LEE.

MORGAN.

PICKENS.

WASHINGTON.

SUMTER.

PARTISAN LEADERS OF THE SOUTH.

PATRIOT LEADERS OF THE SOUTH.

CORNWALLIS now felt himself at liberty to dispatch to the ministry that Georgia and the Carolinas were " British once more." In their eyes he was the one man " on whom rested the hopes of the ministry for the successful termination of the war."

He, with Tarleton, had decided that an iron yoke should be put upon the people of the South. He ordered commanders of all posts " to imprison all who would not take up arms for the king, and to seize or destroy their whole property. Any militia man who had borne arms with the British, and afterward joined the Americans, should be hanged immediately."

His underlings, tory and British, all through the State, bettered by his instructions. They patrolled the country far and near,—burned, ravaged, and put to death whon they would.

" In violation of agreements, the Continental soldiers who capitulated at Charleston, nineteen hundred in number, were transferred to wretched prison ships, where they were joined by hundreds more, taken at Camden.

In thirteen months, one-third of them had perished by malignant fevers. Others were impressed into British naval service, or taken by violence on board transports and forced to serve in British regiments in Jamaica. Of more than three thousand, all but seven hundred were thus made way with."

Yet the South remained unconquered, and moved forward to her independence through the bitterest sorrows of civil war. Members of the same families were arrayed against each other; neighbors outlawed and savagely butchered each other; the land blazed with burning homesteads ; women and children, reared in luxury, were driven from their homes and shivered half clad beside forest fires, while large rewards were offered by the British authorities to those who should inform of the place of concealment of cattle, horses, negroes, plate, bonds and deeds, of the patriots of the Carolinas.

Of South Carolina, Bancroft says: " Left to her own resources, it was through bloodshed and devastation, and the depths of wretchedness, that her citizens were to bring her back to her place in the Republic, by their own heroic courage and self-devotion, *having suffered more, and dared more, and achieved more, than the men of any other State !*"

They rallied to the standards of their patriot leaders : Williams, Davidson, Pickens, Davie, Sumter, and, most illustrious of all, Francis Marion.

Of rich Huguenot blood, he represented the virtues of three generations, and his name deserves to stand next to those of Morgan, Stark and Wayne, among the great field executives of the Revolution. He was small in stature, of delicate physique, and gentle to tenderness. Armed with all knightly virtues of courage, truth and honor, he proved himself the friend and protector of the weak and oppressed ; he wept with the weeping mothers, widows and orphans of his suffering country, and drew to himself the love and confidence of all.

Soon after the fall of Charleston, Sumter had hovered round the British camp so much to their annoyance that Cornwallis dispatched Tarleton to destroy him, saying : " Sumter has certainly been our greatest plague in this country." He was soon, however, forced to recall Tarleton to deal with a still more wary antagonist.

"Colonel Marion," wrote Cornwallis, "so wrought on the minds of the people, that there was scarcely an inhabitant between the Pedee and the Santee that was not in arms against us. They even crossed the Santee and carried terror to the gates of Charleston. They are the same stuff as compose all Americans."

To Tarleton, Cornwallis wrote : "I most sincerely hope you will get at Mr. Marion. I am always sanguine where you are concerned." *

Tarleton himself pays tribute to the "zeal and ability of Mr. Marion," for with all his skill and cunning he failed to trap him.

He was soon again recalled to attend to Sumter, who had just defeated a British detachment under Weymes, and Cornwallis writes : "I wish you would get three legions and divide yourself into three parts. We can do nothing without you." This time Tarleton advanced swiftly, but cautiously, upon Sumter, who, though superior in numbers, promptly retired, and intrenched his force in good position, using some log-houses for barricades. Nothing daunted by his disadvantage of numbers, Tarleton followed boldly, and at last, leaving his infantry behind, he made an unexpected push with only one hundred and seventy cavalry and eighty mounted men. Coming up with them, he attacked vigorously. The Americans inflicted heavy loss upon the enemy, but, unfortunately, Sumter was severely wounded early in the action, and the whole band retreated, and even thought it wise to disperse for the time. Both claimed the victory. Cornwallis makes his acknowledgments to Tarleton in these words : "I will not tire you with a repetition of my obligations to you. I trust you will find that I shall never forget them." To the British ministry he wrote : "It is not easy for Lieutenant-Colonel Tarleton to add to the reputation he has acquired in this province. With a small

* *Tarleton's Campaigns.*

force of cavalry he pursued and defeated Sumter, who had a thousand men, sheltered in log-houses, in a strong position. This action is a proof of that spirit, and those talents, which must render the most efficient service to his country." *

On the approach of Gates' army to Camden, Marion had come into his camp with his tatterdemalion militia brigade. As his men were hatless, Marion "took part with his brethren," and marched hatless at their head.

· They and their commander drew forth only the scorn of that fine gentleman Gates, who had no instinct to discover either ability or nobility in honorable rags. Marion, who knew the heart of the militiamen, and knew how to *fight* and *conquer* with them, might have saved the day at Camden, in spite of Gates; but that *no-general* sent Marion, with Major Horry, on the useless errand of destroying the bridges and boats behind the British to prevent their escape. After Gates' defeat, Marion waylaid a British guard, who were conducting some of the continental prisoners from Camden to Charleston, dispersed them, and released the captives.

Learning the utter rout and destruction of Gates' army and the prostration of the cause, Marion sounded his signals, assembled his little band of faithful hearts about him, and thus addressed them: "Well, gentlemen, you see our situation. Our peaceful land filled with uproar and death, while foreign ruffians, braving us up to our very fire-sides and altars, leave us no alternative but slavery or death. Two gallant armies have marched to our assistance; but for lack of competent commanders, both have been lost. That under General Lincoln, after having been duped and butchered at Savannah, was at last completely trapped at Charleston. That under General Gates, having been imprudently overmarched, is now cut up at Camden. Thus are all our hopes from the north entirely

<hr>

* *Tarleton's Campaigns.*

at an end, and poor Carolina is left to shift for herself. And now, my countrymen, I want to know your minds. As to my own, that has been long made up. I consider my life is but a moment, and to fill that moment with duty is my all. While I live, my country shall never be enslaved. She may come to that wretched state for what I know, but my eyes shall never behold it. Never shall she clank her chains in my ears, and pointing to the ignominious badge exclaim: *It was your cowardice that brought me to this!*"

We are tempted to clip another page from the quaint eloquence of his biographer and brother in arms:

"The Washington of the South, Marion steadily pursued the warfare most safe for us, and most fatal to our enemies. He taught us to sleep in the swamps, to feed on roots, to drink the turbid waters of the ditch, and to prowl nightly round the encampments of the foe, like lions round the habitations of those who had slaughtered their cubs. Sometimes he taught us to 'fall upon the enemy by surprise, distracting the midnight hour with the horrors of our battle ; at other times, when our forces were increased, he led us on boldly to the charge, hewing the enemy to pieces under the approving light of day. O Marion, my friend ! my friend ! although thy wars are all ended, and thyself at rest in the grave, yet I see thee still. I see thee as thou wert wont to ride, most terrible in battle to the enemies of thy country. Thine eyes, like balls of fire, flamed beneath thy lowering brows. But lovely still wert thou in mercy, thou bravest among the sons of men ! For soon as the enemy, sinking under our swords, cried for quarter, thy heart swelled with commiseration, and thy countenance was changed, even as the countenance of a man who beheld the slaughter of his brothers. The basest tory who could but touch the hem of thy garment, was safe. The avengers of blood stopped short in thy presence, and turned away abashed from the lightning of thine eyes. O that my pen were of the quill of the swan that sings for future days, then shouldst thou, my friend, receive the fulness of thy fame."

From this time, date the tactics of this marvellously elastic brigade, which sometimes numbered twenty and sometimes twelve hundred, as the emergency demanded, and as they wielded, by turns, the hoe or the sword.

The government was powerless to maintain military magazines, commissariat, or hospital; without clothes, shelter, rations or pay, this patriot band marched and counter-marched, advanced and retreated, disbanded and re-assembled, manœuvred and dissolved, visible or invisible, as by magic. Every swamp furnished them with a natural hiding-place, whence they suddenly emerged upon their enemy, struck a swift blow, and retired to their fastness from superior forces.

The number and value of these skirmishes with the enemy, escape the page of history, and can never be told. Marion foiled or defeated, in turn, the ablest officers of Cornwallis, sent to stop his career, and utterly baffled Tarleton *by eluding him*. When Greene's army was driven before Cornwallis, out of North Carolina, Marion swept down and harassed his posts in the rear, capturing con· voys, and breaking their communications with Charleston.

Scorn upon any and all insinuations against the valor of the Southern militia of the Revolution. They rendered splendid service, and in the best possible way suited to their circumstances. While every field action of the regular army in the Carolinas, except Cowpens, was attended by disaster and a measure of disgrace, these patriot militia leaders, and their followers, harried and worried the British out of their borders; and the forces of Sumter and Marion swept the country to the very gates of Charleston. Let Guilford Court-House, Hobkirk's Hill, Ninety-six, and Eutaw Springs confess.

As soon as the British evacuated the city of Charleston,

Marion sheathed his sword, disbanded his faithful comrades with the tenderness of a brother, and went back in poverty to his plough, "one of the purest men, truest patriots and most adroit Generals that American History can boast." Valiant in war, he was also wise in the councils of peace. He afterward sat in the senate of his State, and assisted in framing its constitution.

His remains enrich the soil of St. John's parish, South Carolina, and "a plain oblong tomb, gift of a private citizen," marks the sacred spot.

Meantime the hot August breath of that calamitous day of Camden, bearing on its wings the groans of a lost cause and a prostrate people, swept up through the valley of Virginia and came to Morgan's ears. He could no longer hold back; the cause needed every patriot heart and hand to the rescue. To the voice of wailing from the banks of Southern savannahs, was added the spur of the odious treason just enacted on the banks of the Hudson. Nor did he stand upon the order of his going, but to his eternal honor, he went at once, as *Colonel Morgan.* In September 1780, accompanied by an escort of young gentlemen who desired to serve with him, Morgan rode into Gates' camp at Hillsborough, and reported for duty.

THE BATTLE OF THE COLONELS—No. 2.

CORNWALLIS' ambition extended from Georgia to the waters of the Chesapeake. This much he had promised to restore to the British crown. He had fortified and garrisoned the strong interior posts of Camden, Winnsborough, Ninety-Six, and Augusta. With a chain of inferior posts below, on the Santee and Wateree, the rich and fertile country was secured to them. He held, also, the seacoast from Charleston to Savannah.

The excessive heat of summer being passed, Cornwallis thought he might now venture his advance into North Carolina. But the avenger was on his track.

During the summer, British agents had stirred up the Cherokee tribes ; their chiefs had come down to Augusta to meet those agents and receive the presents which were to spur their zeal in their murderous work.

Colonel Clarke, a fugitive patriot from Georgia, with a company of riflemen, assisted by a band of backwoodsmen, attacked and defeated the garrison under Colonel Brown, at Augusta, captured the presents and drove the savages back to their lair.

Colonel Furguson, commander of the British post of Ninety-Six, and next to Tarleton in audacity and cruelty, moved out to way-lay and capture this American detachment.

He fell in with a party of North Carolina militia, under McDowall, whom he pursued and scattered at the foot of the Alleghanies, where Tennessee and the Carolinas meet. The fugitives sought refuge among the dwellers in the uplands, and recounted the sorrows of the plains below

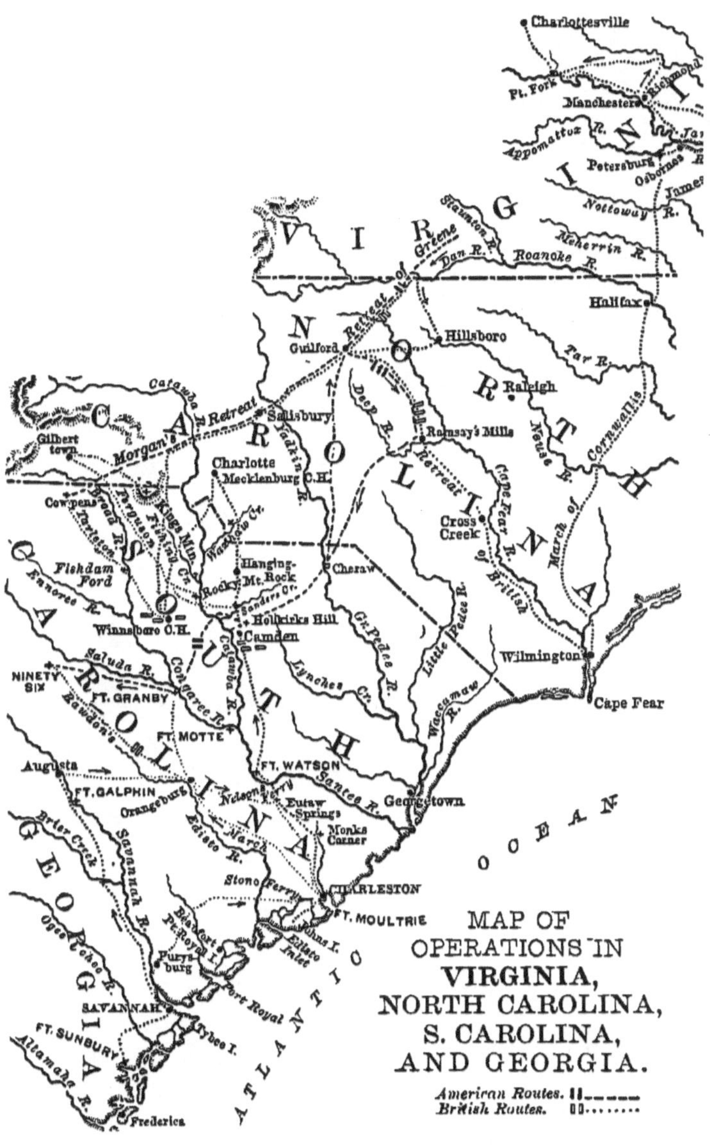

MAP OF
OPERATIONS IN
VIRGINIA,
NORTH CAROLINA,
S. CAROLINA,
AND GEORGIA.
American Routes.
British Routes.
Charlottesville
Ft. Fork
Manchester
Richmond
Appomattox R.
Petersburg
Osbornes
James
Nottoway R.
Staunton R.
Greene
Dan R.
Roanoke R.
Meherrin R.
Halifax
VIRGINIA
NORTH
Hillsboro
Guilford
Retreat of N.
Tar R.
Raleigh
CAROLINA
Catawba R.
Retreat
Salisbury
Ramsay's Mills
Morgan's
Gilbert town
Yadkin R.
Deep R.
Neuse R.
March of Cornwallis
Charlotte
Mecklenburg C.H.
Retreat
Cape Fear R.
Cross Creek
Cowpens
Broad R.
Tarleton
Ferguson
Kings Mtn.
Fishing Cr.
Wateree Cr.
March of British
Fishdam Ford
Rocky Mt. Rock
Hanging-Rock
Cheraw
Kanawee R.
Sanders Cr.
Gr. Pedee R.
Little Pedee R.
Winnsboro C.H.
Hobkirks Hill
Camden
Lynches Cr.
Waccamaw R.
Wilmington
Saluda R.
Congaree R.
SOUTH
Cape Fear
NINETY SIX
FT. GRANBY
Rawdon's
CAROLINA
FT. MOTTE
FT. WATSON
Augusta
Santee R.
Georgetown
FT. GALPHIN
Orangeburg
Nelson's Ferry
Eutaw Springs
Otter Creek
Savannah R.
Edisto R.
March
Monks Corner
OCEAN
GEORGIA
Stono Ferry
CHARLESTON
FT. MOULTRIE
Ogeechee R.
Beaufort
Port Royal I.
Purysburg
Johns I.
Edisto Inlet
ATLANTIC
SAVANNAH
FT. SUNBURY
Tybee I.
Altamaha R.
Frederica

to the liberty-loving sons of the forests, "among whom slavery was scarcely known." The story of the anguish and desolations of an innocent people, touched the springs of sympathy in the hearts of these backwoodsmen.

The spirit of the mountains woke—the spirit of liberty; and these brave hearts and strong hands resolved to leave their homes, descend from the highlands, and strike one blow in the cause of humanity. The men of the Watauga Valley ranged themselves under the leadership of Isaac Shelby and John Sevier, subsequently first governors of Kentucky and Tennessee. Colonel Campbell, of southwest Virginia, brother-in-law of Patrick Henry, hearing of this movement, joined them with four hundred militia.

Colonel Cleaveland, of North Carolina, with his regiment and the fugitives under McDowall, repaired to the appointed rendezvous at Watauga, September 25th, 1780.

" On the next day, each man mounted on his own horse, armed with his own rifle, and carrying his own store of provisions, began the ride over the mountains, where the passes through the Alleghanies are the highest. Not even a bridle-path led through the forest, nor was there a house for forty miles between the Watauga and the Catawba. The men left their families in secluded valleys, distant one from the other, exposed not only to parties of royalists but of Indians."

Furguson heard of this rising of the mountain yeomanry upon his track, and dispatched an express to Cornwallis for reinforcements. The ubiquitous Tarleton was sent to his assistance.

Meantime the patriot leader, James Williams, who was soon to offer up his life, was on the upper Catawba with four hundred and fifty mounted men. He, too, learned by his scouts of the mountain torrent of freemen, descending and swelling as it rolled.

He advanced to meet them, and, near the field of Cowpens, on the Broad River—auspicious spot, so soon to blaze with the glory of our arms—they joined forces and counted thirteen hundred strong.

Williams proposed to guide them at once to Ferguson's encampment. Calling a council, they decided to push on and strike him by surprise. Selecting nine hundred picked men and their fleetest horses, they began their march at sunset. They dismounted but once in thirty-six hours. All night they rode, and the next day, evening, October 7th, 1780, reached the foot of King's Mountain—perpetual monument of the valor of these men.

Ferguson's force of tories, and a detachment of British regulars, numbered upwards of eleven hundred. They were strongly posted on what they thought an impregnable height, "the craggy cliffs cropping out in form of natural breastworks along its sides and on its heights."

But these brave hearts and strong hands had come to do the deed, and they did it. All honor to the militia heroes of King's Mountain, without a leader above the rank of colonel. All honor to the patriot yeomanry of Virginia, Tennessee, North Carolina, South Carolina, and Georgia, who met here to clasp hands and pour out their heart's blood in the cause of human liberty.

They quietly dismounted and formed themselves into four columns. The post of extreme danger was assumed by Colonel Campbell, of Virginia, and Colonel Shelby. They led the two columns that were to attack in front; climbing the mountain, to be received on the bayonets of the British regulars.

But on, and up, they strode—hearts of lions—repulsed at first, they rallied, and gained the height. A death struggle ensued, until the right and left wings in the rear closed round the enemy's flanks and rear, and circled them with a ring of fire.

For fifty minutes the battle raged, until the position of the enemy was no longer tenable. Their leader, Ferguson, being killed, they attempted to escape along the top of the ridge ; but Colonels Cleaveland, Sevier and Williams intercepted them, and they threw down their arms.

The British loss was four hundred and fifty killed or severely wounded, and six hundred and fifty prisoners. The American loss was only twenty-eight killed and sixty wounded. Among these, however, they had to mourn the death of the patriot Colonel James Williams—" a man of exalted character and of a brief but glorious career."

As the battle of Herkimer's Mohawk yeomanry had first reversed the gloom of the Northern Department in 1777, so now the battle of the yeomanry of King's Mountain first reversed the gloom of the Southern Department in 1780.

The mountaineers had moved too swiftly this time for Tarleton. He heard the tidings of the disaster at the forks of the Catawba, and sped back with all haste to Cornwallis' camp. An immediate retreat was ordered. The whole aspect of affairs was changed. It strengthened the hearts of the patriots and dismayed the tories.

' The appearance on the frontiers of a numerous enemy from settlements beyond the mountains whose names had thus far remained unknown to the British, took Cornwallis by surprise ; and their success was fatal to this intended expedition. He had expected to step with ease from one Carolina to the other, and from these to the conquest of Virginia." *

There was nothing now but a swift retreat back into South Carolina, on which he was followed by the militia, who "harassed his foraging parties, intercepted his dispatches, and captured his wagons."

They were delayed by heavy rains at the fords ; Cornwallis fell ill of a fever ; they were without tents, and the soldiers bivouacked in the woods, drenched with rain, in unwholesome air. After a miserable march of fifteen days, they found themselves at the posts from which they

* *Bancroft*, Vol. X.

had set out, near Camden.   Autumn malaria decimated the British regiments in their garrisons faster than the British ministry could replace them.

It was a superb stroke, King's Mountain—a revelation to the British, and it illuminates Washington's meaning when, in the midst of the disasters of the Jerseys, he declared that, if driven from the Atlantic coast, he could retire behind the natural barrier of the Alleghanies, and still hold the continent.

XXIII.—1780.

MAJOR-GENERAL GREENE.

CONGRESS voted a court of inquiry into Gates' conduct of the Southern Department; but he was finally acquitted with honor. He was, however, superseded soon after Camden. That affair taught Congress less confidence in their own judgment and more in that of the commander-in-chief, who, at their request, now nominated General Greene as Gates' successor.

No man owed more to the patronage of the commander-in-chief than did this officer. He was a man of unblemished integrity, and a firm and consistent adherent to the cause of independence; but his order of talent fitted him rather for usefulness in the council-chamber than on the field. We reach this conclusion because, though he entered the army before Boston in 1775 and served to the end of the war, no page of history links his name with any remarkable military achievement. Exception: he crossed the Delaware with Washington's detachment in the attack upon Trenton. His military record at Forts Washington and Lee, at Brandywine and Germantown, shed no lustre upon his arms. He won no laurels at Newport, except in waving the olive-branch between American and French jealousy; but we remember to his honor that he stood faithfully with Washington in the matter of the "Cabal."

After Germantown, Washington induced him to accept the office of quartermaster; but he took it reluctantly, administered it ungraciously, and finally so far forgot himself in his letters to Congress as to draw the pronounced censure of that body ; and, but for the prompt and vigorous intervention of Washington's influence, he would probably have been dismissed the service.

Greene had a vice of letter-writing, and has in these, elaborated himself in a way not conducive to his immortality. His fame would have been more enduring if he had written fewer letters, and also, if Johnson had never written his life.

General Greene came of peace-loving Quaker parentage, . yet he had an inordinate ambition for military glory, and his own reputation was to him a perpetual source of disquiet.

He assumed the duties of quartermaster while the army was yet at Valley Forge, and when the administration of the commissariat was at its worst. There were cormorant contractors and sutlers in those days, who availed themselves of the vicissitudes of values and the depreciation of the currency. Washington writes to the President of Pennsylvania with exceptional warmth : " It is much to be lamented that each State, long 'ere this, has not hunted them down as pests to society and the greatest enemies we have. I would to God that some of the more atrocious in each State were hung upon gallows five times as high as Haman's; no punishment, in my opinion, is too severe for the man who can build his fortunes upon his country's ruin."

Washington hoped much from the integrity and industry of Greene, as the department had been placed " on a centralized system under Greene's immediate authority, with powers almost independent of Congress, and lucrative emoluments for himself, his assistants and subordinates."

But Greene was restive and discontented at his post; he failed to give satisfaction and preferred to return to field service. He writes to Washington : " I have desired Congress to give me leave to resign, as I apprehended a loss of reputation if I continued in the business. I will not sacrifice my reputation for any consideration whatever. I am willing to serve the public, but I think I have a right to choose that way of performing the service which will be most honorable to myself. * * * * I will not deny that the profits are flattering to my fortune, but not less humbling to my military pride. * * * * * There is a great difference between being raised to an office and descending to one, which is my case. There is also a great difference between serving where you have a fair prospect of honor and laurels, and where you have no prospect of either. *Nobody ever heard of a quartermaster in history, as such, or in relating any brilliant action.* I engaged in this business as well out of *compassion to your Excellency* as from a regard to the public." * [He nowhere seems to realize that he served a cause.]

At another date, thus : " Your Excellency has made me very unhappy. I can submit very patiently to deserved censure, but it wounds my feelings exceedingly to meet with a rebuke for doing what I conceived to be a proper part of my duty, and in the order of things. * * * * If I had neglected my duty in pursuit of pleasure, or if I had been wanting in respect to your Excellency, I would have put my hand upon my mouth and been silent upon the occasion : but as I am not conscious of being chargeable with either the one or the other, I cannot help thinking I have been treated with a degree of severity that I am in no respect deserving. Your Excellency well knows how I came into this department. It was by your special request, and you must be sensible there is no other man upon earth would have brought me into the business but you. The distress the department was in, *the disgrace which must accompany your operations without a change,* the difficulty of engaging a person capable of conducting the business, together with the hopes of meeting your approbation, and having your full aid and assistance, recon-

* The italics, wherever occurring, are ours.

ciled me to the undertaking. * * * * * * I have
never solicited you for a furlough to go home, to indulge
in pleasure or to improve my interest, which, by-the-by, I
have neglected going on four years. Neither have I ever
spared myself, by night or day, where it has been necessary to promote the public interest under your direction.
I have never been troublesome to your Excellency to pub-
lish anything to my advantage, although I think myself
as justly entitled as some others who have been more .
fortunate, particularly in the action of the Brandywine.
However, I can speak with a becoming pride that I have
always endeavored to deserve the public esteem and your
Excellency's approbation.

As I came into the quartermaster's department with
reluctance, so I shall leave it with pleasure. Your influence brought me in, and the want of your approbation
will induce me to go out."

It is not very surprising that, two months after this date,
Greene writes : " This is the third time I have wrote since
I have had a line from your Excellency. Should be glad
to hear from you when at leisure, etc." *

That majestic figure, living in the ages rather than the
moments, working for the races yet to be, rather than for
his contemporaries, opposed a matchless patience, alike to
the treachery of Lee, the indifference of Adams, the arrogance of Gates, and the petulance of Greene.

Upon the fall of Charleston, Greene had asked of Washington the command of the Southern Department, but
Congress selected Gates. After the failure of the complot
of Arnold and Clinton, Washington appointed Greene
president of the military court that tried André, and
subsequently Greene solicited the command of West Point.

" October 5, 1780.

" Sir :—A new disposition of the army going to be
* Sparks' Correspondence of Washington, Vol. II, p. 162.

made, and an officer appointed to the command of West Point, I take the liberty just to intimate my inclinations for the appointment. * * * * I hope there is nothing indelicate or improper in the application. I am prompted to the measure from the feelings incident to the human heart," etc. * * *

He obtained it, but had_occupied the post only a few days when Washington was requested by Congress to name Gates' successor. He selected General Greene, desiring him to proceed southward without delay; to which he replied :

"WEST POINT, October 16, 1780.

"Sir:—Your Excellency's letter of the 14th, appointing me to the command of the Southern army, was delivered me last evening. I beg your Excellency to be persuaded that I am fully sensible of the honor you do me. I foresee the command will be accompanied with innumerable embarrassments; but the generous support which I expect from the partiality of Southern gentlemen, as well as the aid and assistance I hope to derive from your Excellency's advice and extensive influence, affords me some consolation in contemplating the difficulties.

"I will prepare myself for the command as soon as I can ; if it was possible, I should be glad to spend a few days at home, before I set out to the southward, especially . as it is altogether uncertain how long my command may continue, or what deaths or accidents may happen during my absence. However, it will not be possible for me to leave this place for several days, if I put my baggage in the least order, or my business in proper train for such a long journey. Nor is my health in a condition to set out immediately, having had a considerable fever upon me for several days," etc.

Washington had not yet received intelligence of the battle of King's Mountain; that event having occurred

October 8th, only five days before he had communicated to Greene his appointment. He returned for answer that the grave aspect of military affairs in South Carolina admitted no delay; that he must set out *immediately*.

Greene writes:

"WEST POINT, October 19, 1780.

" *Sir:*—Your Excellency's favor of the 18th came to hand this afternoon. I had given over the thoughts of going home even if I obtained your permission, before I received your pleasure upon the subject. Before I marched from Tappan I wrote to Mrs. Greene to come to camp, and expect her here every hour. Should I set out before her arrival, the disappointment of not seeing me, added to the shock of my going southward, I am very apprehensive will have some disagreeable effect upon her health, especially as her apprehensions have been all alive respecting my going southward, before there was the least probability of it. My baggage sets out in the morning, if Colonel Hughes does not disappoint me about the horses; and my stay shall not be more than a day longer, whether Mrs. Greene comes or not.

"Your Excellency cannot be more anxious to have me come on, than I am to comply with your orders, especially since the two last articles of intelligence, the sailing of the troops from New York, and the advance of Lord Cornwallis into the State of North Carolina." *

General Greene left West Point, October 20th, and made a sort of leisurely, triumphal procession southward. He addresses the commander-in-chief from Philadelphia, November 3d, and a few days after, finds himself under the hospitable roof of Mount Vernon, and writes thus, by "candle light": "Mount Vernon is one of the most pleasant places I ever saw, and I do not wonder you so

* *Sparks' Correspondence*, Vol. III., p. 123.

often languish to return to the pleasures of domestic life. *Nothing but the glory of being commander-in-chief, and the happiness of being universally admired,* could compensate for such a sacrifice as you make."*

From Richmond, November 19th, he writes: "I am received and treated with all the marks of respect and attention that I can wish. Your letters have been of singular service, and I am exceedingly obliged to you for the warm manner in which you recommended me to the notice of your friends. Your weight and influence, both with Congress and this State, in support of the Southern operations, will be exceedingly important to my success."

To Alexander Hamilton he wrote: "General Washington's influence will do more than all the assemblies upon the continent. I always thought him exceedingly popular, but in many places he is little less than adored, and universally admired. From being the friend of the General, I found myself exceedingly well received."

Notwithstanding all this, the horrors of the situation began to take hold on Greene. Of the Southern people he says: "I believe the views and wishes of the great body of the people are entirely with us. But remove the personal influence of a few, and they are a lifeless and inanimate mass, without direction or spirit to employ the means they possess for their own security.

"I cannot contemplate my own situation without the greatest degree of anxiety. I am far removed from almost all my friends and connections, and have to prosecute a war in a country, in the best state, attended with insurmountable difficulties; but doubly so now, from the state of our finances and the loss of public credit. How I shall be able to support myself, under all these embarrassments, God only knows! My only consolation is, that if I fail, I hope it will not be accompanied with any peculiar marks of personal disgrace. Censure and reproach even follow

* *Greene's Life of Greene,* Vol. III., p. 53.

the unfortunate. This I expect, if I don't succeed. The ruin of my family is what hangs most heavy on my mind. My fortune is small, and misfortune or disgrace to me, must be ruin to them. I beg your Excellency will do me the honor to forward the enclosed letter to Mrs. Greene, who is rendered exceedingly unhappy by my going southward."

Arriving at Charlotte, North Carolina, December 2d, 1780, after a journey of six weeks, Greene relieved Gates, assumed command of the Southern Department, and writes : "To give your Excellency an idea of the state and condition of this army, if it deserves the name of one, I enclose you an extract of a letter from General Gates to the Board of War: 'Nothing can be more wretched and distressing than the condition of the troops, starving with cold and hunger, without tents or camp equipage. Those of the Virginia line are literally naked, unfit for any kind of duty, and must remain so until clothing can be had from the north.'"

Again : "I will not pain your Excellency with further accounts of the wants and sufferings of this army ; but I am not without great apprehension of its entire dissolution unless the commissary's and quartermaster's departments can be rendered more competent to the demands of the service. Nor are the clothing and hospital departments upon a better footing. Not a shilling in the pay-chest, nor a prospect of any for months to come. This is really making bricks without straw." "P. S. This moment accounts have been received that General Leslie landed his troops at Charleston on the 21st December, and on the 24th was at Monk's corner."

This was strictly true, but not at all new. Nor was it peculiar to the Carolinas. The Virginia troops at home were naked ; Sumter's and Marion's band of heroes were in the same state ; yet at this very time, both in Virginia and Carolina, they were in active warfare and doing capital service. How often had the army of the commander-in-chief precisely answered to this description.

The commander doubtless reminded him of this, for Greene replies: "Your Excellency's letter of December 13th, came to hand this day. It is true I came to the southward in expectation of meeting with difficulties; but they far exceed what I had any idea of. * * * We will do all in our power; but the soldiers have no spirit, and it is impossible they should in their present situation. *I wish the enemy would give us a little more time to prepare ourselves.* However, I don't intend to be drove out of North Carolina, if *I can possibly avoid it.*"*

Up to this time General Greene had run his career under Washington's wing, and now, in desiring to command a department extending from Georgia to the Chesapeake, he had overestimated his abilities.

Finding it impossible to subsist his army near Charlotte, he had sent Kosciusko to entrench a position in a fruitful region on the Pedee, at Cheraw Hills. Thither Greene led his army, arriving on December 26th, 1780. Greene writes: "*It is a camp of repose,* and no army ever wanted one more; the troops having totally lost their discipline."

Greene's biographer says that he addressed himself to "disciplining both officers and men, *inviting his officers to his table by turns, and endeavoring to give a higher tone to their habits of thought and conversation.*"†

Useful, but not well timed, in view of the military status; the imminent, deadly emergency at that moment, both in Virginia and the Carolinas. Polishing arms rather than manners was in order, when Arnold was ravaging Virginia and burning her towns; when Cornwallis with his coadjutors Rawdon, Webster and Tarleton were spread over South Carolina holding her fast bound; and Leslie, by

* *Sparks' Correspondence*, Vol. III., p. 208.
† *Greene's Life of Greene.*

Greene's own report, with two thousand fresh troops, had
landed in Charleston and advanced thirty miles on his way
to join Cornwallis.   Aside from that "Camp of Repose,"
what hope to confront this formidable enemy ! Sumter
and Marion were in the field ; below and between Camden
and Charleston, watching, harassing, and wasting the
enemy, and keeping Greene informed of their every movement.

MORGAN TO THE RESCUE.

GATES had hailed the arrival in his camp of Daniel Morgan. It must be said of that officer that he was doing what he could, to re-collect and re-organize the fragments of his broken army.

Our Maryland heroes, Lieutenant Colonel Howard and Colonel Otho H. Williams, were there with their surviving continentals; some of the Virginia line; with militia newly arrived; in all about fourteen hundred men.

Morgan was immediately invited by the North Carolina authorities to take command of their militia, but Gates had another plan. From the two battalions of infantry, he selected four hundred picked men under Colonel Howard; a company of riflemen under Captain Rose; such fragments of Colonels White and Washington's cavalry as had escaped the sword of Tarleton, were united under Lieutenant Colonel Washington, and the command of the whole given to Colonel Morgan,* October 1, 1780, just seven days before King's Mountain flamed with sudden glory.

Upon intelligence of this fine stroke, with the total derangement of Cornwallis' plans and his falling back from North Carolina, Morgan pressed forward also, into South Carolina. At this time Gates received the following resolution of Congress with commission of Brigadier General for Morgan:

* *Graham's Life of Morgan*, p. 239.

"October 18, 1780.

"In CONGRESS.

"Congress took into consideration the report of the Board of War respecting the promotion of Colonel Morgan, and it appearing from the letters of Governors Jefferson and Rutledge, and of Major General Gates, that Colonel Morgan's promotion to the rank of Brigadier General will remove several embarrassments which impede the public service in the Southern Department and that it will otherwise greatly advance the said service,

"*Resolved*, therefore, that Colonel Daniel Morgan be, and hereby is, appointed to the rank of Brigadier General in the army of the United States.

"CHARLES THOMPSON, Secretary."

Extract from the minutes.

Congratulations poured in upon him from brother officers who best knew his worth, and Morgan set his face to the foe. His little force had been in part clothed, but they were without tents, wagons, camp equipage, commissariat or hospital stores. They were expected to find their own provisions, fight and sleep, with no shelter from the storm and no covering from the night dews, "beyond the branches of the trees on the leeward side of a hill."

They soon found something to do. A nest of tories were gathered at the farm of one Rugly, who had received a commission of Colonel from the British, and was recruiting for the king's service. Morgan detached his cavalry under Colonel Washington, to break them up. Rugly hearing of their approach, intrenched himself in a log-house with a line of abattis, etc.

Colonel Washington saw at once that his troop of horse was inadequate to the situation. Fruitful in resources, he improvised artillery, by mounting a pine log upon wheels, disposed his forces as if for a cannonade, and sent a corporal of dragoons with a summons to surrender. Rugly made no parley, but surrendered at once, and Washington marched back with a hundred tory prisoners, provisions, and arms.

Gates' army had meanwhile advanced to Charlotte, where General Greene took command. With a generous consideration for Gates' feelings, he confirmed all that General's standing orders, including those to Morgan. Two weeks later, December 20th, Greene with the main army of about twelve hundred men marched to Cheraw Hills on the Pedee; Morgan with a force of less than six hundred pushed forward to the country between the Broad and Pacolet rivers.

His instructions from Greene were, to take position west of the Catawba, and as soon as joined by the militia he was to act offensively or defensively as his prudence and discretion might direct, "*avoiding surprises by every possible precaution.*" He was directed, if the enemy moved towards the main army at Cheraw Hills to follow them and join forces with Greene. He was also directed to keep Greene constantly informed of the enemy's movements, etc.

Morgan had entertained high hopes of a large reinforcement of militia,—perhaps some of the upland yeomanry of King's Mountain fame,—but the savage tribes were astir, threatening their settlements; they were compelled to remain and stand guard at their own cabin doors. A letter from the patriot leader Davidson explains:

"December 14, 1780

"*Dear Sir:*—My orders from General Greene were, to join you as soon as possible after you crossed the river, which I should have effected before this time, had the troops joined agreeable to my expectations. But the expedition against the Cherokee Downs, and the murders committed in Rutherford and Burke counties have entirely drawn off the attention of the people who were to compose my command, etc., etc.

"WM. DAVIDSON.

"General DANIEL MORGAN."

Morgan felt the more anxiety because every indication pointed to a movement of Cornwallis' army, so soon as he should be joined by Leslie. He had greatly desired to enter at once upon offensive field operations in which were included successive attacks upon Ninety-six and Augusta, and even an attack upon the camp of Cornwallis himself. These plans he was now compelled to relinquish. Unable to do what he would, he proceeded to do what he could, in establishing magazines of supplies at various points in his rear, and organizing a system of military detectives by which he could be supplied with speedy and constant information of every movement of the enemy; reports were to be furnished at least twice in twenty-four hours. He also dispatched Colonel Washington and Major McCall to Fair Forest Creek to break up a large camp of tories. They completely surprised, routed, captured or dispersed the whole body. These tory encounters, though mere accessories to Morgan's general plans, were immensely useful in protecting the families and property of the whigs, and in intimidating the rising of the tories.

But a powerful combination was forming against him, and he foresaw earnest work at hand. Cornwallis well knew the temper of Morgan's steel. Memories of Piscataway and Rahway, rose upon him. He had been stung by Morgan's rifle-balls throughout the campaigns of 1777, 1778 and 1779 in the Jerseys; and he had a British, not an American estimation of the hero of Saratoga.

Cornwallis was anticipating an early advance into North Carolina so soon as Leslie came up; but when he learned that Morgan was afield, and hovering in the vicinity of his important posts of Ninety-six and Augusta, he called for his valiant Colonel Tarleton. There could be no advance without first disposing of Morgan. It was now January 1781.

"WINNSBOROUGH, January 2, 1781.

"*Dear Tarleton:*—I sent Haldane to you last night, to desire you would pass Broad river with the legion and the first battalion of the 71st as soon as possible. If Morgan is still at Williams, or anywhere within your reach, I should wish you to *push him to the utmost.* I have not heard, except from McArthur, of his having cannon, nor would I believe it, except on very good authority. It is, however, possible, and Ninety-six is of so much importance that no time is to be lost.

"Yours sincerely,

"CORNWALLIS."

Morgan's own plan was to get into the British rear ; to push down into Georgia, compel them to return to the defence of their menaced posts, and thus relieve the States of North Carolina and Virginia. A course eminently wise, as future operations showed. It looked a hazardous game indeed, and would have been in other hands ; but Morgan, though modest as valiant, and prudent as modest, could yet measure his own resources. But Greene, who, Johnson says, "never played a hazardous game when a safe one would do," forbade Morgan from going so far from the "Camp of Repose" in the Cheraw Hills.

Their correspondence at this time will best disclose the situation. [The letters are copied from *Graham's Life of Morgan*—the italics are ours.]

General Greene to General Morgan.

"CAMP ON THE CHERAWS, December 29, 1780.

"*Dear Sir:*—We arrived here on the 26th inst., after a very tedious and disagreeable march, owing to the badness
10

of the roads and the poor and weak state of our teams. Our prospects with regard to provisions are mended, but this is no Egypt.

"I have this moment received intelligence that General Leslie has landed at Charleston, and is on his way to Camden. His force is about two thousand, perhaps something less. I am also informed that Lord Cornwallis has collected his troops at Camden. You will watch their motions very narrowly and *take care and guard against a surprise. Should they move this way, you will endeavor to cross the river and join us.* Do not be sparing of your expresses, but let me know as often as possible of your situation. I wish to be fully informed of your prospect respecting provisions, and also the number of militia that has joined you. A large number of tents and hatchets are on the road. As soon as they arrive, you shall be supplied. Many other articles necessary for this army, particularly shoes, are coming on.

"I am, sir, your most obedient servant,

"NATHANIEL GREENE.·

" General Daniel MORGAN."

The annexed, from Colonel O. H. Williams, reached Morgan at the same time:

"CAMP AT CHERAW HILLS, December 30.

" *Dear General :*—I enclose you a number of letters, by a sergeant of Lieutenant-Colonel Washington's regiment, which I hope will arrive safe. We are at present in a " camp of repose," and the General is exerting himself and every body else to put his little army in a better condition. Tents sufficient for a larger army than ours are coming from Philadelphia ; they are expected to arrive early in January. We also expect shoes, shirts and some other articles essentially necessary. General Marion writes the General that General Leslie landed at Charleston with his command on December 20th, and that he had advanced as far as Monk's Corner—probably they mean to form a junction and attempt to give a blow to a part of our force while we are divided, *and most probably that blow will be aimed at you, as our position in the centre of a wilderness is less accessible than your camp.*

"I know your discretion renders all caution from me unnecessary; but my friendship will plead an excuse for the impertinence of wishing you to run no risk of a defeat. May your laurels flourish when your locks fade, and an age of peace reward your toils in war. My love to every fellow-soldier, and adieu.

"Yours, most truly,

"O. H. WILLIAMS.

"Brigadier-General MORGAN."

Morgan, from his camp on the Pacolet, writes to General Greene about the same date:

" *December* 31*st*, 1780.

"*Dear General:*—After an uninteresting march, I arrived at this place on the 25th of December. * * * * The militia are increasing fast, so that we cannot be supplied in this neighborhood more than two or three days at farthest. Were we to advance and be constrained to retreat, the consequences would be very disagreeable, and this must be the case should we lay near the enemy and Cornwallis reinforce, which he can do with great facility.

"General Davidson has brought in one hundred and twenty men, and has returned to bring forward a draft of five hundred men. Colonel Pickens has joined me with sixty. Thirty or forty of the men who came out with him have gone into North Carolina to secure their effects, and will immediately repair to my camp.

"When I shall have collected my expected force, I shall be at a loss how to act. *Could a diversion be made in my favor by the main army,* I should wish to march into Georgia. To me it appears an advisable scheme, but should be happy to receive your directions on this point, as *they must be the guide of my actions.*

"I have consulted with General Davidson and Colonel Pickens, whether we could secure a safe retreat should we be pushed by a superior force. They tell me it can be easily effected by passing up the Savannah and crossing over the heads of the rivers along the Indian line. To expedite this movement, should it meet with your approbation, I have sent for one hundred swords, which I intend to put into the hands of expert riflemen, to be mounted and incorporated with Lieutenant-Colonel Washington's corps.

"I have also written to the quartermaster to have me one hundred pack-saddles made immediately;—should be glad if you would direct him to be expeditious. Wagons will be an impediment, whether we attempt to annoy the enemy or provide for our own safety. It is incompatible with the nature of light troops to be encumbered with baggage.

"I would wish to receive an answer to this proposition as soon as possible. This country has been so exhausted that the supplies for my detachment have been precarious and scant ever since my arrival, and in a few days will be unattainable—so that a movement is unavoidable. Should this expedition be thought advisable, a profound secrecy will be essentially necessary. Colonel Lee's corps would ensure its success.

"I have the honor to be,

"DANIEL MORGAN.

"Hon. Major-General GREENE."

General Greene to General Morgan.

"CHERAW, EAST-SIDE PEDEE, January 8, 1781.

"*Dear Sir:*—Colonel Malmody arrived here yesterday

with your letter of the 31st December. I have maturely considered your proposition of an expedition into Georgia, and cannot think it warrantable in the critical situation our army is in.

"I have no small reason to think, by intelligence from different quarters, that the enemy have a movement in contemplation, and that in all probability it will be this way. * * * * Should you go into Georgia, and the enemy push this way, your whole force would be useless. * * * * *

"If you employ detachments to interrupt supplies going to Ninety-Six and Augusta, it will perplex the enemy very much. If you think Ninety-Six, Augusta, or even Savannah, can be surprised, and your force will admit of a detachment for the purpose and leave you a sufficiency to keep up a good countenance, you may attempt it. But don't think of attempting either unless by surprise, for you will only beat your heads against a wall without success. Small parties are better to effect a surprise than large bodies, and the success will not greatly depend upon the numbers but on the secrecy and spirit of the attack. I must repeat my caution to you *to guard against a surprise*. The enemy and the tories will both try to bring you into disgrace, if possible, to prevent your influence upon the militia, especially the weak and wavering. *I cannot pretend to give you any particular instructions respecting a position*. Somewhere between the Saluda and the north Broad River, appears to be the most favorable for annoying the enemy, interrupting their supplies, and harassing their rear, if they should make a movement this way.

"If you could detach a small party to kill the enemy's draft-horses and recruiting cavalry, upon the Congaree, it would give them almost as deadly a blow as a defeat. But this matter must be conducted with great secrecy and dispatch. Lieutenant-Colonel Lee has just arrived with his legion, and Colonel Green is within a few days' march of this with a reinforcement.

"I am, dear sir, etc.,

"NATHANIEL GREENE.

"Brigadier-General MORGAN."

General Morgan to General Greene.

"CAMP ON PACOLET, January 4, 1781.

"*Dear Sir :*— * * * * * * Sensible of the importance of guarding against surprise, I have used every precaution on this head. I have had men who were recommended as every way calculated for the business, continually watching the motions of the enemy ; so, unless they deceive me, I am in no danger of being surprised. I have received no acquisition of force since I wrote you ; but I expect in a few days to be joined by Colonels Clark's and Twigg's regiment. Their numbers I cannot ascertain. The men on the north side of Broad River I have not yet ordered to join me ; but I have directed their officers to keep them in compact bodies, that they may be ready to march at the shortest notice. I intend these as a check on the enemy should they attempt anything against my detachment.

"My situation is far from being agreeable to my wishes or expectations. Forage and provisions are not to be had. Here we cannot subsist, so that we have but one alternative—either to retreat or move into Georgia. A retreat will be attended with the most fatal consequences. The spirit which now begins to pervade the people and call them into the field, will be destroyed. The militia, who have already joined, will desert us, and it is not improbable but that a regard for their own safety will induce them to join the enemy.

"I shall wait with impatience for your directions on

the subject of my letter by Colonel Malmady, as till then my operations must be suspended.

"I am, dear sir, truly yours,

"DANIEL MORGAN."

Greene to Morgan.

"CAMP ON THE PEDEE, January 13, 1781.

"*Dear Sir :*—I am at this moment favored with your letter of the 4th inst. Since I wrote you I have received letters from Virginia, informing me of the arrival there of General Phillips with a detachment of two thousand five hundred men from New York. This circumstance renders it still more improper for you to move far to the southward. It is my wish also that you hold your ground, if possible, for I foresee the disagreeable consequences of a retreat. If moving as far as Ninety-Six, or anywhere in the neighborhood of it, will contribute to the obtaining of more ample supplies, you have my consent.

"Colonel Tarleton is said to be on his way to pay you a visit. I doubt not but he will have a decent reception and a proper dismission. And I am happy to find you have taken every precaution to avoid a surprise. I wish you to be more particular respecting your plan and object in paying a visit to Georgia.

"Virginia is raising three thousand men to recruit this army.

"I am, etc.,

"NATHANIEL GREENE."

Greene to Morgan.

"HEAD QUARTERS, January 13, 1781.

"*Dear Sir :*—There are six wagon loads of cloth on the way from Charleston to the Congaree River, the property of one Wade Hampton, who, it is said, wishes it to fall into our hands. It will halt on the Congaree at Friday's

Ferry, but in that situation you cannot get at it, and the man, it is said, is willing to move it on towards Ninety-Six, as if to relieve that garrison. To satisfy yourself respecting the matter, you must send a man to Mr. Hampton to inquire respecting the report, and, if true, concert with him a plan for getting possession of the cloth, as it would be of *infinite importance* to get it into our possession (!). You will readily see, from the nature of the thing, that it is not to be considered as plunder, nor must anybody but yourself know anything of the transaction, as it would inevitably ruin the man. Great caution should be taken to guard against those evils.

"I am, etc.,
" NATHANIEL GREENE."

General Morgan to General Greene.

" BURR'S MILLS, January 15, 1781.
[Two days before " Cowpens."]

" *Dear General:*—Your letters of the 3d and 8th came to hand yesterday, just as I was preparing to change my position. * * * * * * I find it impracticable to procure more provisions in this quarter than are absolutely necessary for our own immediate consumption ; indeed, it has been with the greatest difficulty that we have been able to effect this. We have to feed such a number of horses, that the most plentiful country must soon be exhausted. Could the militia be persuaded to change their fatal mode of going to war, much provision might be saved ; but the custom has taken such deep root that it cannot be abolished.

" Upon a full and mature deliberation, I am confirmed in the opinion that nothing can be effected by my detachment in this country, which will balance the risks I will be subjected to by remaining here. The enemy's great superiority in numbers, and our distance from the main army, will enable Lord Cornwallis to detach so superior a force against me as to render it essential to our safety to avoid coming to action. *Nor will this be always in my power.* No attempt to surprise me will be left untried by them, and, situated as we must be, every possible precaution may not be sufficient to secure us. The scarcity of forage renders it impossible for us always to be in a compact body; and were this not the case, it is beyond the art of man to keep the militia from straggling. [So " no more of that."]

"My force is inadequate to the attempts you have hinted at "—[*i. e.,* to surprise Ninety-Six, or Augusta, or Savannah, or attack Cornwallis in his camp, to send a party down upon the Congaree, to kill the enemy's draft and cavalry horses, to stop supplies going to the various British posts, to see after Mr. Wade Hampton's cloth, and to fight Tarleton, Cornwallis and Leslie, individually and collectively, etc., etc., etc.] "I have now with me only two hundred South Carolina and Georgia, and one hundred and forty North Carolina volunteers. Nor do I expect to have more than two-thirds of these to assist me should I be attacked, for it is impossible to keep them collected. Though I am convinced that were you on the spot, the propriety of my proposition would strike you forcibly, should you think it inadvisable to recall me, you may depend on my attempting everything to annoy the enemy and to provide for the safety of my detachment. I shall cheerfully acquiesce in your determinations.

"Colonel Tarleton has crossed the Tyger at Musgrove's Mills; his force we cannot learn. It is more than probable we are his object. Cornwallis by last accounts was at the cross-roads near Lee's old place.

"We have just learned that Tarleton's force is from eleven to twelve hundred British.

"I am, dear General, truly yours,

"DANIEL MORGAN."

"CAMP ON PEDEE, January 19, 1781.
[Two days after "Cowpens."]

"*Dear Sir:*—Your favor of the 15th was delivered to me last night about 12 o'clock. * * * I was informed of Lord Cornwallis'. movements before the arrival of your letter, and agree with you in opinion that you are his object ; and from his making so general a movement, it convinces me that he feels a great inconvenience from your force and situation. General Leslie has crossed the Catawba to join him. He would never harass his troops to remove you if he did not think it of some importance, nor would he put his collective force in motion if he had not some respect for your numbers. *I am sensible your situation is critical, and requires the most watchful attention to guard against a surprise. But I think it is of great importance to keep up a force in that quarter.*

"It is not my wish you should come to action unless you have a *manifest superiority and a moral certainty of succeeding.* Put nothing to the hazard ; a retreat may be disagreeable, but not disgraceful. Regard not the opinions of the day. It is not our business to risk too much. *Our affairs are in too critical a condition and require time and nursing to give them a better tone.* * * * Before this can possibly reach you, I imagine the movements of Lord Cornwallis and Colonel Tarleton will be sufficiently explained, and *you be obliged to take some decisive measures.* I shall be perfectly satisfied if you keep clear of a misfortune. *Though I wish you laurels, I am unwilling to expose the common cause to give you an opportunity to acquire them.*

"As the rivers are subject to sudden and great swells, you must be careful that the enemy do not take a position in your rear where you can neither retreat by your flanks

or your front. I am preparing boats to move always with
the army ; would one or two be of any use to you? They
will be put on wheels and made to move with little more
difficulty than a loaded wagon.

"I am, with great esteem, etc.

"NATHANIEL GREENE."

Here is a most strange military pose. Greene with
twelve hundred men, since reinforced by Lee and Colonel
Green, intrenched in the fruitful region of the Pedee, busy
in the cultivation of the "habits of thought and conversation of his officers." Besides this his pen moved incessantly ; batches of letters issued from the "camp of repose" daily in all directions, to all manner of officials,
civil and military, beseeching for supplies and reinforcements for his army; and it must be said, with very fair
success. Tents, wagons, hatchets, nails, shirts and shoes,
in short, everything drifted that way. The General was
also preparing strong pens for prisoners, forgetting the
old receipt for "cooking a fish." He shows himself every
inch the Quartermaster.

Washington's army was emaciated with the drain
southward. He had sent, after the fall of Charleston, De
Kalb and his efficient Maryland and Delaware brigade.
To Greene's cry of entreaty he now dispatched Lee's fine
corps of cavalry and counselled that the whole energies
of the rich State of Virginia should be turned in that
direction.

Jefferson, then Governor of Virginia, followed these
counsels of Washington until he drew upon himself the
censure of his own people for the defence of the Carolinas
at the expense of Virginia. To Steuben, Washington
wrote : "Make the defence of the State interfere as little
as possible with the measures for succoring General Greene.
Bancroft says : "With a magnanimity that knew nothing
of fear, Virginia laid herself bare for the protection of the

Carolinas." Greene himself wrote to Washington afterward: "Virginia has given me every support I could wish." Further on, in reply to Greene's still urgent entreaty for aid, Washington says that "but a handful of troops remain to him, and should he send any more he would be compelled to accompany and command them, or be left without an army."

We see Morgan with his small force pushed forward, to gorge the British tiger Tarleton, held to a position in which he cannot even maintain his little army intact, but must scatter it to prevent starvation ; forbidden to advance or retreat, and bid to stand and be eaten ; enjoined not to fight, unless with a "manifest superiority and a moral certainty of success ;" above all not to be "surprised ;" and finally to take "decisive measures" with Tarleton. These puerile and incoherent cautions seem singularly misaddressed, to the man who had never been known to be *surprised* from Quebec to Cowpens.

Morgan, as we have seen, had delicately hinted to Greene the propriety of some "diversion in his favor, by the main army," and suggested that Lee's cavalry would be invaluable to him. But Greene saw fit to send Lee entirely in an opposite direction. He was perfectly aware that Morgan was menaced by Tarleton and Cornwallis, and that Leslie was well on his way to join the latter. Steuben, who commanded in Virginia, had sent troops, which he sorely needed at home, against Arnold and Phillips, expressly in order that Greene might prevent the junction of Leslie with Cornwallis.

Johnson says that Greene actually "contemplated striking at Cornwallis' army in their divided condition," but it never developed further than a contemplation. Leslie marched without interruption up through the State, crossed the Catawba and joined Cornwallis on January 18th,—just one day too late—Cowpens was fought on the 17th.

Tarleton had expressly arranged that he and Cornwallis should advance simultaneously upon Morgan, as their design was to capture or annihilate him and his army. Cornwallis confirmed the arrangement, but supposing certainly that Greene, with the main army, more than twice Morgan's force, would not stand an idle spectator of these military movements, but would move out to dispute the advance of Leslie, dared not march northward until Leslie's safety was assured. Cornwallis miscalculated; a masterly inactivity was the rôle of the main army; neither a diversion nor a co-operation was to be attempted, and to Morgan's last appeal, with the intelligence that Tarleton was close upon him with eleven hundred picked British regulars, Greene offers the sole consolation of "boats on wheels."

If Greene had had the grace to loan him the main army and Lee's cavalry for ten days! What then? We might have locked Yorktown.

Professor G. W. Greene, in his "Historical Views of the Conduct of the Revolution," says: "The reconquest of the South, and the brilliant campaigns of '80 and '81, belong exclusively to Greene." A slovenly statement, to say the least. General Greene assumed command of the Southern Department at Charlotte, N. C., December 4th, 1780. Just twenty-seven days of the year 1780 remained, though General Greene's field-service does not commence until February 8th, 1781, when Morgan brought his victorious army from Cowpens to Guilford C. H., and General Huger joined him the next day with the main army from Cheraw Hills.

It would add nothing to General Greene's military fame if it were possible to identify him with 1780,—the year of gloom and disaster at the South : the fall of Charleston, the shame of Camden, and Tarleton's iron heel crushing in upon the Carolinas.

That gloom is broken only by the heroic strokes of Sumter and Marion with the swamp heroes, and by the glory of King's Mountain, October 7th, 1780, five days before Greene at West Point received the intelligence of his appointment to the South.

General Greene was entirely innocent of any of this good work; and the main army lay dreaming in their tents in their "Camp of Repose," a hundred and fifty miles away, on that memorable winter dawn, January 17th, 1781, when Morgan and his handful of heroes, hotly . pressed by Tarleton, turned upon, crushed and captured his army, routed and pursued the hitherto invincible, and won immortal fame.

But we anticipate. Morgan's admirable system of military detection now served him to purpose. He knew every movement of Tarleton and Cornwallis almost as soon as made; and, like a skillful player, penetrated and anticipated their game. Nor did Morgan underestimate his powerful antagonist. He knew that Tarleton had thus far triumphantly ridden down all opposition. Marion alone had escaped, by skilfully declining to measure swords with him. *Morgan did not seek the encounter; Tarleton compelled it.* Morgan resolved, however, to select his own battle-field. "Observing the guarded and deliberate manner in which Tarleton advanced upon him, —so unlike that officer's usual mode of approaching an opponent"—he was confirmed in his suspicion of the plan concerted between him and Cornwallis to entrap him.

He resolved to cross the Pacolet and march towards the upper waters of the Broad River, which would enable the small detachments of militia he had stationed there to join him, and, in case of misfortune, facilitate a retreat toward the main army at Cheraw.

Accordingly he broke up his camp, put his troops in motion on January 15th, crossed the Pacolet and encamped for the night at Burr's Mills, on Thicketty Creek. Here it was that he wrote his last letter to Greene—two days before Cowpens—warning him that it would not be always in his power to obey his instructions by evading a battle.

Tarleton followed, crossing the Pacolet the morning after. Learning this, Morgan immediately put his army upon the march. Pushing on by a mountain road, he passed Hancocksville at noon, turned into a by-path, and, arriving at Cowpens about sun-down, he ordered a halt.— "I'll go no further."

XXV.—1781.

AT THE "COWPENS."

"Their Diomede, brave in battle, prayed: 'Hear me, O daughter of Ægis-bearing Jove, unwearied; if ever favoring, thou stoodest by me in the hostile fight, now in turn befriend me, O Minerva, and grant me to slay this man who boasts, saying that I shall not long behold the brilliant sun." Thus he spoke praying, and Pallas Minerva heard him, and gave strength and daring to Diomede that he might become conspicuous among all the Argives, and might bear off for himself excellent renown. And she kindled from his helmet and his shield an unwearied fire, and standing near him, spoke winged words."

ILIAD, Book V.

LEFT with these fearful odds, the immortal gods came about our hero, and Cowpens, more than any other Revolutionary battle-field recalls the splendid machinery of the Homeric strifes. Thus the old Greek would say it, but, in our "surer word," "God sent his angel."

Cowpens and Trenton stand illuminated with a super-human glory. At Trenton, when the Hessians threw down their arms, "Washington, whose strong will had been strained for seventeen hours, gave way to his feelings, and with clasped hands raised his eyes, gleaming with thankfulness, to heaven."* At Cowpens, after the victory, Morgan, riding over the field, was heard to utter audible thanksgivings to the God of battles.† Tarleton attempts in vain to account for his amazing discomfiture. After suggesting many things which might have inclined the battle otherwise, he says, "but after all *it remains a mystery. It was either the bravery or good conduct of the Americans, or the loose manner of forming, always practiced by the king's troops in America, or *some unforeseen

* *Bancroft*, Vol. IX.   † *Graham's Life of Morgan.*

event, which may throw terror into the most disciplined soldiers or counteract the best concerted designs."

Cowpens offers several further parallels to Trenton. The long series of disasters at the South had exhausted the resources and well-nigh broken the hearts and crushed the hopes of that gallant people. King's Mountain, indeed, had made a rift in the cloud, but there they had contended mainly with an army of tories. Added to the well-appointed army of Cornwallis, Tarleton had struck a terror into the Southern heart like that with which the Hessian soldiers had inspired the Northern patriots after the defeat of Long Island and the reverses of the commander-in-chief in New Jersey. They saw nothing to oppose to such adversaries. As Trenton dispelled the illusion that invested the Hessian with invincible might, so Cowpens broke the spell that held the Carolinas nerveless before Tarleton.

At Trenton and Cowpens, Washington and Morgan equally realized the momentous issues of the hour, and felt the *absolute necessity of success* to the cause. After the landing of Washington's detachment near Trenton, Sullivan "reported to him by one of his aids, that the arms of his party were wet." "Then tell your General," answered Washington, "to use the bayonet, and penetrate into the town, for the town must be taken, and I am resolved to do it."* Then Stark's bayonets rushed forward.

Morgan knew "he walked o'er perils, on an edge, more likely to fall in, than to get o'er." What struggle shook his soul on that battle's eve, we know not; but that he came out from it, strong and calm, we do know.

Himself tells us of the terror that agitated him on that New Year's eve of 1775 before the assault on Quebec. "He was sleeping when the order was given for his regiment to form. Upon awaking his mind became suddenly so impressed with the fearful nature of the enterprise in which

* *Bancroft,* Vol. IX.

he was about to engage, that he shivered through his whole frame, and, for a time, felt quite unequal to the task which duty and honor imposed upon him. He sought out a secluded spot, and, kneeling down, he prayed most fervently for protection for himself and his men, and for a triumph for his country. He rose with courage and confidence, and with cheerfulness took his place at the head of his command." Morgan's own words are : "If ever I prayed in earnest it was upon that occasion, committing myself into the hands of the Almighty and imploring his protection. Having done so, I rose from my knees, dismissed my fears, and led on my men to the assault. I verily believe it was entirely owing to an overruling Providence, in whom I reposed confidence, that I was so mercifully protected, and brought off safely from the extreme dangers through which I passed on that morning."*

Morgan had informed himself accurately of the nature and strength of Tarleton's force. Picked British regulars, twice his number of infantry, three times his number of cavalry, and well served artillery. Cornwallis' army was almost within striking distance. Of artillery Morgan had none, but hoped to offset this ugly odds by the rifle-balls of his skilled marksmen.

His little army included what remained of the gallant brigade of Marylanders under Howard, who on that shameful field of Camden, drove the British left wing before them at the point of their bayonets, and saved American honor. A more daring and effective corps of cavalry for its numbers than that of Colonel Washington, did not exist. Some of his militia had also served short terms among the Continental army.

On the evening before the battle Colonel Pickens reached the camp with one hundred and fifty militia from the Broad River. During the night several other parties came in, fifty in all. Morgan felt himself sustained by officers

* *Graham's Life of Morgan.*

in whom he reposed unwavering confidence, who, in turn, knew how they were generalled, and were well content to steel themselves from their leader's metal.

Notably the gallant Colonel Pickens, Lieutenant-Colonels Washington and Howard of Maryland were towers of strength. True they had fled before Tarleton at Camden, and will again at Guilford Court-House; but now at Cowpens, he shall fly before them.

Morgan's first care was to strengthen his cavalry, so far inferior in numbers to that of his enemy. He called for volunteers, and forty-five men stepped forward. They were equipped and added to Washington's corps. He next directed his baggage to move before daylight toward the fords of the Broad River; and there await further orders. Patrolling parties were dispatched in different directions to watch and report every move of the enemy, who was encamped not far distant. The troops were dismissed to food and rest. Morgan with his officers sat in council; and after that—the council over—what then?

There could be no repose for Morgan. Bodies of militia were arriving all through the night, on which, in part, his hopes depended. Some of these he had never seen before, and they did not know their comrades. Morgan understood the militia thoroughly; gave them full credit for the kind of service they rendered, and knew how to obtain that service from them.

The first sight of such a commander inspired them with confidence; his powerful physique and dignified military presence; his reputation for judgment and courage; the fame of his achievements; above all, the soul of goodness that beamed from his countenance and warmed his genial, friendly manner, drew their hearts to him.

These new unpracticed militia—children in war—must be educated over night and brought into sympathy and brotherhood with his little army. Morgan must impart somewhat of himself to every heart and arm, that they may strike together, as with one heart and one arm, on the morrow.

A volunteer, Major Thomas Young, tells us this anecdote, for which we thank him right heartily. He says :

"I think Morgan never slept a moment that night. He was moving about among the newly arrived volunteers, giving them words of encouragement, inspecting their arms, directing them how best to prepare themselves. He showed a confident and cheerful air, joked with them about their sweethearts at home, predicting the certainty of success and the glory they would win. He promised them, if they would but stand by him, the 'old wagoner' would crack his whip over Ban Tarleton on the morrow. 'Hold up your heads, boys; three fires and you are free ; and when you go back to your homes, how the old folks will bless you, and the girls kiss you for your gallant deeds.'"

Morgan argued favorably from the fact that Tarleton was intoxicated with his long tide of success. Lastly, with the morning came the intelligence that Cornwallis had not yet moved from Turkey Creek ; which meant that Leslie had not come up and he had only Tarleton to fight.

Tarleton's army was in motion at three o'clock on the morning of the 17th, and at dawn an advance guard of his cavalry drove one of Morgan's patrols, who came into camp, after a running fight, and reported the approach of the British. Meantime two troops of cavalry were sent forward with orders to harass the American rear, supposing of course that they were retreating. They returned to announce that the Americans awaited them in battle array.

They were deployed upon the field that Morgan had selected ; since occupied by the iron works of Messrs. Hampton and Elmore in Spartansburg district.

It measured from front to rear about five hundred yards, and was crossed by two eminences ; the first of which,

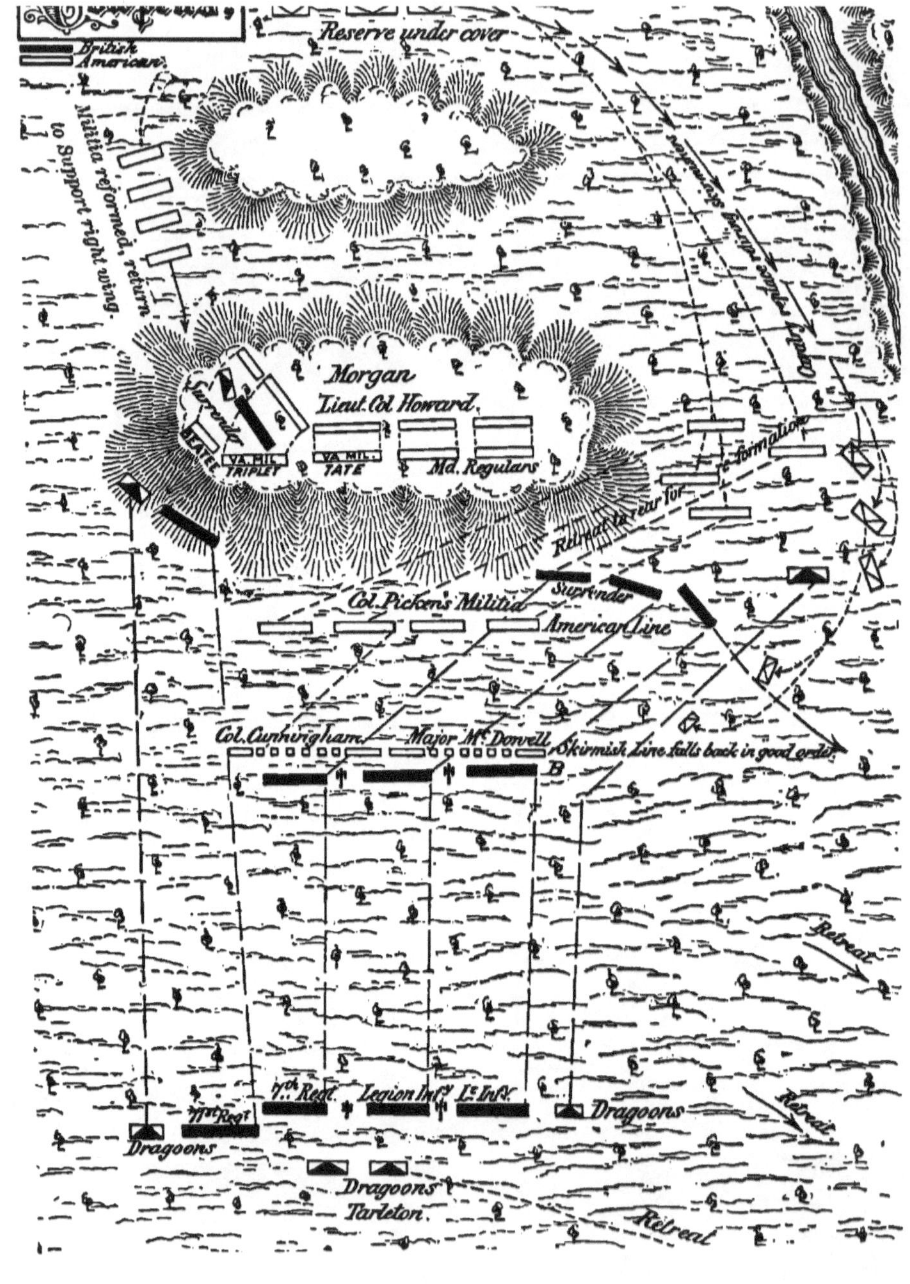

British
American
Reserve under cover
Militia reformed, return
to support right wing.
Morgan
Lieut. Col. Howard.
Surrender
BEATEN
VA. MIL. TRIPLET
VA. MIL. TATE
Md. Regulars
Reenforcements hurried rapidly forward
Retreat to rear for reformation
Col. Picken's Militia
Surrender
American Line
Col. Cunningham
Major McDowell
Skirmish Line falls back in good order
B
Retreat
7th Regt.
Legion Infy
Lt. Infy
Dragoons
Retreat
71st Regt.
Dragoons
Dragoons
Tarleton.
Retreat

gently ascending and stretching to the right and left,
attained its highest point about three hundred yards from
the front. The ground then descended for about eighty
yards, when it gradually rose into a second eminence.
The position was far from the neighborhood of swamps,
free from underbrush, and covered with an ordinary
growth of pine trees; selected with intelligent reference
to the character of his troops and his plan of battle.

Morgan's muster-rolls gave over nine hundred men, but
one detachment had gone with the baggage, another with
prisoners to Salisbury, a third guarded the horses of the
militia in the rear, and a percentage of disabled or sick
·reduced his fighting force to eight hundred. Morgan
himself gives this number. and we take his word.   The
British force reached eleven hundred, with artillery.

On the first eminence, Morgan posted the detachment
that was to bear the strain of the battle—Howard's battalion of Continentals, with the Virginia militia under
Triplett, less than four hundred men. In front of these
were posted the main body of militia, under Colonel
Pickens, about three hundred strong. A hundred yards in
advance of these, were a body of Georgians to the right,
and about the same number of Carolinians on the left,
selected for their courage and skill with the rifle.

Upon the second eminence, a hundred and fifty yards
in the rear of the main body, Colonel Washington was
posted with his cavalry, one hundred and twenty strong.
He was to rally the militia should they fly, and protect
them should they be pursued. Back of these the horses
of the militia were secured to the boughs of· young pine
trees, saddled and bridled, ready for use in any emergency.

They had scarcely taken their several positions, when
Morgan was informed that Tarleton's dispositions were
such as implied an immediate attack. Delay would have
been Tarleton's best policy, and was what Morgan most
feared, but now departed from his mind every doubt of

the result, and a noble confidence inspired his every word and action, and communicated itself to his followers.

While the enemy formed their line of battle, he occupied the short and awful interval to give to the respective lines the necessary directions, and utter a final word of appeal to their courage and patriotism. To the picked body of marksmen in front, his instructions were, to take the cover of the trees, and, upon the approach of the enemy within good shooting range, to show whether or not they were entitled to their reputation of brave men and good marksmen.

They were to retire slowly as the enemy advanced, loading and firing under shelter of the trees, until they reached the main body under Pickens, with whom they were to act. He had set the Georgians on the right and the Carolinians on the left, with the view of exciting a spirit of rivalry. "Let me see," as he turned from the line, "which are most entitled to the credit of brave men." To the main body of militia he then addressed himself. His orders were, to reserve their fire until the enemy approached within fifty yards, when, after delivering two well-directed rounds, they were to retire in good order and take position on the left of the main line, in the rear, firing by regiments as they fell back.

Having concluded these minute directions, he then appealed to their courage and patriotism. He complimented them upon the excellent service they had already rendered, with all the disadvantages of contending with regular troops, and besought them on this day to add to that reputation. ·

He asked but an ordinary display of manhood on their part to render victory certain. He adroitly hinted that flight would but ensure their destruction, while safety, advantage and honor would alike be obtained by a courageous resistance. He assured them that, for himself, he had not a doubt of the result, if they, the militia, would but perform their simple duty. He recalled the glory of his previous battle-fields, in which, at the head of his valiant rifle regiments, he had humbled foes far more formidable than those now before him, and expressed *the mortification he had experienced at having been compelled, in obedience to orders, to avoid grappling with an opponent whom he felt satisfied he could crush whenever he chose.* Rehearsing his orders, with an exhortation to obey them with firmness, he proceeded to Howard's main line. A few brief words were all that were necessary here. They needed no stimulus of spirit-stirring speech to the performance of heroic deeds.

He explained to them his instructions for the·movements of the militia, prepared them to expect the retreat of that body, and his purpose to be accomplished by this maneuvre. He directed them to fire low and deliberately ; not to break on any account, and, if forced to retire, to rally on the eminence in their rear, where, supported by the cavalry and militia, there could be no defeat. He reminded them of their own proud achievements, and charged them that with them rested the final fortunes of the day and the good to be achieved for their country.

Tarleton himself led the attack by moving forward with a small reconnoitering party. A salute of rifle-balls, from the American advance, convinced him that prudence was the better part of valor. He retired and directed a troop of cavalry to charge the line and drive it in upon the rear body of militia under Pickens. The Georgians and Carolinians strictly obeyed the orders they had received,—retired slowly, loading and firing, and joined the main force, after having emptied fifteen saddles.

Tarleton by this time had ordered the advance of his artillery, and, under cover of a warm fire, was forming his right wing. His light and legion infantry, divesting themselves of everything but their arms and ammunition, rapidly formed on the right, and, covered by the fire of a

three-pounder, approached to within three hundred yards
of the militia. The seventh regiment formed to the left
of the light infantry, covered by another three-pounder.
Fifty dragoons on each flank completed the disposition of
Tarleton's main line. The first battalion of the seventy-
first infantry, with two hundred of the legion cavalry,
were reserved at about one hundred and fifty yards to the
rear.

Tarleton ordered a prompt advance of the whole line,
accompanied by a continual fire of the artillery. When
within about one hundred yards of the American front,
they received a close and deadly fire from the militia under
Pickens. Succeeding discharges told well upon them,
especially their officers, not one of whom showed himself
conspicuously but was brought to the ground.

Their pace slackened, and an evident disorder pervaded
their line, but they recovered and continued their forward
movement in the face of the fire of Pickens' rifles.

The militia behaved nobly, they did more than had
been required of them. They now retreated, facing the
foe and firing, to their place on the American left, but,
before they could form in position here, Tarleton ordered
a cavalry charge. This broke their lines, and they retreated rapidly, pursued by the cavalry, to the rear eminence, and to the protection of Washington's legion,—
precisely as they had been directed.

The British, deceived by the apparent flight of the
militia, supposing the victory already achieved, set up a
deafening shout, and with a rapid but uneven pace,
pressed forward upon the main line under Howard. Now
came the tug of battle. The Continentals held their
ground as if rooted to the spot, and rapidly delivered their
fire. The British line faltered, ceased to advance, and
showed rather a disposition to retire; so much so, that
Tarleton hastily ordered up his reserves — infantry and
cavalry—to their support.

Morgan saw, and hailed it as an indication of discouragement and weakness; his clarion tones sent it over the field, inspiring his men and officers with new energy.

At this moment the British cavalry, which had pursued our militia to the rear, had there encountered Washington's legion to their cost. They were now flying back past the American left, hotly pursued by Washington, while the militia, rallied and re-formed by the gallant Pickens, were seen coming round the rear eminence, advancing towards the American right. Howard's division still maintained itself bravely, but the British reserves, infantry and cavalry, were now up, and the whole line again advancing.

The first reinforcements took post on the left, which stretched their line away beyond Howard's right, and threatened a flank attack. For a few minutes, the peril was imminent; but Morgan provided for the emergency. Washington's cavalry, returning from the pursuit of the flying British dragoons, were ordered by Morgan to charge the British reserve cavalry before they could effect their purpose on Howard's right. He himself galloped to the rear to hasten up the militia to the rescue.

Just now occurred what seemed to threaten a calamity, but the military instinct of both Morgan and Howard joined to turn it into splendid victory. Until the cavalry and militia could reach him, a change of front suggested itself to Howard as the best means for a temporary check upon the rapidly advancing foe. He ordered the flank company to perform the evolution which would bring it at a right angle with the main body. The order was misunderstood, and instead, after coming to the right about, they marched to the rear, and the whole body faced about and moved after them. This was agreeable to Morgan's order in case they were compelled to retire. But he now saw the movement with a momentary consternation; galloping up to Howard, they came to an understanding

11

and decided not to rectify the mistake. Instead, Morgan rode back to fix upon the spot for them to re-form ;—this movement also brought them abreast with the advancing militia.

The militia had sent a galling fire into the British reserve under McArthur, not only forcing it to forego its attempt upon the left, but to retire to some distance. Washington, at the same time, made a furious onset upon the cavalry, just as they were about to charge the American flank, broke through their column, wheeled, and charged on them a second time, with crushing effect. They not only fled, but dispersed, and took no further part in the battle.

The British had been thus twice misled, construing the change of position of Howard's line into retreat and defeat. Washington, in their rear, seeing the broken *esprit* of the British line, hastened a swift message to Morgan : "They are coming on like a mob ; give them a fire and I will charge them."

Howard's main line had by this time descended the slope of the first eminence and reached the rise of the second eminence in perfect order, when the word "halt" was given. Then Morgan's clarion voice rang along the line : " Face about, one good fire and the victory is ours."

It was done bravely and well; the on-coming foe recoiled before the deadly fire, and, ere they recovered the shock, Howard thundered, "Charge." In a moment the American bayonets were at their breasts ; Washington's cavalry were at their backs ; the whole body of militia on their left ;—the battle was virtually done. The seventh regiment threw down their arms ; the legion and light-infantry attempted to fly, but the cavalry hemmed them in, and rode them down.

At the feet of our army lay, suppliants for mercy, those who had showed none when ours had asked it from them. " Tarleton's quarters" ran along the line, and it required all the influence of Morgan, Howard, and the officers, to prevent wholesale slaughter.

Their precipitate advance had left their artillery in their rear; forced by Howard's charge to recoil, their artillery was now again in front, and both pieces were quickly captured.

The struggle was still continued by the militia and McArthur's battalion on the right. Fiercely assailed, on front and flank, by Pickens, they fell back, thinking to effect a safe retreat, when Howard wheeled upon them with the right wing of the American line. They were thrown utterly into confusion—the militia rushed upon them, and a hand-to-hand fight ensued. The Georgians took McArthur prisoner; broken and dispirited, deserted by their friends and surrounded by their enemies, they grounded their arms at the summons of Howard. Colonel Pickens received their commander's sword, and the militia took charge of the prisoners.

Tarleton in vain endeavored to rally his legion cavalry, to advance and cover McArthur's retreat. Failing in this, he himself rode forward at the head of his detachment of the seventeenth dragoons, accompanied by fourteen officers of the legion cavalry, with the hope of bearing off the artillery. Approaching near enough to discover that the artillery, as well as the day, was lost, he wheeled to retire. Colonel Washington, seeing the party, rightly conjectured that Tarleton was with this body, and, eager to crown the day by his capture, pursued and charged them.

In his eagerness, Washington and a handful of men rode much ahead of his party, and Tarleton turned upon them. Nothing daunted, Washington crossed swords with Tarleton's aid, and experienced the superiority of his British steel, for his own broke near the hilt. The officer rose in his stirrups to give vigor to the blow that should dispatch our gallant knight, Colonel Washington, when his page Collin, a lad who attended upon and dearly loved Washington, rode up, and discharging his pistol into the officer's shoulder, the uplifted sword fell from his grasp. Another officer, and Tarleton himself, aimed a sword thrust at Washington, now defenceless, but the unseen chariots and horsemen were round about and every blow was parried. The whole detachment now coming up, and Tarleton realizing his danger, decamped at full speed, sending a parting shot at Washington, whose horse received the ball. Morgan dispatched his cavalry and the mounted militia to pursue the flying foe and gather up the stragglers. Unfortunately, they took the wrong road at the outset. The time thus lost could not be recovered, for Tarleton made speed.

The pursuit was continued for more than twenty miles, and though baffled in its main object, Washington in returning swept the country on each side of his route, captured and brought in a hundred additional prisoners.

The American loss was incredibly small—a matter of twelve killed and sixty-one wounded; no officer of rank among either. The loss was chiefly sustained by the Continental troops, particularly by the flank companies of the right.

The British killed and wounded amounted to two hundred and thirty, among whom ten of the killed were officers, and among the prisoners, twenty-seven were officers; while the whole number of prisoners reached fully six hundred. Of the quality of the troops—they were Cornwallis' best.

It was all over in less than an hour.*

We have no idea that Morgan fashioned himself after Shakespeare's royal hero. Doubtless, he never heard of him. The parallel would startle us, did we not know that heroes think and speak and act alike the world over.

Indulge us, reader. To the herald of the French King

---

* For this account of the battle of Cowpens we are indebted substantially to "*Graham's Life of Morgan.*"

sent to Henry V., anticipating the defeat of the latter and demanding to know in advance what ransom he will give, royal Henry answers :

> " Turn thee back,
> And tell thy king, I do not seek him now,
> But could be willing to march on to Calais,
> Without impeachment.
> Go bid thy master well advise himself:
> If we may pass, we will ; if we be hindered,
> We shall, your tawny ground, with your red blood
> Discolor.
> The sum of all our answer is but this,—
> We would not seek a battle as we are ;
> Nor as we are, we say, we will not shun it ;
> So tell your master."

In the chorus to Act 4th, the night before the battle, Henry spends the hours among his troops, steeling hearts and nerves for the morrow.

> " For forth he goes and visits all his host ;
> Bids them good morrow, with a modest smile,
> And calls them—brothers, friends, and countrymen.
> Upon his royal face there is no note,
> How dread an army hath surrounded him ;
> Nor doth he dedicate one jot of color
> Unto the weary and all watched night ;
> But freshly looks, and overbears attaint,
> With cheerful semblance and sweet majesty ;
> That every wretch, pining and pale before ;
> Beholding him, plucks comfort from his looks.
> A largess universal, like the sun,
> His liberal eye doth give to every one,
> Thawing cold fear.   Then mean, and gentle, all
> Behold ! as may unworthiness define—
> *A little touch of Harry* (*Daniel*) *in the night.*

Full surely there must have been those in Morgan's camp, who remembering the brave men loitering idly at the " Camp of Repose " in the Cheraw Hills, gave utterance to words akin to those of Westmoreland: " O that we now had here but one ten thousand of those men in England that do no work to-day."

And as Morgan moves among his men, drawn up in battle line, setting before them the issues of that day, and the glory that awaited them, we hear King Henry's Crispian speech:

        " What's he that wishes so?
My cousin Westmoreland?   No, my fair cousin:
If we are marked to die, we are enough
To do our country loss ; and if to live,
The fewer men, the greater share of honor.
God's will ! I pray thee, wish not one man more.

    *   *   *   *   *

This day is called the feast of Crispian
He, that outlives this day and comes safe home,
Will stand a tip-toe when this day is named,
And rouse him at the name of Crispian.
He that shall live this day, and see old age
Will yearly on the vigil, feast his friends,
And say, to-morrow is St. Crispian.
Then will he strip his sleeves and show his scars,
And say, these wounds I had on Crispin's day.
Old men forget: yet all shall be forgot,
But he'll remember with advantages,
What feats he did that day.   Then shall our names
Familiar in their mouths as household words,
Harry the King, Bedford and Exeter,
Warwick and Talbot, Salisbury and Gloster,
Be in their flowing cups freshly remembered ;
His story shall the good man teach his son
And Crispin Crispian shall ne'er go by
From this day to the ending of the world
But we in it shall be remembered.
We few, we happy few, we band of brothers,
For he to-day that sheds his blood with me
Shall be my brother ; be he ne'er so vile,
This day, shall gentle his condition.

And, gentlemen in England now abed,
Shall think themselves accursed, they were not here,
And hold their manhoods cheap, while any speaks,
That fought with us, upon St. Crispin's day."

The battle won, we hear the royal hero:

"*K. H.* Now herald; are the dead numbered?
Herald. Here is the number of the slaughtered French.
K. H. This note doth tell me of ten thousand French
That in the field lie slain.
In these ten thousand they have lost,
There are but sixteen hundred mercenaries;
The rest are—princes, barons, lords, knights, squires
And gentlemen of blood and quality.
Here was a royal fellowship of death!
Where is the number of our English dead?

[Herald presents another paper.]

Edward the duke of York, the earl of Suffolk,
Sir Richard Ketly, Davy Gam, esquire;
None else of name,—and of all other men,
But five and twenty."

King Henry too gives thanks right christianly :

"O God, thy arm was here,
And not to us, but to thy arm alone,
Ascribe we all ; *When? without stratagem,*
But in plain shock, and even play of battle,
Was ever known, so great and little loss
On one part and on the other? Take it God
For it is only thine!"

And here is our modest hero's letter to his commander
General Greene, in which he praises everybody but himself.

"CAMP NEAR CAIN CREEK, January 19, 1781.

"*Dear Sir :*—The troops I have the honor to command,
have gained a great victory over a detachment from the
British army, commanded by Lieutenant-Colonel Tarleton.

The action happened on the 17th instant, about sunrise, at a place called Cowpens, near Pacolet river.   *   *   *

"Such was the inferiority of our numbers that our success must be attributed to the justice of our cause and the gallantry of our troops. My wishes would induce me to name every sentinel in the corps. In justice to the bravery and good conduct of the officers, I have taken the liberty to enclose you a list of their names, from a conviction that you will be pleased to introduce such characters to the world.

"I am, dear sir,
"Your obedient servant,
"DANIEL MORGAN.

"To General GREENE."

MORGAN'S RETREAT.

THE first news of this crushing defeat reached Cornwallis' camp by the flying cavalry, on the evening of the 17th January. Astonishment and mortification equally possessed him. He had not entertained a moment's anxiety for the result of the encounter, so extravagant was his estimate of Tarleton's ability, with his picked command, to completely crush Morgan.

Tarleton criticises Cornwallis very freely in his "Campaign," for failing to co-operate with him according to pre-arrangement, and says, "it would have prevented the misfortune, or, at least, softened its results." He felt the humiliation and disgrace keenly, and promptly requested Cornwallis either to announce his approbation of his conduct, or to grant him leave to retire until the affair could be investigated.

In reply, Cornwallis writes to him: "You have forfeited no part of my esteem, as an officer, by the unfortunate affair of the 17th. The means you used to bring the enemy to action were able and masterly, and must ever do you honor. Your dispositions were unexceptionable. The total misbehavior of our troops, could alone have deprived you of the glory which was so justly your due."

Again, in his despatches, Cornwallis writes: "His superiority of numbers, quality of fighting material, artillery and cavalry, with advantage of position, left Tarleton no room to doubt of the most brilliant success." To Lord Germain: "The unfortunate affair of the 17th was a very severe and unexpected blow, for besides reputation, our loss did not fall short of six hundred men." To Sir Henry Clinton : "It is impossible to foresee all the consequences that this unexpected and *extraordinary* event may produce, but your Excellency may be assured that nothing but the most absolute necessity shall induce me to give up the important object of the winter's campaign." Tarleton says : "As the defeat of Ferguson, at King's Mountain, made the first invasion of North Carolina impossible, so the battle of Cowpens would probably make the second disastrous."

Cowpens demonstrates all the qualities of field generalship, but what shall be said of the retreat which Morgan conducted from the field to Guilford Court-House?—a distance of more than one hundred and fifty miles—staggering beneath the weight of his spoils : six hundred prisoners, artillery, standards, eight hundred muskets, a traveling forge, wagons, etc.   For the artillery, Morgan had captured them from the British at Saratoga in 1777 ; the British had retaken them from Gates at Camden, and Morgan had again captured them at Cowpens.   What Nemesis watched here ?

The battle over, "far from being intoxicated with his victory, Morgan thought only of the imminent perils that yet menaced him."   It was still within the power of his enemy to pluck from him all the fruits of his victory. He shows now a magnificent poise of courage and judgment.   Instant retreat was imperative.

Before sunset, Cornwallis would hear of the destruction of Tarleton's army.   Leslie was momentarily expected in his camp.   The British army had been for days under marching orders.   Stung by a sense of loss and humiliation, the British commander would surely put forth a stupendous effort to pursue and overtake him, recover his captured light infantry, and punish Morgan's temerity.

The victorious General must resort now to *ruse ;* he

threw out the idea that he intended to cross the Broad River and hold the country north of it. He tarried no longer than to arrange for the burying of the dead and the care of the wounded of both armies. Arms and trophies filled the wagons, prisoners were collected and guarded, and the whole army in motion before noon. At sunset he crossed the Broad River at the Cherokee Ford, and encamped on its north bank.

A few hours rest was all he allowed his army—they were on the march long before daylight. Washington and his cavalry had now rejoined them. Morgan put all the prisoners under his charge, directing them to cross the Catawba by the upper fords. The main body took a more direct road to Ramsower's Mills, on the little Catawba. Morgan turned his ear backward, continually listening for the pursuers on his track ; what, then, was his surprise and joy to learn from his detectives on the 20th that, up to the 19th, Cornwallis was still in his camp. He pushed forward with equal vigor and hope.

Meantime, Leslie had joined forces with Cornwallis on the 18th, after their long and difficult march up through nearly the whole length of the State. On the 19th, the British army moved towards King's Creek, and Tarleton was directed to cross the Broad River and reconnoitre for intelligence of Morgan, of whose movements they were in profound ignorance ; so well had he kept his own counsel. By way of palliating his disgrace at Cowpens, Tarleton had represented Morgan's forces at two thousand. If this were so, it behooved Cornwallis to move warily in his vicinity. Tarleton crossed the river, but learned only that Morgan had marched immediately from the battlefield, crossed the Broad by the upper fords, and the impression prevailed that he intended to hold that part of the country.

Cornwallis now caught eagerly at the hope of cornering him and undoing the work of the 17th. But Morgan's *ruse* was entirely successful ; while he was pushing rapidly eastward toward the Catawba, Cornwallis hurried nearly northwest, toward a point which Morgan had passed two days before.

Vexed, foiled, and out-generaled, he now turned his army in the direction his wily adversary had taken. Encumbered with his splendid baggage-train, he reached the west bank of the Little Catawba at Ramsower's Mills, on the 24th, to find that Morgan had crossed two days before, and doubtless by this time had passed the Great Catawba, and was safe upon its east bank.

It was even so, and Morgan's fears floated down with its tide ; nothing now could deprive him of the glories of that hard-fought field of Cowpens.   As his hopes rose, those of Cornwallis sank.   His boastful promises to the British ministry !—what prospect to make them good?   His military reputation was in eclipse, and if not retrieved by some speedy stroke of arms, would bring upon him the censure of his superiors. " In sight, as it were, of his headquarters, a large detachment of his army had been captured ; yet he had suffered it, together with its arms, standards, cannon, baggage, etc., to be borne off by an inconsiderable force, in a circuitous route, towards a point which he ought to have known would be aimed at, and which was nearer to himself than to his opponent. He made no vigorous, well-directed effort to amend his mishaps until the time had passed for such effort to avail." *

Vexed now to bewilderment, Cornwallis came to the desperate resolution of destroying his supply trains, and burning his baggage, thus disencumbering his whole army for a chase. Nothing but an absolute certainty of success could justify a step which involved the abandonment of his contemplated winter campaign ; but, learning that Morgan had come to a halt at Sherrald's Ford, on the east

* *Graham's Life of Morgan.*

bank of the Catawba, he proceeded to execute his mad resolution.

Morgan had halted to recruit and rest his men, and hoped to get some intelligence from Greene's army.

His health had been but partially re-established, when the urgent appeal of the South brought him again into the field. The exposure of a winter campaign, in the rainy season, without tents or shelter, without comforts or even necessary food, had induced fever and ague, and developed his old enemy, sciatica,—souvenir of his winter in Maine and Canada.

The pain was torture : he was well-nigh disabled. It was now the 23d of January, seven days after Cowpens. Morgan turns his ear anxiously towards the hills of Cheraw, but it is still a " Camp of Repose,"—they did not hear of Cowpens until the 25th.

He writes :

" SHERRALD's FORD, January 23, 1781.

" *Sir :*—I arrived here this morning. The prisoners crossed at Island Ford. I shall send them on to Salisbury in the morning guarded by Major Triplitt's militia, whose time expires this day. Lord Cornwallis, whether from bad intelligence or to make a show, moved up towards Gilbert town to intercept me, the day after I had passed him. *   *   *

" I received your letters of the 13th inst. Would have endeavored to get the cloth [Wade Hampton's], but being obliged to come so far out of the way with my prisoners, puts it entirely out of my power. However, I will communicate the matter to Colonel Pickens ; perhaps he may have some enterprising followers that would undertake it. I have engaged one of his captains to go round and kill the enemy's horses : perhaps he may do the other business. *I intend to stay at this place till I hear from you,* in order to recruit the men and get in good train.

We must be fitted out with pack-horses, for, as I wrote you before, wagons will not do for light troops.

"I have got men who are watching the enemy's movements, and will give you the earliest accounts. I think they will be this way, if the stroke we gave Tarleton don't check them.

"At this time we have six hundred prisoners.

"I have the honor to be, etc.

"DANIEL MORGAN.

"Major General GREENE."

One scents a little covert irony in the following.

SHERRALD'S FORD, January 24, 1781.

"*Sir:*—I have just received your letter of the 19th [two days after Cowpens], and am much obliged to you for your cautions against a *surprise*. Mr. Tarleton might as well have been surprised himself, as been so devilishly beaten as he was.

"I approve much of having boats with the main army, but would not wish to have any with me ; *my party is too weak to guard them.* I am convinced that a descent into Georgia would answer a very good purpose. It would draw the attention of the enemy that way, and would much disconcert my Lord's plans.

"I am convinced by every circumstance, he intends to march through this part of the State towards Virginia, and his making a junction with Leslie, fixes me in that opinion.

"I should be exceedingly glad to make a descent into Georgia, but am so emaciated that I can't undertake it. I grow worse every hour. I can't ride out of a walk. I am exceedingly sorry to leave the field at such a time as this, but it must be the case. Pickens is a very enterprising man, and a very judicious one : perhaps he might answer the purpose.

"I have had no intelligence from Lord Cornwallis this two days. I expect to hear from him every hour. If anything interesting transpires, I will let you know it immediately.

"I have the honor, etc.,

"DANIEL MORGAN.

"Major General GREENE.

"N. B. My detachment is much weakened by this fight with Tarleton. We have near fifty men disabled. We have nothing to drink."

They had cherry bounce at Cheraw Hills, for Morgan's good friend Colonel O. H. Williams writes to him immediately upon receiving the news of his victory,—though Morgan does not receive it for many days after.

"CAMP PEDEE, January 25, 1781.

"*Dear General :*—I rejoice exceedingly at your success. The advantages you have gained are important, and do great honor to your little corps. I am delighted that the accumulated honors of a young partisan, should be plundered by my old friend.

"We have had a *feu de joie*, drank all your healths, and swore you were the finest fellows on earth, and love you if possible more than ever. The General has, I think, made his compliments in very handsome terms. Enclosed is a copy of his orders. It was written immediately after we received the news, and *during the operation of some cherry bounce.* Compliments to Howard and all friends. Adieu.

"Sincerely yours,

"O. H. WILLIAMS.

"Brigadier General MORGAN."

Letters from Morgan to Greene under same date run thus :

" SHERRALD'S FORD, January 25, 1781, Sunrise.

"*Sir:*—I am this moment informed by express that Cornwallis is at Ramsower's Mills, on their march this way, destroying all before him. I shall know the truth of this in a few hours and let you know immediately.

"I am your obedient servant,

"DANIEL MORGAN."

Yet again same date :

"SHERRALD'S FORD, January 25, 1781.

"*Dear General :*—I receive intelligence every hour of the enemy's rapid approach, in consequence of which I am sending off my wagons. My numbers at this time are too weak to fight them. *I intend to move towards Salisbury in order to get near the main army. I know they intend to bring me to an action which I am resolved carefully to avoid. I expect you will move somewhere on the Yadkin to oppose their crossing.*

" I think it would be advisable to join our forces and fight them before they join Phillips, which they certainly will do, if they are not stopped. I have ordered the commanding officer at Salisbury to move off with the prisoners and stores. If you think it right, you will repeat it. I cannot ascertain the enemy's numbers, but suppose them odds of two thousand ; that number if they keep in a compact body, we cannot hurt.

"I am, dear General, etc.,

"DANIEL MORGAN."

"CAMP SHERRALD'S FORD, January 25, 1781.

" *Sir :*—The enemy encamped last night at Ramsower's Mills in force ; they marched near thirty miles yesterday. It is my opinion they intend to make a forced march through this part of the State, and make a junction with Phillips high up in the country. *If so, the position you have taken will be much out of the way. If Cornwallis and*

Leslie have joined forces, we are not able to contend with them. All the Southern militia have dispersed. What numbers General Davidson has I am not able to inform you, as they were only collecting yesterday. *From this information you will be able to dispose of your army in the best manner.* I will do everything in my power; but you may not put much dependence in me, for I can neither ride nor walk. I will continue to give you every intelligence in my power.

> "I have the honor to be,
>
> "DANIEL MORGAN."

Again:

> "SHERRALD'S FORD, January 25, 1781.

"*Dear Sir:*—After my late success, and my sanguine expectation to do something clever this campaign, I must inform you that I shall be obliged to give over the pursuit, by reason of an old pain returning upon me that laid me up four months of last winter and spring. It is a sciatica that renders me entirely incapable of active service. I have had it for three weeks, but, on getting wet the other day, it has seized me more violently, which gives me great pain when I ride, and at times, when walking or standing, am obliged to sit down as quick as if I were shot.

I am not unacquainted with the hurt my retiring will be to the service, as the people have much dependence in me, but the love I have for my country, and the willingness I have always showed to serve it, will convince you that nothing would be wanting on my side were I able to persevere. So I must beg leave of absence till I find myself able to take the field again. If I can procure a chaise, I will endeavor to get home. General Davidson, Colonel Pickens, and General Sumter, can manage the militia better than I can, and will well supply my place.

"I have this moment received intelligence that the enemy are within a few miles from this place, moving on rapidly. *My party are so weak that I think I must give way.*

"I have the honor to be, etc.,
"DANIEL MORGAN."

The next letter is under date of January 28th, twelve days after Cowpens.—No sign or sound of the main army.

"SHERRALD'S FORD, January 28, 1781.

"*Sir:*—Lord Cornwallis encamped on the 24th at Ram-sower's Mills, with his main body from Broad River. My reason for not writing to you for two days was to find out which way they really intended, that I might have it in my power to inform you fully. I am trying to collect the militia to make a stand at this place. I have ordered General Davidson, with five hundred militia, to Beatty's Ford. We are filling all the private fords to make them impassable. The one I lie at, I intend to leave open. I ordered all the prisoners and stores from Salisbury to the Moravian town. I am told they are gone under a weak guard. I hope some of them don't get away. If the enemy pursued, I ordered them to Augusta, Virginia; should be glad if you would give orders concerning them.

"I am a little apprehensive that Cornwallis intends to surprise me, lying so still this day or two; but if the militia don't deceive me, whom I am obliged to trust to as guards up and down the river, I think I will put it out of his power.

"If I were able to ride and see about everything myself, I should think myself perfectly safe; but I am obliged to lie in a house out of camp, not being able to encounter the badness of the weather. However, nothing in my power shall be left undone to secure this part of the country and annoy the enemy.

"I have the honor to be, etc.,
"DANIEL MORGAN."

"Beatty's Ford, January 29th, 1781.

[Twelve days after "Cowpens."]

"*Dear Sir* :—I have just arrived at this place to view our situation. General Davidson is here with eight hundred men. The enemy is within ten miles of this place in force; their advance is in sight. It is uncertain whether they intend to cross here or not. I have detached two hundred men to the Tuckaseega Ford, to fill it up and defend it.

"An express has just arrived who informs me that they have burned their wagons and loaded their men heavily. I am just returning to Sherrald's Ford, where our regulars lie. I expect they will attempt to cross in the morning. I will let you hear every particular,

"I have the honor to be,

"Daniel Morgan."

It was now January 30th, the fourteenth day from the battle of Cowpens; still no sign or sound from the main army.

Morgan lay yet at Sherrald's Ford, hoping to be joined by militia, and hoping against hope for help from Greene. The militia came in slowly; it was the time for preparing the ground for planting; this must be attended to, or starvation of their families was certain. Also, it was Tarleton's and Cornwallis' orders to burn the house of every whig who was absent from home. Notwithstanding the check at Cowpens, the whole on-coming British army was upon them. Morgan saw that there ought to be another battle fought at the Catawba, if they were to accomplish what they had been sent to do, namely, to keep Cornwallis out of Virginia, and drive him back to the sea. But his pigmy force had dwindled. The Georgia and South Carolina volunteers had gone back, while the term of service of Triplett's Virginia militia had expired. Morgan resolved to wait until the last moment of safety, hoping, if Greene brought up the army, to dispute Cornwallis' passage of the river. A heavy rain had fallen on the 29th, and Morgan was safe so long as the river continued unfordable.

Thus matters stood when, on the morning of January 30th, General Greene rode into Morgan's camp accompanied only by one aid and an escort of cavalry. What for? "That way lies" honor. It was not a General that was wanted—it was an army.

We can nowhere find what greeting Morgan gave him ; they parted company before many hours, for the river fell as rapidly as it rose, and Morgan was compelled to move on. Greene had started his army on the 29th of January— it took four days to get it in motion after the news of the battle reached it on the 25th, but it was marching towards Salisbury, not Catawba, under General Huger.

Cornwallis would cross on the morrow ; therefore, on the evening of the 31st, "Morgan, with his force, moved off in silence, and, pushing forward all that night and the next day, gained a full day's march ahead of the enemy." Greene remained at the Catawba. Morgan made for the Yadkin. The march was conducted in a sweeping, drenching winter rain. The Yadkin was rising rapidly, but Morgan had provided for his crossing, by assembling all the boats for miles. Upon reaching the fords, he found hundreds of terrified people flying from the on-coming British army, and the tender mercies of Tarleton. They, too, threw themselves upon Morgan's protection. He gave it—"Great Heart"—sent them all safely across, though his guard on the west bank had a hot skirmish with Cornwallis' advance cavalry, who endeavored to seize the boats, but were driven back.

Morgan marched on towards Guilford C. H., in North Carolina, whither the main army were also now ordered to direct their march. But he now began to be anxious for the comfort of his worn-down, half-starved soldiers. He could neither ride on horseback nor walk, but, on the 5th of February, giving the command to Lieutenant-

Colonel Howard, he took a carriage and rode ahead to prepare quarters and supplies. He accomplished all, and wrote to General Greene :

"GUILFORD C. H., February 6, 1781.

"*Sir :*—I arrived here last evening, and sent a number of prisoners that were here, to join the main body. About four thousand pounds of salted meat, corn-meal and forage equivalent, is promised me. I am much indisposed with pain. When I get everything in as good a trim as possible respecting provisions, etc., I shall move on slowly to some safe retreat and try to recover.

"I am sincerely, etc.,

"DANIEL MORGAN."

Morgan's army reached Guilford C. H., on February 8th, and on the 9th the main army, under Huger, with the cavalry of Lee, arrived, making a force of two thousand, of whom six hundred were militia.

On the tenth of October, Morgan took a carriage and started towards home. His sufferings had become almost insupportable. After a few days traveling, he was forced to stop at the house of General Lawson. Again he set out, and was again compelled to stop and gather strength. His friend, Carter Harrison, received the war-worn hero, and here he remained some time.

XXVII.—1781.

MORGAN AT HOME.

MORGAN reached his home, near Winchester, emaciated to the bone, shaken by tertian ague, racked with torturing pains and oppressed with mental forebodings that his battle-days and deeds were done. That herculean frame, with its iron fibre,—fitting abode for the kingly spirit that inhabited it,—already tottered to its final fall. Both Morgan and Washington seemed physically organized for centenarians, but hard service curtailed them of a quarter of a century.

His hours of painful weariness were cheered by letters of congratulation from brother officers, and acknowledgments of Congress and other public bodies, of the brilliant and valuable service he had just performed. From the House of Delegates of Virginia:

"*Friday*, March 9th, 1781.

"*Resolved*, That Brigadier-General Morgan be requested to accept of a horse with furniture, and a sword, as a further testimony of the high esteem of his country for his military character and abilities, so gloriously displayed in the victory gained by him and the troops he lately commanded in South Carolina," etc.

From Hon. Richard Henry Lee:

"RICHMOND, March 21, 1781.

"*Sir:*—It is with peculiar pleasure that I execute the order of the House of Delegates, in transmitting to you their sense, and through them the sense that your country entertains, of the many signal services performed by you in the various victories that you have obtained over the enemies of the United States, and more especially in the late well-timed total defeat given to the British troops in South Carolina. I am directed to request of you, sir, that you will convey to the brave officers and troops under your command in the action of the 17th of January, the sense entertained by the House of Delegates of their valor and great service on that occasion.

" Having thus discharged my duty to the House of Delegates, permit me to lament that the unfortunate state of your health should deprive the public of those eminent services in the field which you are so capable of performing. Let me hope that it will not be long before return of health will restore you to the army and to your country.

" I have the honor to be,

" RICHARD HENRY LEE, Sec.

" Brigadier-General MORGAN."

From Governor Rutledge to General Morgan.

" CHERAWS, January 25, 1781.

" Dear Sir:—I request that you will be pleased to accept my warmest and most cordial thanks, and that you will present them to the brave officers and men under your command, for the good conduct and intrepidity manifested in the action with Lieutenant-Colonel Tarleton on the 17th of January. This total defeat of chosen British troops, by a number far inferior to them, will forever distinguish the gallant men by whom the glorious victory was obtained and endear them to their country. Colonel Pickens' behavior justified the opinion I have always had of that gallant officer. Enclosed is a Brigadier's commission, of which I desire his acceptance.

" I am, etc.,

" J. RUTLEDGE."

Congress also expressed their approbation by passing a preamble and resolutions of appreciation and obligation to the officers and men who took part in the action of Cowpens. They directed that a gold medal, with suitable inscriptions, should be presented to Morgan, to Colonels Washington and Howard a silver medal, and to Major Triplitt a sword.

It was scarcely over-estimated. In consideration of the respective numbers, quality of fighting material, etc., it was certainly the most brilliant action of the war. Had Greene brought his army with him to the Catawba, the passage of that river by Cornwallis could have been either utterly disputed or made so disastrous as to have compelled that General to fall back into lower South Carolina.

Lest Morgan should be over-much exalted, the envious hastened to discharge their little arrows of criticism and innuendo at the colossus who, for a time, had arrested the attention of the continent. Tarleton, stung by so complete a castigation from one whom he affected to despise, impugns Morgan's judgment, accusing him of temerity in selecting a battle-field disadvantageous to the American army and favorable for the British.

He says : "The situation of the enemy was desperate in case of a misfortune ; an open country and a river in their rear, threw them entirely in the power of a superior cavalry, whilst the light troops [British], in case of a repulse, had the expectation of a neighboring force [Cornwallis' army] to protect them from destruction." Tarleton does not seem to be aware of the recoil of such a criticism.

Morgan, in a few words, justifies himself from the charge of temerity, and establishes the ripe military judgment that fixed upon the field of Cowpens.

"I would not," said he, "have had a swamp in view of

my militia upon any consideration ; they would have made for it, and nothing could have detained them. As to covering my wings ; I knew my adversary, and was perfectly sure I should have nothing but down-right fighting. As to *retreat*, it was the very thing I wished to cut off all hope of. I would have thanked Tarleton if he had surrounded me with his cavalry. It would have been better than placing my own men in the rear to shoot down those who broke from the ranks.

" When men are forced to fight, they will sell their lives as dearly as possible. I knew that the dread of Tarleton's cavalry would give due weight to the protection of my bayonets and keep my troops from breaking, as Buford's regiment had done.

" Had I crossed the river, one-half of the militia would immediately have abandoned me."

Simply, Tarleton had " reckoned without his host ;" he had come to Cowpens to meet his master.

Colonel Lee, who saw himself hopelessly eclipsed by the splendor of Cowpens, ascribes Morgan's determination to fight Tarleton to a " sudden fit of ill-temper, which overruled the suggestions of Morgan's sound and discriminating judgment."

His masterly retreat, before so superior an enemy, was pronounced " miraculous."

Lee likewise accuses him of quarreling with Greene, of showing a disregard for the safety of the main body of the army. Doubtless he had reason for some curious thoughts of his Commanding General, but there is no proof that any jarring words passed between them ; their subsequent correspondence entirely contradicts such an assertion.* For magnanimity Morgan ranks with Washington.

His motives for leaving the service were also impugned ; it was insinuated that his ill-health was feigned. Those

* *Lee's Memoirs and Graham's Life of Morgan.*

12

are the small accusements of small minds, contradicted
by the most obvious facts and motives of the case, and in
direct opposition to the express assertions of Morgan himself. He was of other stuff than that which makes liars
and hypocrites.

Bancroft says : "A severe attack of acute rheumatism,
consequent on the exposure of this and former campaigns,
forced him to take leave of absence. Wherever he had
appeared, he had always heralded the way to daring action.
He first attracted attention at Boston, was foremost on
the march through the wilderness to Canada, and foremost to take Quebec by storm. He bore the brunt of
every engagement with Burgoyne's army, and now he had
won the most extraordinary victory of the war. He took
with him into retirement the praises of all the army and
of the chief civil representatives of the country. Again
and again hopes rose that he might once more appear in
arms; but the unrelenting malady obliged him to refuse
the invitation of La Fayette and even of Washington."

This last was true in effect though not literally ; he took
the field at the urgent solicitation of La Fayette and of
Governor Jefferson, during the siege of Yorktown, but
soon succumbed to his distressing malady.

XXVIII.—1781.

GREENE'S RETREAT ACROSS THE DAN.

TURNING over General Greene's letters to Washington after Cowpens, we read under date of Jan. 24, "Camp of Repose": "The event is glorious, and I am exceedingly unhappy that our wretched condition will not permit of our improving it to the best advantage. I shall do all I can, but our prospects are gloomy. Our force is small and daily declining. We have no clothing or provisions but what we collect from day to day." On January 28, four days after hearing of Cowpens, "I have the satisfaction to transmit to your Excellency a letter from Brigadier-General Morgan, announcing the total defeat of Lieutenant-Colonel Tarleton. The victory was complete and the action glorious. The brilliancy and success with which it was fought does the highest honor to the American arms, and adds splendor to the character of the General and his officers. I am unhappy that the distressed condition of this army will not admit of our improving the advantage we have gained." *

Under date of February 9, Guilford C. H., 1781, General Greene gives the reason for leaving his army and riding in haste into Morgan's camp at Sherrald's Ford. He says: "I set out to join the light infantry in order *to collect the militia* and embarrass the enemy till we could effect a junction of our forces." †

* *Sparks Cor.*, Vol. III, pp. 214–218.
† *Sparks' Cor.*, Vol. III, p. 225.

We have already referred to the difficulty of persuading the militia from their agricultural duties at this juncture, but General Davidson's influence had collected about eight hundred men, who were posted at the different fords of the Catawba. When Morgan found that Cornwallis would certainly cross the Catawba in a few hours, he moved away towards the Yadkin, leaving Greene behind to "collect the militia and embarrass the enemy." General Greene conducted no part of the retreat of Morgan's force, but followed him to the Yadkin two days after.

The patriot leader Davidson, with four hundred militia, took post at McGowan's Ford, a short distance below Sherrald's Ford, where Morgan's army had lain. He resolved to dispute as long as possible the crossing of Cornwallis, or at least inflict as heavy a loss upon him as possible. Greene writes: "The enemy crossed at McGowan's Ford, where General Davidson was posted with the greatest part of the militia, *who fled at the first discharge.* The enemy made good the landing, and the militia retreated. A place of rendezvous was appointed for the militia to collect at, who were posted at the different fords up and down the river above thirty miles. Part of them halted about seven miles short of the place of rendezvous, and were overtaken by Tarleton and dispersed. I waited that night at the place appointed for the militia to collect at till morning; but not a man appeared."* This is an error that does injustice to the militia and to the valiant Davidson who stood to his post and there yielded up his life for his country.

It was a brave risk that Cornwallis took in the darkness of that winter morning, to cross a stream "five hundred yards wide, two to four feet deep, and with a current so rapid as to require the greatest care and exertions on the part of those crossing to prevent being swept away."

Davidson discovered their approach and opened fire

* *Sparks' Cor.*, Vol. III, p. 226.

upon them when they had reached the middle of the stream. Their guide then deserted the British, and this circumstance, which at first appeared to be a calamity, ensured their safety. They no longer followed the ford but kept their way directly across the stream, and landed at a point about four hundred yards above the spot where Davidson expected them. Learning the turn of affairs, he moved upon them and opened a severe fire upon the British advance guard. After a sharp action in which the enemy lost sixty killed and many wounded and swept away by the current, Davidson was mounting his horse to bring off his detachment, when a British bullet pierced him and he fell dead.*

Inevitably, the militia, left without a leader, scattered; and of the eight hundred collected by Davidson, but three hundred reported at the appointed rendezvous at Tarrant's Tavern, where Tarleton was quickly upon them. This dissolved the whole body. We might reasonably expect that General Greene would have been at the ford with Davidson, or at least at the rendezvous at Tarrant's Tavern, ten miles from the Catawba, but he was at neither place; he stopped at the house of a Mr. Carr, sixteen miles away. As "not a man appeared," he rode on to Salisbury and alighted, worn and exhausted, at the door of the tavern. "What, alone! General Greene?" asked an officer who was expecting him.

"Yes, hungry, penniless and alone," added Greene.

Here occurred the incident so often told of Greene, when the landlady brought her little store of gold, hoarded for the dire extremities of those evil times, and gave him all. Likewise, after supper, Greene noticed on the wall a picture of King George, which he turned with its face to the wall and wrote upon it, "Hide thy face, George, and blush."

He followed and overtook Morgan at the Yadkin, and

* *Graham's Life of Morgan.*

writes : " As soon as I arrived at the infantry camp, *I wrote letters* to all the militia officers over the mountains to embody their men and join the army. Very few have joined us."

Greene had written to Lee to hasten his junction with the army, saying, "Here is a fine field and great glory ahead," but after joining all forces at Guilford, equal if not greater than that of Cornwallis, he declined a battle and announced his intention to continue the retreat over the Dan into Virginia, where he expected further reinforcements,—a keen disappointment to his officers, especially those who were fresh from the field of Cowpens and eager again to measure swords with the enemy. Johnson says : " The fallen countenances of his officers proclaimed their disappointment."

Before leaving the army Morgan had indicated his preference for his successor as commander of the light troops. He had named his friend Colonel O. H. Williams.

The question now was, how to make the passage of the Dan, for Cornwallis had gained its upper fords ; but Carrington, Greene's quartermaster and a most efficient officer, suggested that the army cross by the lower fords, on rafts and boats which he had assembled there. Colonel Williams with his light infantry protected the rear, and Greene and his whole army were passed safely over the Dan.

"But for Carrington's energy and punctuality in collecting the boats upon the Dan, the retreat which saved the South, would have been its ruin."* It is somewhat difficult to understand how Greene's retreat saved the South. It would have been "better in the breach than the observance," since it abandoned the Carolinas once more to the British and royalists, who uprose and returned to their evil deeds. Tarleton says : "Having chased Greene's army out of North Carolina, the king's standard

---

* *Greene's Life of Greene.*

was raised at Hillsborough."   Bancroft says: "Seven companies were formed in one day."

From the Dan, Greene wrote: "I wish it was in my power to give your Excellency more flattering accounts from this quarter.   However, my utmost exertions shall be continued to save these States.   I shall be happy if my conduct meets with your approbation, *as my situation affords me no prospect of personal glory.*"   Being heavily reinforced by Virginia militia, Greene recrossed the Dan. Finding his force more than twice that of Cornwallis, Greene essayed a battle at Guilford C. H.

His plan of battle was somewhat at fault, his three divisions being posted at too great a distance to properly support each other.   Likewise concerning the militia. "Greene had always differed from Washington on the proper manner of using militia; the former thought they should be used as a reserve to improve an advantage, but Greene insisted that they ought to be placed in front."* Gates had done the same thing at Camden.   Greene therefore formed his front line of North Carolina militia, who, Hildreth says, were so posted as a punishment for suspected toryism.   "Food for powder!"   At the first fire they fled, throwing away arms, knapsacks and canteens.

The heroes of Cowpens were there, and fought splendidly; by British admission, they were at the point of victory when an ill-timed retreat was ordered, leaving the field, the artillery and the glory, to the British, who pursued for three miles.   Greene retreated ten miles, to Troublesome Creek, and fainted. .

He had, however, accomplished his purpose, which was, he said, "to encumber his enemy with wounded."† A fourth of the British army was disabled, including their best officers—Tarleton, Stewart and Webster, mortally.

The British were so weakened by their victory that Cornwallis fell leisurely back and down towards Wilming-

* *Bancroft,* Vol. X.   † *Johnson.*

ton.   Greene followed as leisurely, as far as Deep River, and there gave over the pursuit,—comes to the conclusion to push "boldly" into South Carolina and let Cornwallis go to "Halifax," or wherever he will.

Johnson relates how "Greene afterwards found out that he might have overtaken and must have destroyed Cornwallis."

Greene communicates to Washington his purpose to "surprise" Rawdon at Camden, and adds : " I shall take every measure to avoid a misfortune ; but necessity obliges me to commit myself to chance, and I trust my friends will do justice to my reputation if any accident attends me." *

Unfortunately Greene wrote letters which, passing through an unfriendly country, fell into hands for which they were not intended, so that Lord Rawdon at Camden fully expected and was ready to receive him. Unable to storm the works, Greene took a strong position near Camden, at Hobkirk's Hill. His force was nearly two thousand. Lord Rawdon, with nine hundred, concluded to surprise Greene, who was taking a not over early, or over "hasty," cup of coffee, on the morning of April 28th. This he did. A sharp action ensued, when Greene retreated, having suffered a loss of three hundred. The British lost about the same number. Greene wrote : "Had we defeated the enemy, not a man of the party would have got back into the town ; the disgrace is more vexatious than anything else."

But Marion had, in reality, taken Camden two days before the battle of Hobkirk's Hill. He had invested Fort Watson, on Wright's Bluff, below. The bluff was forty feet high, and the garrison over one hundred. Marion's men felled trees and built towers high enough to command the fort, and compelled a surrender. This was the connecting post between Camden and Charleston, so

* *Sparks' Correspondence*, Vol. III, p. 279.

that, hearing of its fall, Lord Rawdon at once ordered the destruction of his works and the evacuation of Camden. This was May 10th. On May 11th, Orangeburgh surrendered to General Sumter. On the 12th, Marion and that brave woman, Rebecca Motte, drove the British from Fort Motte. Sumter took Fort Granby, and Lee compelled the garrison of Augusta to capitulate, June 5th.

Greene meanwhile attempts Ninety-Six, and makes fearful work of it;—worse than a blunder, it was a crime.

Attacking the enemy in the rear, and reducing the smaller posts, Marion and Sumter had by July compelled the British to evacuate the strong posts of the upper country, and they were now confined to the narrow district between the Santee and lower Savannah. This was the policy advocated from the first by Morgan ; the sequel proves its wisdom.

Bancroft well says of this campaign : "Whatever was achieved, was achieved by Americans alone, and *by Americans of the South.*" Meantime, the interests of the Southern department had been transferred to Virginia.

Cornwallis, having refreshed his battered army and reinforced at Wilmington, called a council of officers to decide whether to return to the defence of what he had already acquired, or march up through North Carolina into Virginia. Tarleton warmly opposed a march into Virginia, and counseled a return to South Carolina. But Cornwallis was sick of the Carolinas, and hoped new fields would bring him new laurels.

Up through the whole length of the State, harrying and terrifying the people, Cornwallis, with two thousand troops, marched, "with no opposition which an advanced guard under Tarleton did not easily overcome ;" reaching

Halifax, "his troops were let loose to commit enormities that were a disgrace to the name of man." *

Early in May he joined forces with Phillips at Petersburgh, and found himself "at the head of seven thousand effective men, and with entire control of the water, while La Fayette had not a third of that number to oppose him."

* *Bancroft.* Vol. X, p. 485.

MORGAN AGAIN IN THE SERVICE.

AFTER a furlough of two months at home, his health being in a measure reinstated, and, seeing General Greene hard pushed at Hobkirk's Hill, Morgan had resolved to repair at once to his camp. Just at this time, however, May 1781, the alarming state of things in Virginia called for the prompt and vigorous service of all her sons.

In January of 1781, whilst Morgan was before Cornwallis in South Carolina, Arnold invaded Virginia with sixteen hundred men, captured Richmond and destroyed an immense amount of public and private property. In March, Phillips joined Arnold with two thousand British from New York, and the whole country, between the rivers James and York, was wasted and burned. Virginia having drained her resources to strengthen Greene's army, with the hope that Cornwallis would be destroyed or driven back to the sea, was illy prepared to resist the present powerful invasion.

Washington sent La Fayette to the rescue, and though he was urgently pressed to come himself to the help of his own State, he declined to move from the highlands of the Hudson.

He hoped much from the influence of La Fayette. In Baltimore the Marquis was warmly received, and tendered the most elegant hospitalities its citizens could command. He declined these expensive honors, and begged instead, that the ladies of Baltimore would assemble and ply their patriotic needles to clothe his naked soldiers,—himself furnishing the materials. "He drew to his side, as volunteers, gallant young men, mounted on their own horses, from Maryland and Virginia. Youth, generosity, courage and prudence, were his spells of persuasion. His perceptions were quick, his vigilance never failed, and in his methods of gaining information of the movements of the enemy, he excelled all officers of the war, except Washington and Morgan. All accounts bear testimony to his prudence, and that he never once committed himself during a very difficult campaign."* Tarleton bears witness to this in his "Campaign."

Arriving in Richmond, La Fayette addressed Morgan :

"*May* 21, 1781.

"*My Dear Sir :*—Having heard that on your recovery you had set out for the Southern army, I made no doubt you had arrived in South Carolina. But I hear that you are not yet gone, and with the freedom of an old and affectionate friend, take the liberty to request your assistance.

"Lord Cornwallis came without opposition to Halifax, and has now joined forces with Phillips at Petersburgh.

"General Phillips' force consisted of two thousand five hundred regulars rank and file. The force of Cornwallis you will better know than I do, when I tell you it consists of the 23d, 71st, 33d British, one Hessian regiment, the light infantry and guards, Tarleton's Legion and some other corps. They have entire command of the waters. They have much cavalry. We have for the present forty. Our regular force is near nine hundred. Our militia not very strong. We have not a hundred riflemen, and are in the greatest need of arms.

"Under these circumstances, my dear sir, I do very much want your assistance, and beg leave to request it, both as a lover of public welfare and as a private friend

* *Bancroft*, Vol. X.

of yours. Your influence can do more than orders from the Executive. Permit me, my dear sir, entirely to depend on your exertions.

"Another very great reinforcement to our small, diminutive of an army, and which will produce the happiest effects, would be your personal presence on the field. I beg leave, my dear sir, most warmly to entreat you to join us if the state of your health will permit.

"I remain, my dear sir, most affectionately your friend,

"LA FAYETTE.

"General MORGAN."

Also :

"From CHARLOTTESVILLE, June 2, 1781.

"*Sir:*—I have the pleasure to inclose to you a resolution of the House of Delegates, by which you will perceive the confidence they repose in your exertions and the desire they entertain of your lending your aid under our present circumstances. I sincerely wish your health may be so far re-established as to permit you to take the field, as no one would count more than myself on the effect of your interposition. * * * *

"I am with great respect,

"Your most humble servant,

"THOS. JEFFERSON.

"Brigadier-General MORGAN."

Meantime Tarleton had made a cavalry sweep inland, surprised the Assembly at Charlottesville and taken seven members prisoners, thus for the time unseating the civil authority of the State. A fragment of the body addressed Morgan :

"STAUNTON, June 14.

"*Sir:*—* * * * So much is at stake on the field of battle, that it is not only our wish, but that of every member of the Assembly, that you march with what men you have raised, leaving orders for others to follow you. We are truly sensible of the alacrity with which the people on this side of the mountains will join you ; *they wish to be commanded by you.* We therefore entreat that you lose no time in joining the Marquis.

"We are your very humble servants,

"ARCHIBALD CARY,

"BENJAMIN HARRISON."

Morgan responded promptly to these importunate appeals, and having clothed the men at his own expense, sent them forward under Captain Nelson, and wrote to the Speaker of the House of Delegates that he had contracted a heavy debt which he trusted would be assumed by the State.

Hearing of Morgan's approach, La Fayette writes :

"June 12, 1781.

"*My Dear Sir :*—With the greatest satisfaction I have received your letter mentioning the exertions you have made for our support. Your assistance is very necessary to us, and your success in collecting the troops is above my expectation. The sooner they are with us the better, and I shall be particularly happy in taking by the hand a friend for whom I have ever felt the highest regard and sincerest affection. The enemy are opposite to Elk Creek. Our junction with the Pennsylvanians enables us to some resistance, but we are still much inferior to his Lordship. Whatever you think better for the good of the service that comes within the bounds of my power, I request you will either mention to me or have executed in my name. Adieu, my dear sir, with the most perfect regard and attachment.

"Your most humble servant,

"LA FAYETTE."

Having sent forward his cavalry, Morgan marched with

the riflemen he had collected on the 20th of June, and reached the headquarters of the Marquis on the 6th of July. He was immediately invested with the command of all the light troops and the cavalry.

Concerning the Maryland volunteer dragoons, La Fayette wrote to him :

"July 16, 1781.

"*Dear Sir :*—I have attached to your command Major Nelson's corps and the Maryland volunteer dragoons. I beg leave to recommend the latter to your attention. Most of them are men of fortune who make great sacrifices to serve their country. You will not, therefore, put them upon the duties of orderlies, or the common camp duties which can be as well performed by the Continental horse. In everything else, you will find they will answer your expectations. As they are only to be subject to your orders, when you have accomplished the objects mentioned in my letter of yesterday, or when it is decided that Tarleton intends southerly and is beyond the reach of being struck, you will be good enough to order their return to headquarters It is my wish to dismiss them the moment it is in my power.

"I am your obedient servant,

"LA FAYETTE."

Think of that ! from a man who had himself left ease, honors, wife, children, home and country ; who had perilled his life and devoted his private fortune in the cause of an humble people in a distant land, who was struggling to solve the greatest of political problems, and to realize the noblest dream of the noblest dreamers, from Plato to Washington.

The morning after Morgan's arrival in camp, Cornwallis had dispatched Tarleton with a body of cavalry and mounted infantry to attack La Fayette. They encountered a mounted patrol, who fell back upon the main body of riflemen, giving the alarm. They were instantly in position, and upon Tarleton's approach, opened so prompt and vigorous a fire upon him that he beat a hasty retreat.*

A few days after, Cornwallis sent Tarleton upon a distant and dangerous expedition inland, to destroy a magazine of stores which were intended for Greene's army. Wayne and Morgan had well concerted a plan for his capture. Tarleton, foiled in his work of destruction, was returning, and hearing of the danger that menaced him, he destroyed his wagons, made haste to strike a lower route and narrowly escaped capture.† The knowledge that Morgan was again in the field was a valuable check both upon Tarleton and Cornwallis.

On July 30, Morgan and Wayne moved from Goode's Bridge to Deep Creek, as affording greater facilities for menacing Petersburgh or securing a passage into North Carolina. This may be considered "the first of a series of movements which ended in the capture of Cornwallis."

Three weeks in camp, however, convinced Morgan that he had anticipated his restoration to health. His keen military instincts, the imminent peril of Virginia, the expressed wishes of Congress, the Commander-in-chief, and the State authorities, with the earnest entreaties of his cherished friend La Fayette, had stimulated him to the effort; but the exposure of camp life speedily awoke the sleeping virus in his system, and he again succumbed to his inexorable enemy. He journeyed homeward early in August, with the conviction that he had dealt his last blow for the cause he loved so well.

Shortly before this he had written to General Greene:

"CAMP GOODE'S BRIDGE, July 24, 1781.

"*Dear Sir:*—After making use of the cold bath for upwards of two months, I thought myself so far recovered, as to be able to take the field, and intended to have joined

<hr>

Graham's Life of Morgan.   † *Ibid.*

you. But my Lord, making so deep a lunge at the Old
Dominion, that both Houses of the Assembly requested me
to raise as many volunteers as possible and join the Marquis, which I did.

"How are all the old heroes? Washington, Lee, Howard,
etc. I have not time to write them. Please to make my
compliments to them, also to General Huger, Colonel
Williams and your own family. I saw your letter to the
Marquis and was very unhappy at your situation.* That
d—d reinforcement arrived very unluckily. I lay out the
night after arriving in camp, and caught cold. I am
afraid I am broke down. I sincerely wish you every species
of good luck and all the happiness that country can
afford.

"I have the honor, etc.,
"DANIEL MORGAN."

To this Morgan received the following from General
Greene: †

"HEADQUARTERS, CAMDEN, August 26, 1781.

"*Dear Sir:*—Your letter of July 24th, arrived safe at
headquarters, and your compliments to Williams, Washington, Lee, and other gentlemen you mention, have been
properly distributed. Nothing would give me greater
pleasure than to have you with me. The people of this
county adore you. Had you been with me a few weeks
past, you would have had it in your power to give the
world the pleasure of reading a second Cowpens affair.
But alas! the execution failed * * * Great generals
are scarce. There are few Morgans to be found. The
ladies of Charleston toast you. Don't you think we bear
beating very well, and that we are something of the nature
of stock fish, the more we are beat, the better we grow.

"I may say with the king of Prussia, fortune is a female
and I am no gallant. She has jilted me several times this

* At Ninety-Six.   † *Graham's Life of Morgan.*

campaign, but in spite of her teeth, I pursue her still, in hopes the old adage will be fulfilled, a coy dame may prove kind at last.

"I am not well pleased with her rebuffs, but I bear them with patience. I was content with the flogging at Guilford. But I lost all patience with that of Lord Rawdon [Hobkirk's Hill]. In the one I considered victory as doubtful; in the other certain. * * *

"But to add to my misfortune that cursed reinforcement must arrive by two days too soon. [Ninety-Six.]

"But upon the whole we are as well off as could be expected, and the less we are indebted to fortune, the greater our merit. I claim nothing; the army deserves everything.

"Nurse your old bones and stick by the Marquis, until the modern Hannibal unfolds his great designs. While you and Wayne are with him I think he will be well supported, and I shall feel perfectly easy.

"We are trying to collect the militia to give the enemy battle. If we succeed, you may hear of a few being sent to the shades on both sides. The Dominion has been in great jeopardy this campaign.

"With much esteem, etc.,

"NATHANIEL GREENE."

While at Bath Springs he received this from La Fayette:

"MORSTOK HILL, August 15, 1781.

"*My Dear Friend:*—I have been happy to hear your health was better. I hope the springs will entirely recover it: then, my dear Sir, I shall be happier than can be expressed at seeing you with the army. You are the General and the friend I want; and both from inclination and esteem, I lose a great deal when you go from me, and will think it a great pleasure and a great reinforcement to see you again. But let me entreat you not too soon to expose your health. Great services have been rendered by you; great services are justly expected; so that you cannot, consistent with your duty, trifle with your own life. By the time you are called to come, perhaps the scene will be interesting.

"Your influence, my dear Sir, may render us the greatest service. The militia are coming in so slow that I shall soon be left with the Continentals. For God's sake tell them to come on. I do every day, expect a new campaign, and never was worse provided.

"We put on the best face we can. But I confess I dread consequences. * * *

"Could it be possible to procure a quantity of shoes? The whole army are barefoot. These articles I only mention, my dear friend, in case your health permits you to attend to them. I beg you will not take any trouble about them that might give you improper fatigue.

"Lord Cornwallis' army is divided between York and Gloucester. At York they don't fortify; but they do at Gloucester. * * * There is some rumor of a fleet near the Capes, but I do not believe it. Adieu, my dear Morgan.

"Most affectionately your friend,

"LA FAYETTE."

This correspondence, copied from *Graham's Life of Morgan*, covering the time of his connection with the army of Virginia, disposes of the innuendoes concerning Morgan's feigned ill health, and his lack of devotion to the cause.

But a greater trial awaited him, when he learned that Washington was before Yorktown ; the French fleets off the coast, and glory and victory for the American arms.

The war-worn hero essayed to rouse himself, and once more gird on his armor, but in vain.

He sends this greeting to his beloved Commander-in-chief, full of delicacy and magnanimity :

"*September* 20, 1781.

" *Sir :*—At a time like this, when your Excellency's every moment must be devoted to the grand business of America, I know you can have but little leisure for private letters, but the feelings of my heart will not permit me to be silent; I cannot avoid congratulating your Excellency on the present favorable appearance of our affairs.

"I cannot avoid telling your Excellency how much I wish you success, and how much I wish that the state of my health would permit me to afford my small services on this great occasion.

"Such has been my peculiar fate, that during the whole course of the present war, I have never on any important event, had the honor of serving particularly under your Excellency.

"It is a misfortune I have ever sincerely lamented. There is nothing upon earth, would have given me more real pleasure, than to have made this campaign under your Excellency's eye, to have shared the danger, and let me add, the glory too, which I am almost confident will be acquired. But as my health will not admit of my rejoining the army immediately, I must beg leave to repeat to your Excellency, my most earnest wishes for your success and for your personal safety. I have the honor to be, with sentiments of the highest esteem,

"Your Excellency's obedient humble servant,

"DANIEL MORGAN."

To which Washington very handsomely replies :

"Before YORKTOWN, October 5th, 1781.

" *Sir :*—Surrounded, as I am, with a great variety of concerns on the present occasion, I can yet find time to answer your letter of the 20th ult., which I have received with much satisfaction, not only as it is filled with such warm expressions of desire for my success on the present expedition, but as it breathes the spirit and ardor of a veteran soldier, who, though impaired in the service of his country, yet retains the sentiments of a soldier in the primest degree.

Be assured that I most sincerely lament your present situation, and esteem it a peculiar loss to the United States that you are at this time unable to render your services in the field. I most sincerely thank you for the kind expressions of your good wishes, and earnestly hope that you may be soon restored to that share of health which you may desire, and with which you may again be useful to your country in the same eminent degree as has already distinguished your conduct.

"With much regard and esteem,

"I am, sir, your most obedient servant,

"GEORGE WASHINGTON."

YORKTOWN.

THE day of human liberty was indeed about to dawn, and the faithful watchers and toilers, through the long night of bloody strife, felt the glow of that dawn in their hearts.

Cornwallis, at first posted at Portsmouth, whence he commanded a way of retreat into North Carolina, made a false step in leaving it for Yorktown. This was a most advantageous position so long as he could command the sea, but losing the maritime superiority, it must inevitably become untenable. He looked, of course, for co-operation and succor from Clinton at New York.

On the day that Cornwallis took post at Gloucester and Yorktown, Washington, near New York, had been assured of the co-operation of the French fleet under De Grasse; this determined his course southward, with the allied land force of French under Rochambeau and his own army.

While divisions and jealousies confused the councils of Cornwallis and Clinton, perfect accord joined the hands and strengthened the hearts of the French-American land and naval force. De Barras, commander of the French squadron at Newport, gracefully put himself under the orders of De Grasse, his junior; and when the latter, with twenty-eight ships of the line, entered the Chesapeake and disembarked three thousand men under the Marquis de St. Simon, he quickly notified La Fayette that, though his senior both in years and service, he wished to place himself and his forces under his orders as a Major-General in the United States service.

Cornwallis had fortified the posts of York and Gloucester during the first week in August, and on the 30th of the same month, DeGrasse held the Chesapeake and the sea. September 5th, the British Admiral Graves was dispatched from New York to restore the balance, but De Grasse engaged him at the mouth of the Chesapeake, and, after an action of nearly three hours, remained master of the situation. The British loss was so great that Graves was compelled to return to New York five days afterward.

Washington had brought his forces through Pennsylvania and Maryland to the head of the Chesapeake, whence the French fleet was to convey them before Yorktown.

Leaving them at the Elk River, " Washington, with the Counts Rochambeau and Chastelleux, riding sixty miles a day, on the evening of the ninth of September, reached his own seat at Mount Vernon. It was the first time in more than six years that he had seen his home. From its lofty natural terrace above the Potomac, his illustrious guests commanded a noble river, a wide expanse, and the height—then clothed in forest—within a generation to bear the Capitol of the United Republic."

Two days they sojourned there, and the fourteenth brought them to Williamsburgh, where La Fayette welcomed his beloved General as "Generalissimo of the combined armies of the two nations, to scenes of glory."

Washington had succeeded in deceiving Clinton as to his real intentions, up to the latest moment before setting his army in motion southward. He had caused to be erected, in the vicinity of New York, large army bakeries, and had also allowed letters to Rochambeau, concerning the projected attack upon that city, to find their way into Clinton's hands.

Finding himself completely outwitted, in order to draw Washington's attention, and, if possible, his forces, from Virginia, Clinton planned an expedition of fire, plunder, and murder, into Connecticut, putting Arnold in command. The destruction and cruelty were without parallel, but Washington did not stir a man from before Yorktown.

The allied forces speedily erected around Cornwallis a wall of fire. His only hope was to hold out until Clinton could detach a fleet to his aid. A letter in cipher signified that the fleet would sail from New York not later than October 5th, and urged him to hold out. They worked to strengthen their defences, but the Americans and French were equally zealous, advancing their parallels and erecting batteries, which they crowned with more than a hundred guns.

The 5th of October came and passed without sign of the fleet. Their repairs were still uncompleted. Another cipher letter assured Cornwallis that they would sail on the 12th of October. But he had begun to despair. The enemy's parallels and trenches were daily circumscribing him, and his works were crumbling before their effective fire.

At Gloucester, the British were shut in by dragoons under the Duke de Lauzun and the Virginia militia.

Tarleton had made one sortie with hope of breaking through the besiegers, but they were ridden down and driven back. Tarleton's horse was captured, and his rider narrowly escaped.

Two strong redoubts remained to be taken by assault. Washington assigned one to the French, the other to the Americans. They received their orders with the greatest enthusiasm. The French officers and soldiers had equally imbibed the love of freedom, and were proud to be the defenders and saviors of the young Republic.

There was also much emulation between the attacking

parties as to which should first achieve the capture of the redoubt assigned them. The American column was led by the gallant and gifted Alexander Hamilton, who in after years performed all the brilliant promise of his youth. He was accompanied by the courtly young Colonel Laurens, who always sought the post of danger.

The French column was led by Count William de Deux Ponts and the Baron de l'Estrade.

Their officers addressed them a few words of inspiration ; the attack was made with the greatest impetuosity, and the redoubts carried at the point of the bayonet, with little loss to the American column ; the French suffered more.

Cornwallis, seeing the sufferings of his men, crowded into a small space, with over a thousand disabled by wounds and camp-fever, listened to the counsel of his officers and resolved to attempt an escape on the night of the 18th October. The sick and wounded were commended by letter to the mercy and generosity of Washington, at the very time the British were perpetrating the most atrocious cruelties in Connecticut.

The army embarked in small boats on the James River, when a sudden and violent squall drove the boats down the river and threatened them with instant destruction.

With difficulty they relanded and returned to their camp, feeling that the hand of Providence was against them. On the 18th, Cornwallis sent a flag to Washington with proposals to arrange for a capitulation. On the 19th, the posts of York and Gloucester were surrendered. The land forces became prisoners to America, and the seamen to France. The shipping and naval stores fell to the French, the field artillery to the Americans—one hundred and six pieces, of which seventy-five were brass. The talents and bravery displayed by the allies won them immortal glory, and they enhanced it by the humanity and generosity shown to their prisoners.

The French officers, in particular, honored themselves by the most delicate consideration of their enemies. Lord Cornwallis in his public letters acknowledged this.*

On the day of surrender, Cornwallis was too much indisposed to leave his tent, but sent his sword by General O'Hara. Lincoln, who had surrendered his sword at Charleston to Cornwallis, was appointed by Washington to receive that of Cornwallis. The rigor of the British on that occasion was well remembered, and Washington required the capitulating force to march out with colors cased. Yet, as the prisoners filed past the American lines, we remember his charge, "Don't huzza, boys; posterity will huzza for you."

Tarleton, who was in command of the post of Gloucester at the time of the surrender, communicated to the French General Choisé his apprehensions for his personal safety if put at the disposal of the American militia.†

He got safely away, and on his return to England was immediately promoted to the rank of Colonel, and became so popular, that in 1790 he was sent to parliament free of expense from his native town. In 1817, he was advanced to the rank of major-general, and the next year created a baronet.‡

* *Botta's American Revolution.*   † *Lee's Memoirs.*
‡ *Cyclopedia Americana.*

AT LAST.

THE names of Washington, Rochambeau, La Fayette and De Grasse were on every tongue. The shouts of victory from the field of Yorktown reached Morgan in his home near Winchester, and drew forth his heartiest congratulations to his Commander-in-chief, and to his friend La Fayette.

Shortly after, occurred a painful and needless misunderstanding between Morgan and Washington. The Virginia troops commanded by the former were disbanded after the surrender at Yorktown, and the government, unable to discharge the balance due them, issued certificates of the amount with promise of future payment. But many of the soldiers were sick or disabled by wounds, ragged, penniless, or at a distance from their homes. Their pressing necessities encouraged unprincipled speculators to prey upon them, by offering to cash the certificates at shameful discount. This coming to Morgan's knowledge, he earnestly advised them to retain their certificates, as the public faith was pledged for their payment, offering, at the same time, if any were compelled to part with them, to double the sum offered by these speculators, and also a promise to hold them subject to their redemption should they desire it.

The speculators, foiled of their profits, circulated injurious accusations, charging General Morgan with the meanness they had themselves sought to practice upon the soldiers. It came to Washington's ears. He ceased

to correspond with Morgan, openly expressed his want of
confidence in him, and when they met, treated him with
coldness.*

Morgan was wounded to the soul ; suspecting the cause,
and feeling how undeserved was the implied censure, he
sought an explanation. Washington told him frankly that
he could esteem no man who "labored under the charge of
profiting by the necessities and distresses of the soldiers."
Morgan then stated the facts of the case, giving him the
testimony of numbers of the soldiers, which at once convinced Washington how entirely he had been deceived ;
he promptly expressed his regret at having entertained
accusations against a man so high in his esteem, without
first hearing his version of it. A tithe of the long-suffer-
ing and misplaced confidence thrown away upon Arnold,
would have saved Morgan from a wound sharper than the
steel of an enemy.

Morgan never recovered his health, but ten years of
quiet prosperity in the bosom of his family had somewhat
built up his constitution and quite repaired his fortunes.
He directed the plough as successfully as he had wielded
the sword. By State grants and purchases he became
possessor of not less than two hundred and fifty thousand
acres of land on the Ohio and Monongahela rivers. He
had built a stately mansion and called it "Saratoga,"—
abode of a refined and Christian home-circle,—his estima-
ble wife, their two daughters—the elder married to Colonel
Neville, the younger to Major Heard—and their children.
With ease and dignity they dispensed the largest hospitalities to the best society that Virginia could boast.

Morgan appears again in public life during the "Whis-
key Insurrection" as major-general of the Virginia militia.
In 1797 he represented the counties of Frederic and
Berkeley in Congress. He was also a member of the Congress called by Washington in 1797 to take into considera-

* *Graham's Life of Morgan.*

tion the threatening complexion of affairs between America and France, and was named in connection with a high command, in event of war with that country. While at his post during the regular session of Congress in 1798, his health again gave way. He sank into a confirmed invalidism from this time.

During his whole career, even in his wild young days, Morgan had always expressed and manifested the greatest respect for religion. During the late years of his life, he had been a regular attendant of the church of which his wife had long been a member. He now became a communicant, and for the fuller enjoyment of religious privileges, left his country residence and removed to Winchester. A strong friendship had sprung up between General Morgan and his pastor, Rev. Dr. Hill, of the Presbyterian church. He was in constant attendance upon him during the latter years of his life, and to his manuscripts Morgan's biographer, Mr. James Graham, is largely indebted for some of the most interesting facts of our hero's early life, which Dr. Hill had from his own lips.

And now this happy warrior, having struck all his valiant blows for God and humanity, rested a little space from his labors and waited for his final furlough. "They also serve who only stand and wait," for now he girded on his spiritual armor and made full proof of that nobler courage with which the Christian warrior triumphs over his last enemy.

After a wearisome confinement of a year to his house, and of six months to his bed or easy-chair, he sank under his infirmities and expired July 6, 1802, in the sixty-seventh year of his age, "having served his generation."

In the military escort at his grave were seven members of the rifle company with which Morgan marched to Boston in 1775. Their war-worn rifles fired the last salute over his grave.

His biographer says of his Revolutionary services :

" Whether we regard their extent, their value, or their brilliancy, they were not surpassed by those of any other officer in the army, except the Commander-in-chief himself.

" He participated in, or had the direction of, nearly fifty contests with the enemy, eight of which were general engagements, and in no instance did he fail of entire or partial success. Throughout his long military career, he never experienced a surprise, though the nature of the service in which he was chiefly engaged subjected him constantly to such a contingency.*

"In person he was more than six feet high, and well proportioned ; of an imposing presence ; moving with strength and grace ; of a hardy constitution, that defied fatigue, hunger and cold. He could glow with intensest anger, but passion never mastered his power of discernment; his disposition was sweet and peaceful, so that he delighted in acts of kindness, and never harbored malice or revenge. His courage was not an idle quality, it sprung from the intense energy of his will, which bore him on to do his duty with an irresistible impetuosity. His faculties were quickened at the approach of danger. An instinctive perception of character assisted him to choose those whom it was wise to trust, and a reciprocal sympathy made the obedience of his soldiers an act of affectionate confidence.

" Wherever he was posted in the battle-field, the fight was sure to be waged with fearlessness, judgment, and massive energy. Of all the officers whom Virginia sent into the war, next to Washington, Morgan was the greatest ; yet she raises no statue to the incomparable leader of her light troops." †

It is idle to mention any name with that of Washington,—a greatness so many-sided and symmetrical as to be unique. But if we consider military genius alone—as a

* *Graham's Life of Morgan.* † *Bancroft,* Vol. VIII.

field executive—Morgan towers above all. That insufferable military caste, which it seems must be endured because it cannot be cured, had thus far kept him manacled under his inferiors. Cowpens was his single opportunity to show the reach of his genius. He exhibits here that marvellous power of sympathy which put him in *rapport* with those he commanded, and by which he so multiplied and communicated himself to his troops that he worked his divisions as if they had been his own limbs. His army individualized.

It would seem eminently proper that centennial honors to Daniel Morgan should not devolve upon any one State. No State can establish its claim to him. His track of glory reaches from Quebec to Cowpens.

Leaving Canada,—Maine, New York, New Jersey, Pennsylvania, Virginia, North and South Carolina, may well contend for the honor of honoring him. He belongs to the continent.

Rising from the humblest obscurity to the noble height he gained, he, more than any other of that wonderful Revolutionary group, illustrates the genius and forecasts the possibilities of the New World.

Virginia! dear old Dominion,—mother of States, hallowed ground indeed,—holding in thy bosom the sacred relics of Jefferson, Henry, Morgan and Washington! From such precious seed what heroic harvests may we yet gather!

9 783337 182458